I0545768

Fear of the Unknown

Michael Elia

First published 2017
by Rowanvale Books Ltd
The Gate
Keppoch Street
Roath
Cardiff
CF24 3JW
www.rowanvalebooks.com

A CIP catalogue record for this book is available from the British Library.
ISBN: 978-1-911240-31-0

CHAPTER 1

The sun shimmered through the clouds and the haze over the mountains, pastures and meadows of the Bavarian Alps. Green hills and towering stony mountains were teaming with flowers, buttercups and edelweiss, and the long, tender grass was kept neatly trimmed by the cows, sheep and goats. The weather was hesitating to rain as a few drops of water spat towards the grass and flowers, but no heavy rain was destined to descend towards the pastures and meadows on that clear day as a rainbow of many blurred colours shone between the clouds and hills and then melted into the atmosphere.

On a farm below the base of the mountains, Marion Weisberg was watching the pastures, the flowers, the cattle and sheep, the shimmering rainbow and the hills. Travelling the roads to the north were many vehicles closing in on the city of Munich. Marion's sharp eyes spotted a helicopter gliding southwards from Nuremburg, then across Germany's frontier with Austria towards Vienna. She took a lungful of clean, unpolluted air in her mouth and nostrils. The breeze threw her long, slightly curly black hair across her face and forehead and whistled against her slender, wiry body. She wore blue Levi's jeans, a green T-shirt and a black leather jacket she had bought in Frankfurt. Marion looked younger than her twenty-eight years, and people often commented on her uncanny resemblance to the American film star Karen Allen, famous for acting alongside Harrison Ford in *Raiders of the Lost Ark* and Jeff Bridges in *Starman*.

Marion smiled again as her husband, Klaus, joined her by the fence surrounding the farm. He looked good in jeans and a navy blue jumper. He was blond with some stubble and glasses, and, facially at least, he was the spitting image of the English film actor Kenneth Branagh. Klaus wore black jeans, and a navy blue jumper, and his hand groped Marion's shoulder as he lowered his mouth towards her face and kissed her. His facial hair tickled Marion's cheek and she chuckled slightly.

'Haven't you forgotten something, darling?' Klaus said, his voice low and loving.

'I know, the appointment in Munich Hospital,' Marion said lightly. 'With Doctor Adolf Kringer. I never forget appointments — not like you.'

'You forgot our last appointment with Doctor Kringer three months ago,' Klaus objected. 'Remember? You fell asleep and had a nightmare about that terrible wolf attack thirteen years ago. How do you expect to overcome your paranoid phobia if you don't even attend appointments?'

'Okay, have it your way,' Marion said.

'You've forgotten more appointments than me. You forgot to visit the optician about changing your glasses.'

'Well we won't fall out about it,' Klaus said, his voice more serious. 'Anyway, I've mended the battery on our car, so let's go to this appointment.'

'Anything you say, Klaus,' Marion said, humour evident in her voice, her beaming smile and her sharp eyes. 'How are Mavis and Mildew?'

'I fed them an hour ago,' Klaus told Marion. 'Those terriers are lucky to have me. You see, I get up early, unlike you. I've been on this planet for thirty-four years, and in all that time I've never been late getting up. I value my work; has an ethos to it.'

'Now you're being pompous,' Marion complained lightly. 'But give me two more months working at Munich Zoo and I'll judge for myself whether I've overcome my terrors. Then I'll get up earlier and put in more hours at the zoo. That's *if* the wild animals don't turn me into dinner.'

'Marion, these terrors of yours are nothing to joke about,' Klaus said, frowning. 'Every time a dog barks at you in the street or the zoo's lions and tigers come towards the bars of their cages, you panic like a child. It means you have to do fewer hours at the zoo: your salary is reduced so we can't go out to restaurants like we used to. We may even have to sell the car and use public transport. But the worst thing is, you're still having terrible nightmares about that wolf attack in the Bavarian Forest. And the dreams won't go away until Doctor Kringer comes up with a solution.'

'I prefer not to think about my phobias,' Marion said. 'Anyway, Doctor Kringer will come up with something.'

'I wish I had your confidence in doctors,' Klaus said doubtfully. They walked slowly across the garden, and Mavis and Mildew darted towards them and jumped up at their legs. Marion smiled down at them; she only feared large dogs.

* * *

Doctor Adolf Kringer had just concluded an appointment, and he sat quietly in his office at Munich Hospital. He was a tall, very slim man in his fifties with short grey hair, a handsome face and a long beard that hung down towards his black suit jacket and white shirt underneath.

There was a knock at the door.

'Come in,' the doctor called abruptly, and the door opened.

'Klaus and Marion Weisberg for you, doctor,' the secretary announced.

'Thank you, Helgar,' Kringer said. 'Come in, both of you.'

'It's good to meet again, doctor,' Klaus replied.

'Now, Marion, we've been seeing each other for a year, and I heard that you still haven't overcome your terror of dangerous animals,' Kringer observed. 'Is this true?'

'Yes, it is,' Marion replied.

'I keep telling her that wolves almost never attack humans, and they're not dangerous,' Klaus informed Kringer. 'But I can't rationalise her terror. I've even told her that there has never been an authenticated incident of a wolf attacking a man or child in the whole of Europe or North America. And that applies to most so-called dangerous animals. Humans are more dangerous to wolves than wolves are to humans.'

'You cannot rationalise such terror unless you've been through the same experience,' Kringer told Klaus. 'When you've suffered such a horrific experience as Marion did, it stays with you for the rest of your life. Only careful psychology and therapy can totally overcome these phobias.'

'I *want* to overcome them,' Marion said adamantly. 'It's not fair of me to blame all wolves or other dangerous animals for what happened to me, because wolves have as much right to roam the forests as we do. It was my fault that I was attacked, because I ventured into the wolves' territory and interfered with their cubs. But if I see a wolf now, I can't help but shake and scream. I've come to believe that wolves are bloodthirsty killers, ready to attack humans at any time, any place, and nothing I've done has altered that belief. The nightmares keep coming back, and my phobias are stopping me from working at Munich Zoo. Every time I see a large animal,

I panic, and then I have to finish work early. My employers are very understanding, and so is my husband whom I work with. But my pay has had to be reduced due to time I've had to take off, and if I don't overcome this terror within two months, the zoo manager will ask me to leave the job.'

'I see an interesting scenario here,' Kringer told the young couple. 'When people have phobias, it is almost always terror of spiders, scorpions, snakes, or even cats and dogs, and sometimes frogs or toads. But I've never had anybody come to me with a terror of *all* large animals. It's 2004 now, and the world is more educated and enlightened; most people know not to fear or hate these animals, but accept them as part of the balance of nature. It takes somebody to be attacked by an elephant, crocodile, tiger, bear or wolf to really hate these animals, and even then that person does not extend that hatred and fear to *all* dangerous animals. Yours is a very severe case, Marion.'

'So what's your point, doctor?' Klaus demanded.

'I'm sorry to have to say this, but your wife's phobias will take years to overcome,' Kringer explained, 'and that's *if* they can be overcome at all. Personally, I do not see this ever happening; if Marion hasn't made any progress in the year she has been seeing me, then she will never make any progress. It is difficult enough to cure a simpler phobia of spiders, snakes, frogs, or even dogs, but to cure a paranoid terror on this scale seems impossible. So no, I cannot cure Marion's phobias. Only one person can do that, and that's you, Marion. It's now time that we put an end to our sessions and for you to stop seeing me, for there's nothing more I can do. And I now have to see my next patient.'

'Is that all?' Klaus growled angrily. 'You're not going to give her any treatment, therapy or medication?! Do you know what it's like to live with a wife who is terrified of everything that moves? What it's like for her to have to suffer from these phobias?'

'Klaus, calm down,' Marion begged her husband. 'Leave it. The doctor is right, only we can deal with it!'

'No, Marion, you need help!' Klaus shouted. 'Thank you for wasting a year of our time, doctor.' Klaus stormed outside the office, and Marion followed him.

* * *

Marion and Klaus lay in their bed, frustration gripping Klaus's mind as he pondered over Doctor Kringer's lack of concern. Marion was aware of her husband's pain and anger as she lay on her side. She rolled over and kissed his face.

'You're not still mad about today, are you?' she asked softly. 'Doctor Kringer is only one psychologist among many. We can go to Nuremburg, Frankfurt, Hamburg, Leipzig or Berlin — or even abroad. Don't give up, Klaus. We've got to settle this.'

'I know, Marion,' Klaus replied. 'I know. But what if we never find a psychologist? What if the phobias can never be cured? It's going to mess up our entire lives.'

'No, it won't,' Marion insisted. 'The nightmares will eventually go away. All I have to do is avoid contact with large animals. Listen, tomorrow we go on holiday to Regensburg. I'll stay in a hotel whilst you take Mavis and Mildew and pitch a tent in the Bavarian Forest. That way, we're compromising. I'll stay in the city, but you don't have to lose out on your trip to the forest. I know you've always wanted to visit the Bavarian Forest.'

'But where will we get the money to stay in a hotel and cover our meals?' Klaus asked. 'Hotels in Regensburg are expensive. You're not exactly earning large sums of money, sweetheart.'

'I still have money left to me in my father's will,' Marion said. 'Let's go for it.'

'That sounds like a brilliant idea,' Klaus said. 'But I want to tell you this…'

'Go on,' Marion answered slowly, swiping her hair away from her forehead.

'No matter what happens — whether you lose your job at the zoo, or we run short of money, or you never cure your terrors — you'll always be the only woman in this country, in this whole world, who matters to me. My love for you is like the light of the moon and stars; it will not falter before the darkness. Even if we have nothing else, we still have each other. And when you need me, I'll be there for you.'

Marion smiled and rested her head against Klaus's chest, and in ten minutes both of them were unconscious.

* * *

The morning approached as the dim light of the moon and stars gave way to the sun's brilliance. The ocean-blue sky and its clouds overlooked the green pastures and snow-covered summits of the Bavarian Alps. The farm was so still and quiet that you might imagine you could hear a leaf floating to the ground or an insect landing on the window. The only faint noise was from traffic passing through Bavaria, heading east towards Munich or west towards Swabia and Baden Wurttemburg.

Marion and Klaus were still asleep in their room. Marion's face was shiny with sweat as her worst nightmare tormented her subconscious mind. The towering trees of the Bavarian Forest loomed overhead, as Marion tried to fight off the she-wolf as it tried to maul her. But the wolf's dagger-like teeth snapped her arm at the elbow and stripped what little flesh and skin covered her wiry arm. Marion's eyes were big, her pupils dilated in sheer terror, and her throat was tortured by a rising nausea. Urine soaked her leg in her terror, drenching her pants and jeans. She was screaming, 'Leave me alone! Leave me alone! Somebody help me!' The wolf's dagger-like teeth shredded her hands, but then she kicked the devilish beast in the stomach, winding it. Her right arm and hands were covered in blood and her face was soaked in the wolf's saliva where her fangs had almost savaged her face and throat. Marion scrambled to her feet and tried to flee. The wolf's savage teeth sank into her right buttock and thigh, and she screamed and yelled in agony. And at that moment, the teachers in Marion's group came to her rescue and beat the wolf with their canes so that she fled back towards her cubs in the den.

'No!'

'Marion!' Klaus called, shaking his wife awake. He held her as she jumped back into reality. 'Marion, it's all right. It's all right.'

'Oh God, no!' she cried out, her eyes big with her crippling terror and her mouth agape. 'Shit! God, help me!' She fell against her husband's chest as he embraced her with his strong arms and massaged her head and stroked her hair with gentle hands. 'Don't leave me, please!' she mumbled.

'You'll be fine, love,' Klaus reassured her gently.

After getting ready, they packed their bags and drove north towards Regensburg. As the car reached sixty miles per hour, Klaus turned to Marion.

'Do you want some music on, love?' he asked her.

'No thank you, darling,' Marion said sadly.

'Come on, Marion, be happy,' Klaus insisted. 'We're on holiday. You and I need a break.'

'How can I be happy?' Marion said, her

voice heavy with tortured emotion. 'This is a pain in the neck.'

'What's a pain in the neck?' Klaus said. 'I know that nightmare was distressing for you, but they will go away eventually.'

'How do you know?' Marion snapped suddenly. 'What if they never go away?'

'Forget about it,' Klaus said. 'Come on, let's have some music. How about Ludwig van Beethoven?'

'Damn you, Klaus!' Marion said. 'It's easy for *you* to take it easy.' They drove along the autobahn with the rolling hills, pastures and meadows stretching either side of them.

After a seemingly endless journey, they reached Regensburg, and pulled up outside a small hotel only ten miles from the Bavarian Forest. After settling Marion into her hotel room, Klaus took the two terriers and sat on the top deck of the coach that would transport a group of tourists towards the forest. The tour guide starting relaying some information about the forest.

'We are going to spend a few days pitching tents and exploring the Bavarian Forest,' he began. 'This forest was set up as a national park in 1970 and contains several species of deciduous and coniferous trees. Recently, the Bavarian Forest became joined to the Bohemian Forest on Germany's border with the Czech Republic, after the Czech Republic broke away from what was the Communist state of Czechoslovakia. The Bohemian Forest extends into the Czech Republic where the forest becomes Sumava National Park. So we have Sumava National Park covering the east swathe of forest, Germany's Bohemian Forest covering the central swathe and then the Bavarian Forest stretching west towards the city of Regensburg, the forest where we're heading now.

'Together, these three forests make up the largest wooded area in central Europe, and the biggest forest in Germany next to the Black Forest on the border with France. When heading off alone, beware of wolves, feral dogs and wild boars. Wolves rarely attack people, but the feral dogs might, and the wild boars are the most dangerous wild animals in Germany. Last year, three people had their legs crippled by wild boars charging, but normally they mind their own business if you stay out of their way. The Bavarian and Bohemian Forests are threatened by acid rain, which has destroyed over fifty percent of the German forests, not to mention French, Czech and Polish forests. Such is the modern industry we have around us today.'

They reached their destination and the other tourists pitched their tents close to the outskirts of the forest. However, Klaus intended to spend the night deep in the forest and feel how wild, tranquil and lonely the place was. He took the terriers on a long hike eastwards through the imposing wilderness with its towering deciduous and coniferous trees, flowers, mosses and grasses. Klaus and the terriers then made their way south-east until they ended up on the south side of the forest, where it overlooked the surrounding landscape. This wilderness area was one of the last traditional forests in Europe, and was not only larger than the Black Forest, but far less commercialised and more like a true wilderness. Merging with oaks, beeches, birches, hazels and chestnut trees were limes, pines, spruces and yew trees. Klaus ventured amongst the trees as they towered above the forest floor, with scattered flowers of many colours, mosses, different grasses and bushes. The singing of birds and the rutting of deer and wild boars echoed between the trees. There were also game birds, rabbits, hares and squirrels — not to mention dangerous herbivores and predators roaming around.

Klaus halted and called his dogs back suddenly; ahead of them were the forest's four dominant herbivores: a powerful wild boar, a muscular bull, a large billy goat and a huge ram.

Klaus briefly thought that too many feral creatures were ruining the wilderness areas of Europe, but his fear was even more overpowering than his anger. The four powerful beasts were feeding peacefully, paying no attention to Klaus. Suddenly, the wild boar glared at Klaus, his mouth full of acorns, beechnuts and sweet chestnuts. The bull also looked up, and Klaus swore he saw cold fury in its eyes. The goat and the ram were not so sinister, but they would still take action if the other two animals charged.

Klaus stood rooted to the spot, not moving an inch; to run away would be fatal. Wild boars and bulls would easily outrun a man. The sweat streamed down his face and soaked his beard. His glasses were misted up, so he took them off slowly, not daring to make any fast movements. The terriers were even more petrified than he was, for they instinctively knew the wild boar's savage reputation when cornered or provoked. But none of the beasts charged. The boar and the bull finally lumbered away, followed by the other two beasts. Klaus was relieved that Marion was not there with him to encounter this, for she would have freaked out and made the situation worse.

He led Mavis and Mildew in a different direction, due east. They halted again when they spotted the carcass of a red deer ahead of them. It was being consumed by a lynx. This small wild cat lacked a reputation for attacking humans, unlike the big cats, but Klaus exercised caution and ordered the dogs to heel nevertheless. He remembered attending a breeding programme in Byelorussia four years ago that bred not only lynxes, but also bears, wolves and wolverines to restock the populations of large predators in the forests of Russia, the Ukraine and Byelorussia.

Klaus' mind returned to the present. He guessed that this lynx had killed the deer only an hour ago, and then he strolled stealthily towards some thickets in the distance. Then four mustelids of the weasel tribe came over to dine on the leftovers: the badger emerging from his sett, the weasel and the polecat speeding through the long grass and the pine marten darting down from a tree. Although vicious killers, none of them fought over the carcass; there was plenty of carrion to feed all four. The badger's black body was camouflaged against the darkness with only his striped face giving him away, whilst the weasel and the pine marten were almost invisible and the polecat's facial markings barely showed him up in the grass.

Mavis and Mildew barked at the badger, who bared his teeth at them in fury.

'Come on,' Klaus whispered to the terriers, and they hurried off. They then came upon the spectacle of a feral cat fighting with a tawny owl over the carcass of a rabbit. The cat, with its impressive claws, hissed and spat, the owl struck out with its talons, and then there was a violent tug of war over the rabbit. After twenty seconds of this, the rabbit was torn apart and the owl flew off with one half of the carcass whilst the cat fed on the remaining half. Klaus could clearly see that he was one of those domesticated cats who had become wild, the reason they were called feral cats, as was the case with dogs, bulls, oxen, goats and sheep. When the fierce feline spotted Klaus, he disappeared into the darkness.

Klaus set about pitching his tent.

The Bavarian and Bohemian Forests are two of the few areas in Germany where wolves still survive, and they were now on the prowl. Hidden inside his tent, Klaus heard fighting between wolves and feral dogs, but it was soon over. A little unnerved, Klaus tried to reassure himself that, despite Marion's terrifying experience thirteen years ago, wolves were not bloodthirsty killers of humans, and they did not deserve the fearsome reputation with which they had been branded. Many naturalists had approached wolves and come to no harm, and the same thing was true for feral dogs.

The howling and baying of wolves and dogs became faint in the night, as did the grunting of wild boars, the snuffling of a badger and the ghostly hooting of a tawny owl. Klaus also knew that, across the German-Czech border, in the Sumava Forest National Park, bears roamed the forests and mountains as well as wolves. The brown bear had long been extinct in Germany, but many remained in the remote areas of Eastern Europe. Klaus knew that they too were not dangerous if left alone. He had heard of odd occasions where bears had wandered across the border into Germany's Bohemian Forest, but they had never attacked humans, neither had wolves or lynxes. Klaus finally succumbed to sleep and the terriers relaxed; they were not even disturbed by the rustling in the grass of the weasel, the polecat and the pine marten.

* * *

The even slopes were covered by lush grass and delicate flowers.

In contrast to the serene surroundings, hidden amongst the trees, a mortal battle of life and death continued as predators fought rival predators, herbivores fought rival herbivores and, of course, predators fought herbivores.

Four feral beasts — a bull, an ox and two horses — fought over a pond to assert who was going to drink first, but the horses came off worst. The bull and the ox repelled the horses with their horns, forcing them to flee across the meadow, and then the ox took the first sip from the pond.

A little way off, a golden eagle, a goshawk and a peregrine falcon fiercely contested a roe deer carcass killed by a large mountain fox. All three of them were aggressive birds of prey, but the eagle was the largest and most powerful of the three. He repelled the hawk and the falcon and proceeded to feed, but he was then to lose the carcass to the feral pig. The pig fiercely charged the eagle before the bird of prey ascended towards the sky, then the pig began to feed.

It was early morning and the distant howling of a wolf pack resonated through the forest along with the faint screeching of an owl. Klaus was wide awake and unleashed his terriers, who ran on ahead of him. Soon, they caught sight of a large mountain fox in the distance — bigger, heavier and longer in the legs than its lowlands cousins. Then they saw four other foxes, similar to the first. Terriers had been bred by humans for fox-hunting, and Mavis and Mildew followed their natural instinct upon seeing the five red beasts ahead of them. They gave chase and pursued the foxes down the entrance to their den. And this was to be their undoing.

In the distance, Klaus was calling them.

* * *

Marion was eating breakfast in the hotel lounge when the receptionist approached her. Marion noticed a glum look on the woman's face and her features rearranged themselves to express fear.

'Mrs Weisberg, it's your husband on the phone,' the receptionist said. 'Some bad news. He's calling from a phone box at the campsite near the Bavarian Forest.'

Marion abandoned her breakfast and headed for the phone at the reception area before yanking the phone up from the desk.

'Klaus, is that you?' Marion said apprehensively. 'I heard there's some bad news.'

'It's Mavis and Mildew,' Klaus said, his emotion coming out in his voice. 'They were mauled by five foxes. They pursued the foxes into their den, following their instincts, and the foxes turned on them. The dogs didn't stand a chance. The foxes were large mountain foxes — almost as big as small Dobermans — and they outnumbered the terriers.'

'But Mavis and Mildew will be all right, won't

they?' Marion said, her voice weak. 'How are they?'

'They're seriously injured and have lost a lot of blood,' Klaus said frantically. 'The head of the tour is taking me to the vet's outside Regensburg, and I want you to head there now. The receptionist will know where the vet's is.'

'Okay, I must go now,' Marion said. She pushed the phone down. 'Oh shit!' she exclaimed. She turned to the receptionist. 'I need a taxi to take me to the vet's outside Regensburg. My two terriers have had an accident.'

* * *

Marion joined Klaus at the vet's twenty minutes later, and her face was contorted by sheer horror.

'What happened? Give me details,' she said worriedly.

Klaus held his face in his hands, fighting back tears, and then he recounted exactly what had happened.

'It was morning in the Bavarian Forest. The terriers and I were sleeping in our tent,' he explained. 'I packed my tent and then I led Mavis and Mildew outside the forest to some pastures and hills. I saw many animals, all deadly creatures, but I never imagined for one second that foxes were dangerous. Mavis and Mildew saw the five foxes when walking down a hill, and they chased them.

I called the dogs to come back, but they ignored me. They entered the fox den, and a fight broke out. The foxes turned savage and they viciously attacked Mavis and Mildew. Both dogs suffered broken legs, bite wounds to their necks and they lost a great deal of blood when the arteries and blood vessels in their legs were ruptured. It was horrible. They managed to escape from the fox den, and I was horrified by their injuries. However, I don't hate these foxes because they were only defending themselves and their cubs, like that female wolf who attacked you when you were fifteen.'

'Are Mavis and Mildew okay?' Marion asked desperately. 'Tell me they'll be okay! Please!'

Then the vet came out of his operating room and approached the young couple, his face betraying a tortured look of sadness. Marion and Klaus knew exactly what that look meant.

'What is it?' Marion asked immediately. She glanced at his name badge. 'Mr von Trapp, are Mavis and Mildew okay?'

'I'm afraid I have some bad news,' von Trapp began. 'The terriers had to be put down. I couldn't save them. Their injuries were far too severe and they had lost too much blood. I hate putting animals to sleep, but it was the only way. I'm sorry.'

'No!' Marion exclaimed. 'Shit, no!'

'I didn't expect this to happen, my love,' Klaus said slowly. 'It was my fault. I should never have taken the dogs into the forest.'

'How serious were their injuries?' Marion asked, sheer horror torturing her face. 'Are you sure you couldn't save them?'

'I did everything I could,' von Trapp told her. 'But their injuries were very severe. Mavis had one broken leg, a crippling injury to her back and bite wounds to her throat. The arteries and blood vessels in her leg were ruptured and she lost a lot of blood. Mildew suffered two broken back legs with severed arteries and blood vessels, injuries to her back, the side of her neck and her throat.

'Those foxes didn't mess about, and we can't blame them. Because they are bred for fox-hunting, terriers naturally go for foxes. Fox terriers kill far more foxes than foxes kill them, but that's because the foxes they prey on are normally the smaller lowland foxes, not the large mountain foxes. The mountain foxes are much larger and heavier, with longer legs, bigger heads and stronger jaws. They are nearly as big as a small Doberman, and they are strong and fierce enough to kill a roe deer or a dog that is a little bigger than a terrier.

'However, this is still a very unusual occurrence. Even the largest foxes normally flee from terriers, and will not attack a terrier unless cornered. Plenty of people have come to me with dogs injured in fights with other animals, but never a fight with a fox. They get injured by other dogs or cats, and very occasionally pet dogs in European countries get mauled in fights with bears, wolves and lynxes, but again that is very rare. Wild boars and badgers can kill large dogs, and very rarely I have known of dogs being attacked by packs of weasels, stoats, polecats and martens. But I have never heard of dogs being injured or killed by foxes.'

'But it was still my fault,' Klaus said. 'I should never have taken Mavis and Mildew into the forest or the hills. I should have known something like this would happen.'

Marion was overcome by tortured emotion; she scrambled off her seat and ran out of the clinic. 'No, no, no!' she yelled, and then, blinded by tears, she sprinted into the road. A Volkswagen Beetle screeched towards her at great speed, and failed to stop in time. Marion span round just as the car slammed violently into her, throwing her onto the pavement. She hit her head against the concrete and felt her leg and arm break. There was an unbearable pain in her chest, and her last thought was that four of her ribs must be fractured. Then, concussion took over and she slipped into unconsciousness.

'Marion!' Klaus screamed as he darted out of the clinic and towards his wife. The driver of the Volkswagen jumped out of his vehicle and sped towards Klaus, who was gently touching Marion's bruised face. Von Trapp emerged from the clinic. All three men gazed in shock at the scene, unable to speak.

CHAPTER 2

One of the wards of Regensburg Hospital was very quiet, apart from the slight squeak of a wheelchair moving somewhere nearby. Marion lay in bed critically injured and unconscious. Klaus was with her. Her brother, Lukas, her sister, Eva, and her mother were all sitting by her bed. Her mother was gently holding her hand, tears flowing down her face. Klaus and Lukas comforted her.

'She'll be fine, Rachel,' Klaus reassured her.

'No, she won't,' Rachel said fearfully. 'When my husband had a stroke, I prayed that he would recover, but he never did. And Marion's life has been marred by tragedy. First, there was that wolf attack when she was fifteen, triggering her terror of all large animals, and then there were the deaths of Mavis and Mildew — and now this! A broken leg, a broken arm, four fractured ribs and possibly brain damage from hitting her head! I would rather she died than be reliant on a machine.'

'You mustn't think like that,' Lukas told his mum sharply. 'Marion is strong. She's a fighter. She'll come through this just fine. I know she will.'

'Let's hope so,' Klaus agreed.

* * *

Marion began the long dream that was to transform her life, travelling through darkness before she found herself in a small boat on the Pacific Ocean off California. She was dressed in a T-shirt, shorts and trainers. Then she glanced with horror towards the blue sea as two enormous and enraged sharks advanced towards her boat, darting through the clear water with fearsome brute power and lightning speed.

Marion was more terrified of sharks than all other lethal killers of the natural world, and these two individuals were the great white and the tiger shark, the two shark species with the worst reputation for blood-chilling ferocity and man-eating. Their huge heads emerged at the surface and they bellowed, roared and grunted with psychotic savagery, petrifying Marion. This was like a scene from *Jaws*. Their huge teeth gnashed and crunched with ruthless hatred and speed as their bodies and tails thrashed through the water. The giant, razor-sharp teeth were powerful enough to bite through a surfboard, crush bones or sever a human's leg or arm, and their eyes were cold and evil. They exploded out of the water again as they lunged towards Marion's boat, and each shark tore a chunk of the boat away. Marion screamed hysterically as water trickled into the boat from both holes, and the two giant sharks lashed out with their powerful bodies and tails, and continued biting and ripping the strong wood away with their massive red jaws and lethal teeth like giant razors. She continued screaming as the great white smashed his body against the boat again, shattering the planks, and she felt defenceless against the awesome strength, speed and blood-chilling savagery of both beasts.

Joining the great white shark and the tiger shark came three other lean beasts: the blue shark, the bull shark and the hammerhead shark. It seemed they wanted to share the spoils, and Marion, in her panic, fell overboard into the water. The boat was in pieces, and the great white and the tiger shark lurched through the water towards her, hostile eyes focussed and teeth ready for the kill. Marion was drowning in the water, and she thought she was going to die.

Marion awoke from her nightmare petrified and sweating. Sat opposite her in a straw chair bound together by lion skins was a well-built man in his forties.

Marion glanced at him with big, dilated eyes and clenched teeth. 'Where am I? Who are you?'

'You are in the dreamworld, and I am Chief Jomo,' the man answered.

'The dreamworld?' Marion said blankly.

'What do you mean?'

Jomo smiled. 'You were run over by a car in your homeland, and now you are in a coma,' he explained slowly. 'This is the dreamworld you are in, and it is your destiny to conquer your terror of everything you fear. The universal fear of all mankind.'

'I see,' Marion said. 'And I'm in Africa. Where in Africa?'

'In a tribal village in east Africa,' Jomo replied. 'In Rwanda, where the savannas meet the jungles.'

'Will I come out of this coma alive?' Marion asked.

'That depends.'

'On what?' Marion said fearfully.

'On whether you make it through the Integrity Test,' Jomo said calmly. 'But the Integrity Test is far off. First you have to master your fear, and then you have to learn the skills necessary to pacify dangerous beasts. Only then can you take on the Integrity Test — but there is still no guarantee that you will survive the ordeal. Many people have tried, and they died trying; their fear clouded their judgement.'

'I'll never conquer my fear,' Marion said, defeated before she began.

'You mean you *think* you'll never conquer your fear,' Jomo said, a glum smile on his lips. 'But if you have confidence and faith in yourself, that faith will give you special powers. The Bible says 'Faith can move mountains'. Have you heard of faith-healers, of whom Jesus Christ was one?'

'I don't believe in Jesus or the Bible,' Marion told Jomo. 'But I've heard of people with amazing healing powers. I don't know how they do it.'

'Faith,' Jomo repeated. 'With faith, your body is a natural healer. With faith, you can also calm an aggressive animal or human. Aggressive animals or humans play on their victim's fear. An animal smells fear. But with faith, you will conquer your fear so your body will adopt a relaxed, submissive and unthreatening posture, and most animals who see this will be put off from attacking you. You are terrified of many animals. But this terror is fear of what *can* or *might* happen, rather than fear of what really *will* happen — fear of what *can* be dangerous rather than what really *is* dangerous.

'In truth, most animals will not harm you unless you do something stupid or threaten or surprise them. And they will definitely attack you if you show fear or aggression, or if you run away. You cannot outrun a wild animal — nor can you fight it off. Humans are not made for fighting the way animals are. Fear is your worst enemy. If you conquer your fear, faith and confidence will come in no time. If faith enables faith-healers to cure people of a crippling illness or disease, then that same faith will enable you to pacify the most savage and deadly of animals — even sharks, who are the most ferocious of all so-called "dangerous" animals.'

'Are you trying to patronise me?' Marion snapped.

'No,' Jomo replied. 'The sharks that attacked your boat and devoured you in your nightmare were drawn towards you by your fear. Your screaming and your terror fed their aggression and killer instinct. Had you been calm and still, and had you not screamed or shown terror, the sharks would have just left you alone. To a greater or lesser extent, the same principal applies with aggressive humans. They play on their victim's terror and his or her screaming and aggression. But although sharks are among the most dreaded of all animals, very few actually attack people and even fewer kill people. Plenty of people have swum in shark-infested waters and come to no harm. This is because they were still, calm and passive, and they did not scream or splash or fight like the shark's prey. But your terror of those five sharks was very real. And they fed on your terror. Your terror drew them towards you.'

'I don't believe any of this bullshit!' Marion said, her anger increasing.

'Watch me and you'll learn,' Jomo told her wisely. 'Come outside with me.'

Marion followed him outside the hut and then they walked towards the end of the village. A large black Doberman barked, growled and snarled at Jomo with psychotic fury and hatred. Marion shuddered and sweated; she stood rooted to the spot, and covered her mouth with her hand so as not to scream. A sick, nauseous feeling tortured her gut and she whimpered as she watched the chief approach the dog. Jomo was passive and submissive, approaching the dog with caution and without fear and his hands fondled the beast's shoulders, back and neck. He talked to the dog softly and calmly.

'You're a good boy now,' he said. 'Nobody is going to hurt you.'

The dog's growling and snarling turned into a low whimpering sound as the Doberman rolled onto his back and Jomo caressed its chest and stroked his head. Marion was shocked. She remembered a scene in *The Next Karate Kid* where Mr Miyagi pacified an aggressive dog. When she had watched the film, she failed to believe that this was possible, but now she knew some people really could calm down vicious animals.

'How did you do that?' Marion demanded. 'That dog could've mauled you badly. And, by magic, you stopped him.'

'Faith, not magic,' Jomo repeated. 'But before you begin training, you will have to learn to understand the animals better. And this will be through encountering the spiritualism, worship, myths and superstitions surrounding the dangerous animals of Africa, Asia, the oceans, South America, North America and the Arctic. And through understanding the myths, worship and spiritualism, you will respect these animals in the same way that ancient tribes and different cultures have learned to do so. The dreamworld will not be like your world. Countries and continents will be joined in a way that they are not joined in reality. There will sometimes be imaginary borders, like a border between Africa and India, India and Siberia, Asia and South America. Your reality will be distorted, and animals will appear more savage than they normally are in the real world.'

'I see,' Marion replied, her voice shaking with fear. 'And if I wanted to travel from America to Europe, I only have to cross a border without the Atlantic Ocean in between?'

'In the dreamworld, anything is possible,' Jomo said. 'You can go from East Africa straight to West Africa without passing through the central regions in between. You can travel from South America to Canada or even the Arctic without Mexico and the United States in between. Countries, oceans, deserts, forests and mountain ranges can be eliminated and then reconjured at our convenience.'

'Okay,' Marion said. 'But how am I supposed to conquer my fear? I mean, where do I begin?'

'The spiritualism, worship and myths of dangerous animals in each continent occur in four stages,' Jomo began. 'The first stage is involved cult worship. Next, you'll learn of the different superstitions, legends and myths that relate to the animals. You will then find out how animals were exploited and used for food, clothes and medicines. Finally, you will be taught how to calm down a dangerous animal. There are similarities and differences between each continent in the cult worship, superstitions and legends and how animals are used for human benefit. There are also differences and similarities in how aggressive animals are calmed; our method involves food.'

Marion still failed to believe Jomo, but dared not argue with this intelligent warrior chief. Then she caught a glance of this middle-aged man waving his hands and chanting.

'What are you doing?' she needed to know.

'This is a combination of faith and magic,' Jomo said, as he stopped chanting. 'I cast a spell to make scenes enter our vision and become reality. This is the cult worship, the first stage of your training. And as these scenes come into our vision, I'll explain what they mean to you.'

Marion was amazed. She saw a scene full of elephants, as she herself and Jomo were stood between the savannas and the rainforest. The elephants were feeding on tree vegetation and drinking at the river, as well as showering themselves and their calves with their hose-like trunks. Marion was shaking with fear and brought her hand to her mouth, but Jomo caressed her hand with his right hand and held her gently with his left, his left arm draping around her back and shoulders in a reassuring manner.

'Fear not,' Jomo begged her gently. 'These elephants will not harm you. I'm here to protect you if anything happens.'

Suddenly, Marion felt safe in the arms of the

muscular black man with his long, formidable spear, and confidence came to her in a matter of minutes.

'This is beautiful,' Marion said. 'And I don't feel afraid. Tell me more about these elephants, Jomo.'

'African elephants are the largest of all land animals,' Jomo said. 'Only whales and whale sharks in the oceans are larger than elephants, but on land the African elephant is by far the largest beast, followed by the Indian elephant, then the hippo, then the rhinos and the yeti or abominable snowman.'

'The yeti!' Marion exclaimed. She lacked belief that the yeti existed.

'You'll find out about the yeti later,' Jomo informed her. 'First concentrate on these elephants. We believe that these are not only the largest and strongest of all land animals, but also intelligent and wise. Look at those female elephants nurturing their calves.'

Marion watched with awe and wonder, her teeth slightly clenched. 'I know they are intelligent, but why are they wise?' she asked.

'Because, for all their great size and strength, they are extremely gentle,' Jomo explained. 'And if one member of the elephant herd is attacked or injured, the rest of the herd will rally to its aid, even if it means putting their own lives in danger. Watch those black rhinos and white rhinos attacking that elephant in order to drink at the river. Then see how the other elephants react.'

Three black rhinos and two larger white

rhinos attacked and gored the male elephant, the rhinos trumpeting, wailing and screaming with gut-chilling savagery and hatred. The elephant was seriously injured and screamed in his pain and distress. The other elephants charged the five rhinos with fearsome power, speed and ferocity. Marion was horrified, not seeing any wisdom in this battle, only that the elephants were protecting their own kind.

'They really care about each other and gently nurture their own kind,' Jomo said, 'which is why they are wise.'

The elephants trumpeted and bellowed like the rhinos, and both species fought a running battle. The rhinos reared up on their hind legs and kicked out with their front hooves, as well as lowering their horns to fend off the attacking elephants. However, the elephants surrounded and outnumbered the rhinos, like a pack of wolves attacking a deer, and plunged their tusks into the rhinos.

The rhinos retreated and decided to drink farther downriver. Then the gentleness of the elephants emerged again, as the enormous beasts tended to and cleaned the injuries on the wounded male elephant, and the females nurtured their frightened calves. As the injured bull heaved from his wounds, the other elephants used their delicate trunks to gather clay from the riverbank and apply the clay to the bull's wounds.

'What are they doing?' Marion needed to know.

'Applying styptic clay to this elephant's

injuries to stop the blood flowing from his wounds,' Jomo replied. 'And it works. The clay stops the flow of blood and helps to heal an elephant's injuries. This proves an elephant's intelligence, wisdom and gentleness. They are almost equal to us humans in intelligence and reasoning ability. They also have very good memories. An elephant never forgets.'

'I've heard that an elephant never forgets,' Marion said, and chuckled. 'What about those dead elephants over there? What happened to them?'

'That is supposedly the elephants' graveyard, where it is assumed that old elephants with large tusks go to die,' Jomo explained. 'But the tusks are missing, see? This proves that they were massacred by poachers. An elephant herd may also be wiped out by drought when the rivers and waterholes dry up, causing them to die of hunger and thirst.'

'I see,' Marion said, a slight chill in her voice.

'Turn round and you'll see how we use tamed elephants to round up wild ones,' Jomo said.

'Why do you round up wild elephants?'

'So they can work in our corrals and build huts and lodges for us natives and the white men. They tear down trees to produce wood, and then we convert the wood into buildings.'

Marion turned round and watched the tamed elephants surrounding wild forest elephants and herding them into the enclosures called corrals. 'This is fascinating,' she said. 'Are elephants worshipped by native Africans?'

'No,' Jomo replied slowly. 'But elephants in India, China and south-east Asia have always been worshipped, and still are, to some extent. But you'll learn more about that when your dream takes you from here to Asia. And now I'll show you another few scenes involving native tribesmen taking on a variety of dangerous animals.' The vision was transformed into a colourful view overlooking the savanna and the river. In order to prove their manhood, a group of Maasai warriors hurled their spears and the two rhinos died as the spearheads became embedded in their hearts.

Next, Marion was shown another group of warriors throwing spears at an elephant, killing it.

A third scene involved the Maasai warriors stalking an African buffalo. The buffalo was a lethal adversary as deadly as any elephant or rhino, but he realised his danger too late. The buffalo charged, but the warriors sent their spears and arrows flying into the enormous beast and killed him.

The fourth scene showed a group of young Maasai warriors in Kenya. Two lions bellowed and roared with savage aggression and rage at the sight of the warriors with their weapons. The huge beasts charged forwards with awesome power and explosive speed, their solid muscles rippling. The Maasai warriors hurled their spears towards the lions, and the massive cats were slain.

Marion was terrified of the beasts that were charging the tribesmen. However, she was also horrified at how these animals were being ruthlessly slayed with spears and arrows, for beneath her fear of these fearsome beasts lay a sentimental sympathy and compassion.

Jomo turned towards Marion. 'The last two scenes I want to show you will be of Maasai warriors killing a huge male gorilla, a vicious warthog and a savage bush pig,' she said.

Marion gulped and her teeth chattered. The next scene appeared before her. She watched as a warthog and a bush pig hurtled across the grass with lethal power and lightning speed, the bush pig larger and more vicious than the warthog. Both wild pigs screamed and squealed as they charged, but the Maasai warriors sent their spears thudding into their flanks and continued butchering the beasts until they died.

In Marion's eyes, the warthog and the bush pig were as lethal as the wild boars she had seen in Europe; the bush pig's charge, especially, seemed as deadly and savage as that of the lion or the buffalo. The last scene took place in the jungle, where several tribesmen had cornered a huge gorilla. The gorilla was defending some smaller females, but he was not the dominant silverback male. Even so, he let out a deafening roar, his clubbed fists like giant hams pounding his deep chest and his huge muscles rippling through his massive arms and body. Marion held her breath as the tribesmen killed the gorilla with their spears.

'Why was killing these animals necessary?' Marion wanted to know. 'I fear many animals, but I hate animal cruelty even more.'

'Killing animals is a way of life for us,' Jomo told her. 'As you eat pork, chicken, beef or lamb in your country, we have to kill these animals to survive. We kill a few elephants, but not too many. They provide us with meat and ivory. We trade the ivory for food, clothes and medicine to sustain our families. We hunt rhinos, buffaloes and gorillas for the same reasons, to support ourselves with meat and medicine. We also hunt rhinos to prove our manhood, but this is a more common situation in South Africa. We kill hippos, warthogs and bush pigs for both meat and trophies, like a hippo's tusks. But the most common animal to be killed as a token of manhood is the lion. The Maasai tribes in Kenya and many other tribes in Africa kill lions to prove their manhood, bravery and strength. A boy does not become a man until he has killed a lion.'

'But that's cruel, Jomo,' Marion said.

'To you Europeans it is cruel,' Jomo replied. 'But not to us Africans. There is much that you do not know about the world's tribes and their ways and customs. But you will learn.'

'What is the next scene?' Marion asked, sighing.

'The next scene involves the hippo,' Jomo told her. 'It begins with how the hippo changed its diet from animals and fish to vegetation. Legend has it that the hippo was eating too many animals and fish from the river, so the gods cast a spell on the hippo which changed its canine teeth into tusks. And every time the great beast passed dung from its anus, it had to spray off the dung with its tail so the gods could search the dung for animal bones or fish bones. If there were no bones coming out with the dung, it meant that the hippo was not guilty of eating animals or fish. Watch the hippos over in the river spraying the dung about with their tails.' The hippos swatted the dung with their tails, but no fish or animal bones came out. The hippos were innocent. Then the hippos yawned at each other.

'Those hippos look exhausted,' Marion said. 'They're yawning.'

'They're not exhausted; they are becoming aggressive,' Jomo explained. 'Hippos are always at their most dangerous when they are yawning and showing off their tusks. It means that they intend to fight other hippos or attack lions, crocodiles or humans. Different animals have different ways of demonstrating dominance or aggression to other animals or humans. The elephant spreads out his ears and raises his trunk and tusks. The rhino rakes the ground with his hooves and lowers his head and horns. The buffalo lowers his horns to protect his head and body, rather like the rhino. The lion sweeps back his bushy mane, curls his lips and exposes his fangs. The gorilla bashes his chest with his fists whilst screaming and roaring. And the hippo opens his mouth, exposing his fearsome tusks. If yawning does not deter other hippos or crocodiles, then the hippo will bellow and roar; his war cry is far more savage and deafening than those of the elephant or the rhino. When two bull hippos fight, they do so with extreme ferocity, and cow hippos will fight to defend their calves — rather like elephants, rhinos or buffaloes will. When a hippo yawns, always give the beast a wide berth. But walk away slowly, do not run! Remember, a hippo can run much faster than a human, and that applies to all wild animals.'

'Wow,' said Marion, mulling over the new information. She saw the hippos yawning at some crocodiles, and the crocodiles wisely retreated. She turned to Jomo again and asked, 'Where does the cult worship of dangerous animals come in?'

'First of all, elephants, hippos, rhinos, buffaloes and gorillas are not worshipped by Africans,' Jomo informed her. 'But lions and crocodiles *are* worshipped. I've already told you that all five herbivores, plus lions and crocodiles, are hunted for meat, medicines and trophies, and rhinos and lions are hunted as a token of manhood. Warthogs and bush pigs are also hunted for their meat, heads and tusks. Amongst religious communities like the Bantus, the buffalo is respected, revered and sacrificed at sacred ceremonies. However, the Zulus of southern Africa think that the buffalo can possess the soul of a human being. Watch the Bantus and Zulus worshipping and revering the buffaloes whom they have killed.'

Marion witnessed the Bantu ceremony, as the black men sacrificed the buffalo meat to their god, and then the Zulus eating buffalo meat. And shortly to follow, she watched the souls of dead Zulu warriors leaving the Zulus and passing into the buffaloes, the huge, muscle-bound beasts congregating in a herd.

'And what is the scene after that?' Marion asked.

'The next scene takes place in the jungle, on the imaginary border between the Congo and Cameroon,' Jomo said. The vision changed, and they found themselves in the rainforests bordering Cameroon. 'And here is where gorillas share their range with baboons and their cousins, the drills and mandrills. There are gorillas throughout central and western Africa, and baboons can be found throughout the whole of Africa, both in the rainforest and out on the savanna. Drills can be found in Nigeria and Cameroon, whereas mandrills live in Gabon and Cameroon. Africa has many other species of apes and monkeys, but only four species of Africa's primates are really dangerous to humankind: gorillas, baboons, drills and mandrills. Fortunately, they are not usually dangerous to humans, only to predators like snakes, leopards and black panthers. But watch this next scene.'

The rainforests resounded with the roaring of the male gorillas, and the screaming and barking of the baboons, drills and mandrills. A group of humans approached the gorillas, but the gorillas showed the humans what fruits were edible and passed the fruits to the humans. And the gorillas and humans treated each other as friends and companions. Over the border in Cameroon, the baboons, drills and mandrills were being greedy and devouring antelope carcasses and fruits like gluttons. This showed the baboons and their cousins to be selfish and inconsiderate of each other.

'What does all this mean?' Marion enquired.

'It means apes and monkeys represent the good and bad attributes of human beings in the eyes of white people,' Jomo answered wisely. 'That was far back in time when the white men first colonised West Africa. They also represented greed, selfishness and inquisitiveness. You can see the baboons, drills and mandrills being selfish, and greedily tearing the antelope carcasses and gorging on fruits. Added to this, baboons are very savage and aggressive. Drills and mandrills are even more ferocious and quick-tempered, and gorillas are also reputed to be extremely fierce, but this reputation is not as evident to native Africans as it is to the white men. We respect gorillas, baboons, drills and mandrills. And although gorillas are known to be aggressive and savage, the native tribes of the Congo regard them as the friends and companions of humans, showing the humans what fruits and leaves are nice to eat. That's why you saw those gorillas showing the humans what fruits and leaves were edible and sharing the vegetation food with the humans.'

'So, in many ways, the gorillas are like humans. They are cousins of humankind,'

Marion said thoughtfully.

'You're right, they're very much like humans,' Jomo answered, smiling. 'Many villages in the Congo used to believe that gorillas were not animals at all, but were people of the forest. They believed they were humans who had lost the power of speech, and so they referred to the gorillas as "the great tribes without speech".'

'It's all very fascinating,' Marion told Jomo. 'Which other animals feature in your spiritualism?'

'We will come to that later,' Jomo replied. 'First we'll return to our village in Rwanda and have a rest. Then I'll explain more superstitions, legends and myths surrounding our lethal creatures. Let's go!'

Marion and Jomo made their way through the jungle until they were back in Rwanda, and then they found themselves in Jomo's tribal village. They spotted his tribe worshipping some crocodiles, feeding them with chunks of meat and treating the massive reptiles with great respect. Then the men retreated as the crocodiles watched them with evil and sinister eyes.

'Why are your men feeding the crocodiles?' Marion asked Jomo.

'Because some tribes in Africa worship crocodiles and treat them with enormous respect,' Jomo explained, 'whilst other tribes hate and dread these reptiles as man-eaters and as messengers of evil. My tribe is one of those that worships the crocodiles. We do so because we believe the beasts have a fertility role, and because we believe the crocodile is an ancestor spirit.'

'Do you really believe that?' Marion said.

'The beliefs of tribes and cultures all over the world are different from Western beliefs,' Jomo replied. 'Who is to say who is right and who is wrong? We have ways and means of proving that medicines cure illnesses, how bone and horn from gorillas and rhinos can be turned into medicines and how animals represent certain roles, like the crocodile representing fertility and being an ancestor spirit. Look over there, at the river to the south.'

Marion watched as myth and fantasy became reality. Crocodiles who had died a hundred years ago were suddenly reincarnated as men and women. Other crocodiles who were alive in the present day were passing dung onto the crops in order to make the crops fertile.

'Now I see it all,' Marion agreed. 'The crocodiles' dung makes the crops fertile, and the men and women shown here are descended from crocodiles who died long ago.'

'There is more,' Jomo pointed out. 'The crocodile's appearance itself makes the crops fertile. That's why my tribe is worshipping these crocodiles now, for their presence and the dung they produce will guarantee my tribe a good harvest. And when people die, their spirits become crocodiles again. A man has died in that hut over there to the north. Watch his spirit leaving the hut and turning into a crocodile.' Marion gritted her teeth with sheer amazement and wonder as she witnessed the man's spirit passing outside the thatched hut and becoming a crocodile. The crocodile emerged and joined the other crocodiles.

'Jesus Christ!' Marion exclaimed. 'Is it really true?'

'It is true,' Jomo said evenly. 'But not everybody's spirit becomes a crocodile, for some spirits become other animals, like buffaloes and lions. When a chief dies, his spirit enters a lion's body and he becomes a lion. So, if I were to die tomorrow, I would become a lion.'

Marion swore, then shook her head and said, 'Going back to the role of fertility, which animals have that role other than crocodiles?'

'Only one: the leopard,' Jomo said. 'In Africa, the leopard is a highly respected and revered totemic animal. In some countries, totems have been built for leopards as they have also been built for lions and crocodiles. In the western parts of Africa, the big cat is a storm god, and its growling warns of rain and thunder. You see, in Africa we need rainfall as much as we need sunshine. If the weather were too hot, our crops would die, but rain keeps the crops and the land healthy. Just look at the spotted leopard over there with the black panther.'

Marion glanced at the two big cats as they growled and snarled.

'So the leopard and the black panther

represent rain and thunder, and the crocodile represents the fertility itself?' Marion said, her voice full of wonder.

'That's right,' Jomo replied. 'But we're also terrified of the leopard and the crocodile. The leopard embodies aggression, cunning and courage; it is more devious and dreaded than the lion. The black panthers are the most aggressive and cunning of all leopards. The crocodile is even more terrifying — not only as a voracious man-eater, but as messengers of evil. As well as bringing fertility, these crocodiles bring evil and disaster. These crocodiles will let evil and wickedness run loose on the village and its people.'

'Oh m-my God!' Marion stammered. 'What am I supposed to do? Will the village survive this catastrophe?'

'We'll see,' Jomo said half-heartedly. 'But you must stay protected in my thatched hut when the evil runs loose. Do not venture outside the hut. My tribesmen and I will use whatever means possible to ward off the evil that these crocodiles cause.'

Chief Jomo and Marion retreated into Jomo's hut. Marion felt exhausted. She fell into her bed, whilst Jomo sank into his bed of lion skins with his spear by his side. His wife brought some fruit to him.

'No, Miriam, I do not want this fruit,' Jomo told her. 'I do not have much of an appetite.'

Miriam made her way outside the hut to replace the fruit at the village market, and then she returned to the hut and lay down on the bed beside her husband.

Marion tried to ignore the anxiety, the feeling in her throat – the fear, dread and worry. Eventually, she succumbed to sleep.

* * *

Marion awoke to hear women screaming, men shouting and the crocodiles roaring and snarling. Miriam was also awake, but Jomo wasn't present in the hut. Marion dared not leave her bed, for she was petrified as dread chilled her blood and numbed her legs and body. She now saw the reason behind the belief that crocodiles were messengers of evil, wickedness and disaster. Miriam was also terrified and cowered in her bed.

Finally, Marion summoned enough courage to jump out of bed and to witness what was going on. Curiosity had overcome her, and she felt that whatever was happening outside could not have been worse than waiting to see the outcome in the hut.

She was wrong.

Pure mayhem and disaster had broken loose on the village. There were dead bodies everywhere.

'Oh my God!' Marion cried as she saw Chief Jomo's body being torn apart by a massive crocodile.

The other tribesmen were confronting the crocodiles, but the devilish reptiles were violently strong and incredibly fast, and more crocodiles came on the scene.

Disease had befallen those dead men and women in the village and near the river on that terrible black night, and the malicious reptiles closed in on the corpses like submarines on a convoy of ships. The crocodiles devoured the dead and dying humans, and they were roaring, snarling and hissing at the warriors as the armed men hurled their spears towards them.

Two men defended Jomo's body. The reptiles thrashed around and lashed out at the men with their tails. Three of them fastened their teeth into three men who were knocked down. These crocodiles were massive and had strong, thrashing tails that were powerful enough to break a man's legs with one blow. Their monstrous heads were armed with immense, vice-like jaws and bone-crushing teeth that would tear off a man's leg or arm as a crocodile spun round in a death-roll. The crocodiles turned suddenly against these three men with lethal speed and power, wrenching off their arms or legs, and Marion witnessed this terrifying spectacle with utter horror. A chill ran down her spine and into her stomach, her heart hammered and her legs trembled like the ground beneath a herd of stampeding elephants.

But worse was to follow.

Hippos closed in on the village like lions to a buffalo. The crocodiles retreated and dived into the river upon their approach, knowing the hippos were even more awesome and ruthless than they were. The women sobbed over the bodies of the dead and dying, but the armed men confronted a new danger.

Uniting with the hippos were white rhinos, black rhinos and buffaloes from the savanna, with warthogs and bush pigs taking up the rear. A hostile chorus of hatred echoed through the savanna and rainforest as the beasts snorted, bellowed and screamed. The sounds jarred Marion's nerves and turned her stomach. In her terror, she ran towards the hut's toilet bucket and threw up. Urine flowed down her legs and sweat soaked her forehead and body. She ran towards the window again and could not help staring through this hole in the hut.

The hippos' gaping mouths were as big as caves, with huge tusks that would easily smash large boats to pieces. The rhinos had hooves that could break all a man's bones and great horns that could destroy a truck in seconds. The beasts' eyes were cold and sinister. The buffaloes were enormous black beasts with savage red eyes and horns longer than a bull's, but despite their immense size would easily outrun the fastest human.

The village's warriors were surrounded by all these lethal giants, but Jomo's son, Guamo, a muscular, bearded twenty-seven-year-old, was taking control of the situation.

'Give them all of your crops,' Guamo insisted. 'That's what they're after.'

Marion remembered Jomo telling her how the fourth stage of each period of her training was how to calm down aggressive animals, and the Africans used food to pacify or appease dangerous beasts; meat or fish for predators, and vegetables, plants or fruits for herbivores. There was no time for the tribesmen to argue so they cut bushes with their machetes and hurled the vegetation to the rhinos. Then they collected the vegetables, fruits, bamboo and cereals from the village market and flung them to the hippos and wild pigs. The men finished by throwing wild grasses and bamboo to the buffaloes.

The formidable beasts were eventually appeased by the feast. Their rage faded, and Marion fainted. The village was saved.

Miriam hurried over towards the unconscious Marion and slapped her face to bring her round. She called Guamo, her and Jomo's son. The bearded black man hurried into the hut and tried to help revive Marion, but she remained unconscious.

CHAPTER 3

Thunder ripped across the sky as rain fell upon the land. The crops were fresh for the harvest, and as soon as the rain came to a stop the women brought in the harvest. The men killed some of the livestock, just as the cows, sheep and goats gave birth to youngsters. Marion watched all this with interest. Then, the new chief, Guamo, approached her from behind.

'The leopard, the black panther and the crocodiles served us well,' he began. 'They gave us the rain and thunder and protected the fertility of the crops.'

Marion turned and saw a look of sadness on the young man's face behind his exterior of confidence.

'You must be upset about your father's death…' she said quietly.

'I am upset,' Guamo told her. 'But I know that his life as a lion will be even better than his life as a chief.'

Marion turned towards Jomo's grave and saw the warriors leaving lion claws in the grave. 'Why are they placing lion claws into your father's grave?' she asked.

'Putting lion claws into a chief's grave guarantees that the chief's spirit will be reincarnated as a lion, and this lion will protect the land and control the fertility of crops and livestock, ensuring the tribe's survival,' Guamo explained. 'Now, watch my father's soul leaving his grave and entering a lion's body.'

Marion caught a glance of Jomo's spirit passing out of his body, flowing through the air and then entering the huge, muscle-bound body of a male lion.

'This lion and the rest of his pride will be protected by the village people,' Guamo said. 'If this lion were killed by the villagers, it would spell doom on our crops and livestock because he protects the village and the farmland. That is why people protect but also avoid him. But there are superstitions about lions that are held by individual tribal people in most of eastern and central Africa, especially Kenya. Some humans believe that lions speak our languages and are able to plot like humans. Another belief is that a lion which kills humans possesses powerful magic.'

'This is fascinating,' Marion said. 'Carry on.'

'To take this belief in magic further, there used to be the belief that the beasts are wizards and witches who have transformed themselves into lions and lionesses,' Guamo continued. 'There is also a belief that a dead man can dig himself out of his grave and become a lion. There are many other beliefs like these. For example, some people think that a magic charm made from a lion's claws and worn around your leg makes you immune to a bullet fired from a rifle. There are also beliefs connecting leopards and hyenas to witchcraft — but we will come to that situation later.'

Marion and Guamo stared into space, lost in thoughts of humans transforming into lions and coming back from the dead. Then thunder tore across the sky again.

'It appears that another storm is coming,' Marion observed. 'I hope your crops and livestock stay fertile.'

'The new crops have been sewn and the young livestock have been born,' Guamo said, smiling. 'Now we must go inside the hut, and you can help my mother with the cooking.'

'Cooking would give me great pleasure,' Marion told him, also smiling.

The two of them retreated into the hut.

Marion, Miriam and Chief Guamo were eating ostrich egg with a mixture of vegetables and the meat of ostrich and warthog. The ostrich meat was tough and tasted like beef, whilst the warthog meat was similar to pork.

'This is a delicious meal,' Marion enthused. 'Miriam, you sure are a great cook.'

'You must also take some credit,' Guamo praised Marion. 'I enjoyed watching you helping Mother in the kitchen.'

'I'd bet you did,' Marion said between mouthfuls of food.

Guamo grinned. 'But I must tell you another piece of cult worship, again concerning the lion,' he said. 'Lions are symbols of strength, bravery, courage, leadership and ferocity. Tribal chiefs and political leaders see themselves as lions and have lions as their emblems. King Richard the First, who ruled England in the twelfth century, was called Richard the Lionheart. Lions and wild boars appeared on medieval coats of arms and shields, and some African chiefs wear lion skins when hunting game or going into battle. In some parts of Africa, as well as Asia, there are totems for lions, tigers and leopards, as all three big cats symbolise strength, bravery and leadership.'

'That explains more why the lion is called the king of beasts,' Marion replied. 'But the true king of beasts is the tiger, if you ask me. The tiger is larger, stronger, more cunning and savage than the lion. But people see the lion as a gentleman and don't feel the same way about the tiger.'

'To some Asian cultures, the tiger is a gentleman, whilst to other cultures he is cruel and treacherous,' Guamo told her. 'But to all cultures, the lion is a gentleman. And now the storm has ended, and the crops and livestock are fertile. It is time that I gave you a tour of the savanna and jungle, so you feel like a free woman who knows the area. A woman who is not tied to the home.'

'Is this another educational trip?' Marion enquired.

'It is,' Guamo answered. 'For you, the cult worship has ended, and the real superstitions and legends have begun. You must get plenty of rest. Our trip will begin in the evening. And now I must rest.'

'Be my guest,' Marion said.

Marion set off with Guamo that evening, and the atmosphere and smell of the savanna evoked feelings of awe, wonder and apprehension in Marion — awe and wonder because she admired the spectacle and beauty of the savanna and its wildlife, and apprehension because many lethal beasts roamed the wilderness, ranging in size from elephants, hippos and buffaloes down to a honey badger, a lynx-like caracal and a serval. The honey badger is related to the badgers and weasels of Europe, whilst the other two killers are smaller wild cats. Marion's terror was very real, and Guamo placed a reassuring hand on her narrow shoulders.

'You'll be fine,' he promised. 'These animals are not dangerous. The most peaceful creatures are the zebras, antelopes, impalas and gazelles. Also, the giraffes are gentle; they keep the leaves of the trees in check.' The zebras gathered in a herd with the antelope, impalas and gazelles while the giraffes consumed the leaves of the trees until the trees were bare. Then the zebras and giraffes drank at the river alongside the warthogs and bush pigs. Marion could see some hippos submerging themselves in the muddy-green depths of the water. Elephants and buffaloes joined the other beasts. Nearby, a pride of lions and lionesses tugged at the remains of a fresh zebra carcass.

'Those are Jomo's lions. You see that male lion eating the first share of the zebra? He is my father,' Guamo informed Marion. 'My father's spirit will be our guardian angel. The male lions always have first share of a kill before the lionesses can eat, and then it's the cubs' turn.'

'I see,' Marion replied.

They strolled further across the savanna. As darkness began to draw in, they saw a honey badger and some smaller wild cats of Africa. The honey badger fought a savage battle with a python and finally killed the large snake, this proving the honey badger's strength, ferocity and reckless boldness. A caracal and a serval fought viciously against an eagle and a hawk, both wild cats hissing and spitting like snakes, their razor-sharp claws slashing. The fierce birds cut swiftly through the air, lowering their fearsome talons as they swooped down. However, the caracal finally killed the eagle with a powerful blow from his right paw, whilst the serval repeated this swift, hammer-like blow against the hawk with his left paw. Both birds of prey were in heaps on the grass, and the cats tore them to pieces with their vicious claws and fangs. They were strong, bold and fierce, but the honey badger was the most powerful and savage small predator in Africa.

'These killers are amazing!' Marion exclaimed, her voice a mixture of wonder and fear. 'Which of these three should I fear the most?'

'None of them,' Guamo reassured her. 'They

will avoid you if you avoid them. However, honey badgers are the worst of the three; they are not only brave enough to kill a python, as we have seen, but they have been known to bring down an adult buffalo several times their own size and weight. Not even lions, leopards or hyenas will face a honey badger.'

Marion shuddered at the thought of being faced with an enraged honey badger, and then she turned to Guamo again. 'So what exactly is the purpose of this walkabout?' she asked nervously.

'For you to confront your fear,' Guamo told her.

Marion gasped, but Guamo went on before she could say a word.

'You will do this by facing the five top predators of Africa after the crocodile. The crocodile attacks and kills humans without provocation, but these other killers are not man-killers by nature. They are the lion, the leopard, the hyena, the African hunting dog and the jackal. The jackal is the smallest and least dangerous of the five, but lions and hyenas are the top predators of Africa.'

'Oh no, Guamo!' Marion protested. 'I cannot overcome my fear!'

'"Cannot" is not an African word,' Guamo said. 'If you are strong-willed, there is a way. There is nothing more powerful than the human mind; not even the body is as powerful as the brain.'

'V-very well, but I'm going to end up in a predator's belly,' Marion stuttered, chewing a nail.

'Fight your fear,' Guamo said firmly. 'Remember, fear is your worst enemy. Now come with me to the top of this hill and lie low. You will see two leopards: the spotted leopard and the black panther. Both are large males weighing a hundred and twenty pounds.'

Marion trembled, but trusted in Guamo to protect her should the leopards carry out an attack.

Guamo and Marion crawled through the sharp elephant grass; Marion's face and hands were cut by the grass, which sliced through delicate skin like knives. Her blood mixed with sweat and was chilled by the freezing African night. They watched a gang of women chanting in a circle. Close to them were five hyenas.

'I thought we came here to see leopards,' Marion said softly. 'But all I see are weird women chanting, surrounded by five hyenas.'

'These women are witches,' Guamo explained. 'You may not have noticed, but in the jungle there are plenty of old people lying dead. Well, these hyenas are the spirits of those old people, for old men and women who die may be reincarnated as hyenas. In African spiritualism, hyenas are messengers of evil, like crocodiles, and they are carriers of witches and wizards. Those hyenas next to the witches are evil; they are going to carry the witches on their backs.

'Now, you want to know about leopards. Well, these witches are also casting out evil souls from their own bodies so they can pursue wickedness in the form of a leopard or a black panther. But the leopards started life as humans. At night, some humans transform themselves into leopards. They are called wereleopards.'

Marion watched as two black men appeared — the wereleopards. Her mind flashed back to medieval European myths about werewolves, men who became wolves at night. It seemed European mythology was linked to African mythology sometimes.

'Now watch,' Guamo whispered, fear emerging in his voice. 'The witches have two white men as their prisoners. They're going to use the wereleopards to kill the men.'

'We must stop them!' Marion whispered back, horrified.

'No!' Guamo asserted. 'You should not mess with witches or magic. We are only two humans against five witches. No man or woman can fight magic.'

'Oh no,' Marion sighed.

'Now be quiet,' Guamo whispered urgently.

The white men were petrified as the black men altered their physique; one became a huge leopard while the other became a large black panther.

The leopards hissed, spat and snarled with venomous hatred and fury, and then darted towards the white men. They lunged, their claws ripping into the men as their fangs tore at their throats. The white men were dead in ten seconds. Marion gasped and turned her face away with horror, and Guamo comforted her.

'This must be very traumatic for you,' Guamo said softly. 'But it was necessary to convey to you how witches and their souls and the spirits of dead people can commit evil in the form of leopards and hyenas. However, you must remember it was not leopards who killed those prisoners; it was men who are wereleopards. Real leopards are not a threat to humans if left alone, and the same thing applies to hyenas. It is wereleopards and werehyenas who kill people, just as werewolves are believed to in Europe.'

The witches suddenly turned to face them, eyes burning with hatred.

'Quick — we must escape!' Guamo shouted.

In their terror, Marion and Guamo jumped to their feet and ran down the hill into the jungle. They could hear the witches racing after them on their hyenas and knew that they could never outrun the beasts. The hyenas were laughing and baying with malicious hatred as the witches urged them to attack, and Marion's blood froze when she heard the chilling cries. She knew that, in some areas of Africa, hyenas had a fearsome reputation and were even considered to be dominant over lions and crocodiles. A hyena's jaws could easily bite off a human's limb, tear a zebra to pieces or even fatally wound a buffalo.

'I can't move,' Marion gasped, once they were deep in the jungle. She leant against a tree, panting. 'I'm finished. You must go on without me.'

'No, I will not leave you. We will face the witches and hyenas with help from African hunting dogs and jackals.'

'What?!'

Guamo looked around but could no longer see the witches. Reassured, he said, 'I must explain more mythology to you, this time about wild dogs. In African spiritualism, hunting dogs and jackals are useful friends and heroes to humans; they are intelligent and resourceful. White people generally dread the world's wolves and wild dogs; they think they are bloodthirsty, evil killers. This applies not only to wolves and coyotes in Europe and North America, but also to hunting dogs in Africa, dholes in Asia and jackals in both Africa and Asia. However, native tribes and cultures from Africa, Asia, Australia and North America regard wild dogs as friends, companions and heroes. To most white people, African hunting dogs have a reputation for savagery; they have even been called the hounds from hell. But these hunting dogs and jackals will save us from the witches and hyenas. The hunting dogs will outnumber and kill the hyenas whilst the jackals attack the witches. And now, you must stand your ground with me.'

Marion's sweat stuck to her slender body and soaked her hair. As she trembled like somebody with a fever, nausea came up from her stomach to her throat and her eyes were filled with terror.

To Marion, there were no beasts on Earth worse than hyenas and wild dogs; she remembered the vicious wolf attack in the Bavarian Forest thirteen years ago. To her, hyenas and hunting dogs were worse than wolves, yet now she was being asked to accept that the beasts were on her side and would save her and the young chief. She bit her lip.

The hyenas had caught up to them now. She could hear them laughing and baying with bloodlust as they came into view, their evil eyes glowing amber and their dreaded, gnarling teeth jagged and powerful. The witches sneered with malice, and Marion raised her hand to her mouth to prevent herself from screaming or being sick. Guamo's hand squeezed her shoulder briefly, then he raised his spear and prepared to fight.

Suddenly, the atmosphere was ignited by the bloodthirsty barking of the jackals and gruesome growling of the hunting dogs. Marion whipped around and saw the savage wild dogs emerging from the savanna to confront the hyenas. Their eyes burned with ferocity, their jaws snapped at the air and their sinuous muscles rippled under their skin. The hyenas were more powerful, with stronger jaws and teeth, but the twenty hunting dogs outnumbered them by four to one, and there were five jackals to every witch. The barking of the jackals and the savage snarling of the hunting dogs made Marion feel numb with terror. She threw up. Her sweat chilled her body as she gasped for breath, fighting the foul taste left in her mouth.

'Back, you bastards!' Guamo yelled, partly to deter the hyenas but also to bolster his own courage and edge the wild dogs on to attack the hyenas and witches. The hyenas and hunting dogs lunged towards each other as the jackals charged the witches, and a blood-curdling battle was fought across the savanna. The hyenas killed five hunting dogs with their dreaded jaws and teeth, but the fifteen survivors tore the hyenas to pieces with their terrible teeth.

The jackals mauled the witches, and the evil women fled into the jungle with gaping wounds. Only three hyenas survived the battle — though they had broken legs and torn flanks. They limped slowly across the savanna, easy targets, but the hunting dogs and jackals did not give chase; they had seen a new danger.

The two wereleopards had found them.

They came into Marion's view from the jungle. The leopards snarled, making Marion's blood curdle. Guamo gripped his spear even tighter. Marion was frozen and could not move a muscle, but Guamo raised his spear defiantly.

'Back, you bastards!' he yelled, repeating the words he had screamed to the hyenas and witches. But the snarling of the wereleopards developed into an aggressive screaming sound, much like chainsaws cutting into wood. Of all Africa's predators, only the savage bellowing of crocodiles is dreaded more than the fiery screaming of leopards.

The wereleopards screamed again, but with their superior numbers the hunting dogs and jackals were not deterred. Even Guamo was not intimidated, and the leopards hesitated a little way off, eyeing their enemy.

From the savannas of Africa to the steaming jungles of Asia, wild dogs are dominant over leopards and black panthers; their strength is in their numbers. To a solitary predator like the leopard, avoiding injury is essential because even a minor wound can affect its ability to hunt and kill prey.

Marion saw the wereleopards hesitate and her heart fluttered in hope. She knew that, for all their reputation for cowardice, the jackals had been very bold and fierce in attacking the witches and would be good allies to the hunting dogs in defying the wereleopards.

Sure enough, the hunting dogs and hyenas growled and snarled in fierce hatred, and the wereleopards turned tail and darted back into the jungle.

Marion took some deep, steadying breaths and then fell against Guamo's broad chest. She began to sob and whimper. Guamo embraced her to his muscular body, caressing her back and shoulders and fondling her hair.

'You'll be fine,' he assured her. 'Now that the witches are gone, those wereleopards will never bother us again. They are like real leopards, in a way: they go out of their way to avoid trouble.'

Marion's tears soaked her face. 'Can we go back to your village?' she pleaded.

'Your wish is my command,' Guamo said. They thanked the wild dogs, who made their way back across the sunbaked savanna. In the distance, Guamo spotted some lions and lionesses watching them. These were Jomo's lions, he felt sure. He smiled slightly and slowly led Marion back to the village.

* * *

The following morning, Marion awoke and climbed out of bed to join Guamo and Miriam. She made her way towards the two of them and then sat down in a comfortable chair. It was a strong chair, made from forest vines and lianas and held together by a lion skin, but despite her comfort the previous night's chain of events on the savanna still plagued her.

'Did you sleep well?' Guamo asked her.

'I did, thank you,' Marion replied. 'Why are you looking at me like that?'

'Because we have reached the third stage of your education,' Guamo informed her. 'We have completed cult worship, superstitions and legends. Now I must tell you how we use dangerous animals for food, clothes and medicines.'

'That sounds more appealing than that incident we had last night with the hyenas and leopards,' Marion said bitterly.

'I had to assess you,' Guamo told her. 'I

needed to see the extent of your fear of other animals. Your terror made you freeze and vomit. I can see there is much work to be done. But if you have faith, in time you will master your fear.'

'I'm listening,' Marion said.

'Look, here I have hands cut from dead gorillas,' Guamo began. 'As a tribe, we kill very few gorillas — only enough to meet our needs. These gorilla hands transfer the gorilla's power to humans. If we possess these gorilla hands, we will be strong and powerful.'

'I see,' Marion replied, not really believing this superstition. But then she felt the gorilla's power flowing through her as Guamo passed the gorilla hands to her. She began to believe the young chief.

'In this pot we have the powdered bones of a gorilla's fingers,' Guamo said. 'If you rub the powder into a cut on your skin, the powder will heal it. Here, try it.'

Marion took a handful of the powder from Guamo and rubbed the substance into her arms and hands, which had been severely cut by the sharp elephant grass the previous night. She also smeared the powder into the scratches on her face. She was shocked to find that all the cuts healed in no time. The superstitions about medicines from cultures throughout the world seemed to have some degree of truth in them.

'This is amazing!' Marion exclaimed to Guamo. 'I feel stronger physically, emotionally and mentally, and the cuts on my face, arms and hands have stopped hurting. You're amazing, Guamo!'

'No, nature is amazing,' Guamo replied modestly. 'Our faith also makes us strong. If you believe that a substance will cure an injury or disease, then it will work. If you don't believe in the substance, then it won't work. Also, some sort of substance in the bones of animals is very good for injuries or diseases. In China and south-east Asia, people believe that rhino horns and tiger bones make good medicines. We Africans also use rhino horn for the same purpose; we believe that if we drink powdered rhino horn with water, the substance will protect us from diseases and injuries when we face dangerous animals.'

Marion dared not call into question Guamo's beliefs; she drank the powdered rhino horn with water when he handed it to her. The horn had no taste, and the powder was so fine that it did not irritate her throat or stomach.

Suddenly, she felt much more powerful and confident. She turned to Guamo and Miriam, a question burning in her eyes.

'I need to ask you something,' she began. 'Are you aware that it is now illegal to hunt rhinos and gorillas? They are both endangered species.'

'You are right,' Guamo replied. 'But we only kill one in every hundred rhinos or gorillas. Poachers are the real threat; they massacre these creatures in their thousands. Tribal beliefs in medicines are very strong and uncompromising. We have been using these animal products for centuries, and despite our hunting activities the rainforests and savannas were always teeming with elephants, rhinos, buffaloes and gorillas. The situation only went wrong when white men from Europe and America came to Africa, competed with large animals for land, killed too many animals and massacred African tribes. The slave trade began, and black workers were exploited and maltreated to suit the white men's greed and arrogance.

'After the Second World War, African countries gained independence, but we Africans were never taught by the European colonists how to run countries democratically, or to manage the land for farming and livestock or protect wildlife. Africa has been marred by wars, dictatorships, droughts, famines and diseases, but there is still a vast majority of African countries where most people live normal, happy lives. Yet it was the white men who first brought the problems of wildlife destruction and poaching to Africa, and now many black poachers massacre thousands of wild animals in order to get money to feed their families. The top wildlife dealers make the most money. Ancient tribes like mine kill very few animals, only enough to meet their needs. The beliefs about rhino horns and tiger bones having medicinal properties are far more powerful in China, Nepal and south-east Asia, as well as Manchuria and Siberia, where poachers kill Siberian tigers. But my tribe does not trade with the Asians, for we only kill wild animals to support ourselves. And we don't sell rhino dagger handles to the Middle East, unlike some dealers.'

'I see,' Marion said slowly. 'Which other animals are used in African medicine?'

'The crocodile,' Guamo replied. 'African tribes hunted crocodiles for meat and medicines until the nineteenth century, but crocodiles are not hunted for this purpose anymore. Other animals are still hunted for their meat. The lion is still hunted for its meat and its heart, which we believe gives people great strength, courage and bravery. For breakfast we have a selection of meats for you to try; they come from an elephant, a rhino, a hippo, a buffalo, a warthog, a bush pig and a lion — all powerful, brave and dangerous animals. We do not eat meat from leopards, crocodiles, baboons or gorillas. Try some lion meat, along with a piece of its heart. They will make you strong, brave and confident.' Marion chewed and swallowed a plateful of well-cooked lion meat and lion heart, and it was very tough to eat. She screwed up her face at the taste, but then began to feel physically and mentally stronger.

Next, Marion was offered elephant meat, rhino meat and hippo meat. This selection of different meats was very tough and fatty, but she forced herself to swallow each mouthful, and then Miriam offered her the meat of a buffalo, a warthog and a bush pig. She found these slightly more appealing, but her stomach soon began to ache because her appetite was not accustomed to African food.

'That was a fine selection of different meats,' Marion said politely. 'Can I have some cooked vegetables, please? And then perhaps some fruit?'

'It will be our pleasure,' Miriam enthused. Marion was given a plateful of couscous with sauerkraut vegetables, and then finished her feast with a half-ripe banana.

'Did you enjoy your meal?' Miriam asked her.

'You'd better believe it!' Marion exclaimed with excitement. 'This sauerkraut is far better than any I've ever had in Germany, and the couscous beats any I've ever had in the Middle East! But my stomach is hurting like crazy; I guess I'm not used to this kind of food.'

'Meat, fish and vegetables from tropical countries are produced differently to meat and vegetables in the West,' Guamo told Marion. 'The process of cooking food is very different. The meat of wild animals has harder muscle than the meat of farm animals which produce beef, pork, lamb or chicken, and this meat requires longer, more thorough cooking. And we don't have refrigerators or ovens like you Europeans. We cannot keep meat and vegetables cold or hot for very long, so the bacteria in the air gets to the meat. Now, you should take a nice, long sleep and give the meats and vegetables a chance to adapt to your body. But there are two points I must make before you sleep off the food. Firstly, do you notice that we have elephant and hippo tusks made of ivory in this room?'

'Yes, I do,' Marion answered. 'They look very impressive. And you also have lion skins and leopard skins. And buffalo horns. I trust that you hunt these wild animals as sparingly as you hunt rhinos and gorillas?'

'Yes, we do,' Guamo replied. 'And we have always hunted elephants, hippos and buffaloes, plus lions and leopards. Also crocodiles, which brings me to the second point.'

'Go on,' Marion said.

'In the corner of this room are the liver and intestines of a crocodile,' Guamo said, pointing. 'These organs from the crocodile contain powerful magic which skillful witchdoctors use to cast spells. These spells kill any humans or animals who threaten the witchdoctor in possession of these organs. However, one must always try to diffuse dangerous situations by pacifying aggressive animals or humans; we use food to appease dangerous animals about to attack. Only if all else fails should one cast a lethal spell upon an aggressive animal or human.'

'But I've never killed an animal in my life, and certainly never another human being,' Marion objected. 'That's murder.'

'I said only as a last resort,' Guamo replied. 'It is sometimes necessary as self-defence.'

'So you're going to teach me how to cast spells with a crocodile's liver and intestines?' Marion joked. 'Huh, that's rich. You can't be serious.' She chuckled and then succumbed to fits of laughter before falling off her chair. When she got up again, Guamo and Miriam were frowning and looked rather offended by her mindless, hysterical laughter.

'I will prove to you that I'm serious,' Guamo snapped. 'Your training will begin tomorrow.'

'Look, I'm sorry, Chief,' Marion said, her amusement now turning to embarrassment as she realised how much she'd upset her hosts. 'No hard feelings. I'm a European woman who is not used to all these tribal superstitions. So you're serious? You're going to teach me how to kill an enemy with magic? Magic from those crocodile organs over there?' She pointed to the liver and intestines.

'Your apology is accepted,' Guamo said calmly. 'Have a day's rest to sleep over the different meats, vegetables and couscous. Tomorrow, we'll train you to be a witchdoctor.'

Guamo vacated the hut and Miriam began washing up the bowls from their meal.

'Huh,' Marion muttered to herself. 'The situations I get into... Me, a witchdoctor? That's a laugh.'

Her stomach was still painful so she returned to her room and climbed into her bed. Within ten minutes, she was asleep.

* * *

Guamo spent three days training Marion in the use of the crocodile's organs. On the last day, to her amazement, Marion used the magic to kill three cattle and four sheep.

She knew that crocodile magic really was no joke at all. Marion shook hands with the four witchdoctors assisting Guamo in training her, and then the bearded chief turned to her again.

'The magic of the crocodile's liver and intestines is very strong, powerful and dangerous,' Guamo reminded her. 'It is a lethal weapon if misused, more deadly than a knife or even a gun. I must emphasise that you must never use the crocodile's organs against a human or an animal except as a very last resort. You must go out of your way to diffuse aggressive situations first; you can do this by offering food, and through maintaining a submissive, passive, non-threatening posture.

'I will teach you deep breathing exercises and correct body postures. That way, you will be calm, confident and level-headed in the face of danger, and any animals you come across will smell no fear. Most animals will be put off attacking a human who is confident and level-headed. But if all else fails, then and only then must you use the crocodile magic.'

'Then let's begin,' Marion said, her eyes determined and her jaw set.

Over the next four days, Guamo instructed Marion in deep breathing and non-threatening postures and body language.

The day after her training had finished, Guamo told Marion they were going on a trip to Benin in western Africa.

'Why are we going to Benin?' Marion asked.

'To give you a relaxing holiday, and to visit the palace of the oba. Benin is one of the most relaxing countries in Africa.'

'What is an oba?'

'An oba is an African king or lord. So, the oba of Benin is the king or lord of Benin,' Guamo explained. 'Now, I am going to cast a spell to shorten our journey. In this dreamworld, it is possible to alter the position of countries, landscapes, terrain and even the pattern of time. It is even possible to walk on air or water here.'

'It's like being in a science fiction movie,' Marion said, chuckling. 'I feel like I'm in a parallel universe on a planet similar to Earth, but slightly different.'

'You have summed it up very well,' Guamo enthused. 'And now I will perform the spell.'

Moments later they were in Benin.

'The palace is over there to the south,' said Guamo. 'But first, I must take you to my brother's hut — follow me.' He led her to a large hut on the edge of a jungle. 'He's not home at the moment, but he won't mind us having a look inside,' Guamo said.

'What's in there?' Marion asked.

'You will see.'

They made their way through the hallway into a gallery that closely resembled a museum. Marion was awestruck by what she saw.

There were the horns of elephants, hippos

and rhinos taken as trophies. The hippo tusks were the longest, but those of the rhinos and elephants were equally as impressive. Towering above Marion and Guamo were the stuffed bodies of the horns' owners: an elephant, a hippo, a white rhino and a black rhino. Behind these giants were the enormous stuffed bodies of lions and lionesses.

'All these trophies have been legally killed,' Guamo reassured Marion.

After leaving the hut, Marion and Guamo strolled through jungle to the nearby palace. They entered the impressive building and headed through many galleries to the main museum where they saw more stuffed lions, as well as gorillas, baboons, drills and mandrills. There were more ivory tusks, taken from dead elephants, and rhino horns, some of which had been crafted into ornaments. Guamo was staring at a stuffed leopard in the corner — a behaviour which Marion noticed immediately.

'Look at all these ornaments and wonders,' Marion said. 'They are incredible, and all you're looking at is that stuffed leopard.'

'That's because the oba of Benin had a special interest in leopards,' Guamo replied. 'My father and I told you that lions have long been emblems of strength, courage, majesty and ferocity, and have symbolised the power of African leaders and chiefs... Well, the oba of Benin treated the leopard, with its boldness, savagery and cunning, as the symbol of chieftainship. Like lions, leopards are also symbols of being brave, vicious, aggressive and cunning; they are the embodiment of aggression and courage amongst native peoples throughout Africa and Asia. Just look at the leopard, its sinuous muscles and the aggression and cunning in his eyes.'

'It is beautiful,' Marion said, her voice full of wonder.

'The oba also had a fascination with crocodiles. Look at that wall over there. It is decorated with a crocodile plaque.'

Marion glanced towards the wooden plaque with a crocodile carved into it. 'Hmm, I'm not particularly impressed — but then again, I hate crocodiles,' she admitted. 'I'm more impressed with the stuffed leopard. But it's a shame this leopard had to be killed just to become a trophy. I must admit, I feel the same way about all these animals, from elephants, hippos and rhinos down to baboons, drills and mandrills. And especially gorillas, because they are one of humankind's closest relations. Killing a gorilla is almost as evil and terrible as killing a human being, I feel.'

'But all these animals and trophies were hunted over a hundred years ago,' Guamo pointed out. 'Back in a time when nobody gave animal rights even a second thought. Now it is illegal to kill any of these animals.'

'Thank God for that.' Marion sighed. 'I used to hate and dread all these dangerous animals, but now your training has given me more confidence, and I'm beginning to feel differently towards them. I feel a mixture of compassion and sympathy for the animals you've shown me — even crocodiles, hyenas and wild dogs.'

'That's a positive sign,' Guamo said, smiling with pride.

They wandered the palace for ten more minutes, chatting and admiring the building, before leaving to have lunch with Guamo's brother.

* * *

Back in Rwanda, Marion spent the next five days relaxing, practising deep breathing exercises and correct body postures for diffusing aggressive animals, training in how to use crocodile body parts as weapons and using food to appease animals. As far as the food technique was concerned, she practised with vicious dogs owned by some of the villagers and she found that feeding them meat and fish was extremely effective in pacifying them.

Marion's first real test in pacifying animals finally came. She stood nervously alongside Guamo, the four witchdoctors and the rest of the villagers.

'So your first test to calm down Africa's deadly creatures has come,' Guamo began. 'But to carry all this food, you will need a truck. My brother, Kofi, whom you have already met, will drive the truck as you throw the food to the animals. How are you feeling?'

'Very tense,' Marion said with honesty. 'But eating the lion meat and lion heart has given me tremendous strength, courage and confidence — as does carrying these crocodile organs, though I hope I'll never have to use them.'

Guamo smiled and gave her a small nod, then they said goodbye, and Marion climbed into the back of the truck, which was open to the air. The smell of Africa wafted through Marion's nostrils: a mixture of the sunbaked savanna, the damp, murky smell of the rain-soaked jungles and the villagers' oiled bodies. Feeling open to attack and vulnerable, Marion forced into her mind and heart the mental strength and courage of a lion. She was sat amongst masses of vegetables, fruits and meat, and the meat's stench soon overpowered the other aromas of Africa and made Marion feel nauseous.

Kofi pushed his keys into the ignition and pressed the accelerator; the truck veered and jerked before gliding south, over the savanna grass towards the muddy-green river where hippos and crocodiles dwelled in their dozens. A massive bull elephant charged with enormous power and speed, his ears spread out like fans and his trunk raised between his shining ivory tusks. His feet thundered across the savanna grass, flattening it into the dusty soil, and his bellowing roar echoed through the atmosphere. Marion's adrenaline raced through her body and sent blood rushing through her heart and brain, but the lion's meat gave her the strength. She kept a cool head and looked around. Beside her, amongst the meat and vegetables, were some branches from an acacia tree. Marion's experience at Munich Zoo had taught her that African elephants loved acacia leaves. She picked up the branch and hurled it into the elephant's path. The elephant immediately halted in his tracks and began eating the leaves.

The truck drove on towards a river, and an enormous bull hippo appeared. It bellowed with far greater ferocity than the elephant. His eyes conveyed fierce aggression and rage, and his gaping, cavernous mouth opened to expose giant tusks. At the same time, a crocodile lunged towards the truck with lightning speed and strength, his powerful tail thrashing with the force to break a man's leg and his vice-like jaws and teeth ready to catch hold of one of Marion's arms and dislocate it with a bone-breaking twist of his body.

Marion hurled a meat carcass to the crocodile and some dried reeds to the hippo, and both the hippo and the crocodile retreated into the river's murky depths. For those ten petrifying seconds, Marion's heart had dropped to her stomach.

The next three animals they encountered were a huge white rhino, a massive black rhino and an enormous buffalo. All were armed with ground-churning hooves and deadly horns. The rhinos charged with as much power and speed as an elephant, their huge heads and horns lowered as they bellowed with aggression. The buffalo also charged, grunting with a savage fury that would put any elephant or lion to shame.

Marion had no time to be petrified; she grabbed the last two acacia branches and tossed them into the path of the oncoming rhinos. The beasts stopped dead in their tracks and started chomping on the juicy leaves. Then Marion reached for some bamboo stems she had seen and threw them to the buffalo, and the fearsome black beast also halted. Marion sighed and took deep, steadying breaths. Kofi yelled words of encouragement from the driver's seat, and her lips formed a small smile.

Then her next adversary came racing into view: a large lion weighing over 500 pounds. He was truly an awesome beast; Marion could not help but admire the way his body churned with thick muscle and sinew and his bushy mane flowed in the breeze as he ran. Then her eyes focused on his. With sharp claws, exposed teeth and death in his stare, she felt petrified as the lion charged towards her.

The lion roared with rage and Marion was jolted out of her terrified paralysis. She wrenched half a zebra carcass towards the edge of the truck, spun it round and used all her strength to kick the heavy weight to the ground. The zebra carcass crashed into the lion's path, persuading the big cat to feed on it. It was clear to Marion that this lion had only attacked the truck because of hunger, as did most lions who viewed humans as prey.

Facing a crocodile or a lion was terrifying enough, but Marion found out with relief that she would not have to confront the savagery of hyenas, hunting dogs and jackals, or the controlled ferocity of leopards and black panthers.

However, Kofi told her that some wild pigs and baboons were up ahead. They were even more petrifying than suffering attack by hyenas, wild dogs or leopards. Marion shuddered as a bush pig and a warthog charged, squealing with vicious hatred, their tusks gleaming like scimitars and their bodies rippling with muscle. They hurtled through the grass with the strength, speed and ferocity of a wild boar. Marion flung three lots of cabbages, carrots and turnips to the wild pigs, and they began gnawing at these root vegetables greedily. Marion breathed heavily, her eyes closed, and suddenly she tasted vomit. Sick splattered on the dry, sun-burned grass, and Marion gasped at the burning in her throat.

The truck veered round and raced north-west towards the jungle. Marion watched the acacia and baobab trees flash by as the sun imposed its scorching heat onto the dry grass. Before long, the truck entered the rainforest along a basic mud path and dropped its speed from fifty miles per hour to ten. Finally, they came to a halt.

Marion instantly saw why.

They were surrounded by three enormous male gorillas, one of them a dominant silverback, along with four savage baboons and three vicious mandrills. The gorillas pounded their enormous chests with their muscular arms and enormous fists, and then screamed at the truck, their teeth flashing like daggers as they charged with brute power and speed. The baboons and mandrills were also violently strong with rippling muscles and teeth as fearsome as a leopard's fangs, and they followed the gorillas' example by screaming their war cry and charging.

Marion felt cold sweat drip down her forehead and sting her eyes. She grabbed some leaves and roots from beside her and threw them towards the baboons and mandrills, who instantly fell upon the food. She then turned to face the gorillas, who still seemed hell-bent on tearing her to a pulp with their gleaming teeth and ham-like fists. She threw some bamboo and fruits to the gorillas, and then lobbed the last ten bananas to the baboons and mandrills. The rainforest was suddenly peaceful, free of the primates' screams.

Marion felt strangely numb as the adrenaline left her body. Kofi vacated the truck and climbed into the vehicle's open area to join her, and she slowly came back to life. She cheered and grinned, immensely proud of how brave she had been to face these lethal killers of Africa and diffuse their blood-curdling savagery with food.

Kofi embraced her. 'Don't scream and cheer too much,' he said, amused. 'It will make the gorillas and baboons aggressive again. Ah, they've gone off into the jungle.

But you did great. My father and my brother would be proud of you.'

'I'd bet they would,' Marion said, grinning.

They leapt off the open area of the truck and climbed up into the front seats of the vehicle and drove back to the village.

Guamo embraced Marion with pride, amazed at how the scared young woman had begun to overcome her fear and hatred towards Africa's deadliest killers. 'I can't tell you how proud I am. However, you have a long way to go before you overcome your terrors completely,' he reminded her. 'You have used food to calm down animals. Now you will have to learn many other calming methods and techniques, and your first destination will be Asia. You will leave for Nepal tomorrow.'

'It's a shame,' Marion sighed, her face frowning. 'I'll really miss Africa.'

'Then take one last look at Rwanda,' Kofi said. 'Watch the splendour and majesty of Africa in all its glory.'

Marion looked around, trying to memorise the scenery and atmosphere, and then turned to Chief Guamo with a barrage of questions she felt she had to ask before she left.

'Apart from pythons and venomous snakes, Africa has many dangerous or fearsome animals,' she observed. 'Will you tell me how many animals I must treat with caution?'

'There are many, but we'll start from the largest and work our way down to the smallest,' Guamo suggested. 'First, there are the herbivores. The largest of all land animals are elephants, hippos and rhinos. Elephants are only dangerous when they have young, or when the males go through the mating period called musth. When an elephant goes through musth, he will attack any animal, man, vehicle or hut that gets in his way, and will trample crops. However, normally elephants are intelligent and gentle animals and show no hostility towards humans. Hippos are by far the most lethal beasts in Africa, and they kill more people than any other African animal. The hippo is very territorial. If humans in boats venture into the territory of hippos, then the hippos will attack them without mercy. When enraged, a hippo is as savage as an elephant, a rhino and a lion put together, and its giant tusks will crush and smash the strongest and hardest of boats. Sometimes hippos trample crops and attack villages, causing terrible destruction to buildings and people. I knew one man who had his left leg bitten off by a hippo.'

Marion gasped, imagining having her leg torn off by the savage beast.

Guamo nodded gravely and continued. 'Then there are rhinos, who are not as dangerous as hippos. The larger white rhinos are not as fearsome as black rhinos, but both species may attack a man in self-defence. However, if people leave them alone, rhinos will generally not attack people. Both white rhinos and black rhinos are endangered species, and humans pose more of a threat to them than they do to humans.'

Marion saw some elephants and rhinos feeding in her peripheral vision. None of them showed any hostility to humans because they had always been treated with respect and caution.

'Okay,' Marion said. 'Which animal is next among the top man-killers?'

'The next animal is the African buffalo,' Guamo told her. 'Alongside hippos, buffaloes are the worst man-killers in Africa. If you surprise a buffalo or approach a buffalo herd, they will charge without warning or hesitation. Although they are not intelligent, they can be very cunning. Big game hunters rate buffaloes as the most dangerous big game in Africa because when a buffalo has been wounded he will allow the hunter to pursue him through thick bush and then lie hidden in ambush before mauling the hunter. Many huntsmen have been killed in this way by buffaloes. Not even lions or crocodiles will attack a healthy buffalo, only going for the young, weak or sick animals.'

Marion watched the herd of buffaloes dining on the thick grass, and they too conveyed no ferocity to the humans. But she knew that this placid appearance was very deceptive. They were extremely savage wild beasts who would follow their natural instinct in order to protect their territory or their families, and they were more than capable of making devastating attacks on humans.

'Right, we've dealt with buffaloes,' Marion said quickly. 'Which animals are next?'

'Crocodiles,' Guamo replied. 'Next to hippos and buffaloes, crocodiles kill more humans than any other animal in Africa. Crocodiles are primitive killers; they lack intelligence and are extremely savage. You were petrified of the five sharks who attacked your boat, but crocodiles are far worse than sharks. They have no fear of humans and will attack without provocation. Most animals fear humankind and hate the taste of human flesh, but not the crocodile. His killing power is awesome and his speed is like lightning. You never know when a crocodile will attack until it's too late, for they tend to be submerged in murky waters.'

'I am terrified of both sharks *and* crocodiles,' Marion admitted.

'Then we come to lions,' Guamo went on. 'Watch those lions over there, eating a zebra.'

Marion admired the grace and power of a pride of lions and lionesses as they feasted. 'They're beautiful,' she said.

Guamo smiled. 'Yes, they are — but they're also deadly. Lions very rarely attack people, but they should always be treated with caution, especially lionesses with cubs. Most lions who kill humans have turned to this habit through being injured by bullet wounds inflicted by hunters. But we need to get the problem of man-eating lions in perspective. Some lions become man-eaters, but not many. Leopards, however, are more cunning and savage than lions. Do you see the two in the baobab trees over there, a spotted leopard and a black panther?'

Marion squinted and saw the sinuous power and beauty of the leopard and the black panther among the leaves.

'Leopards and black panthers are the fiercest and most cunning of all big cats, and they provoke more terror in humans than lions. Fortunately, the leopard has a marked fear of humans, and very few become man-eaters. Although they don't grow very large, they can kill a man in a matter of seconds.'

'This is all very scary,' Marion said, still eyeing the two beasts in the baobab trees. 'Are there many other savage beasts?'

'Yes, many,' Guamo told her. 'But they are very rarely dangerous to humans, and most are not dangerous at all unless provoked. For example, warthogs and bush pigs are not a threat to humans, but a few cases have occurred of humans being injured or killed by these wild pigs. One man I knew was put in hospital after a bush pig crippled his right leg and then ate his kidneys, liver and stomach. He died soon after. But, on the whole, Africa's wild pigs will avoid humans.'

'People also have a fear of gorillas,' Marion pointed out. 'Especially the male silverback gorillas.'

'You're right, they do,' Guamo agreed. 'But contrary to the horror stories of their deadly ferocity, gorillas are intelligent and gentle animals. A few people have been attacked or killed by gorillas, but this was usually when a male gorilla was defending himself or his family. When the silverback gorilla or a troop of male gorillas charges, it is worse than the charge of an elephant or a rhino. This is because when the male gorilla is enraged, his face is furious and will make you petrified. No other animal has a face that can express emotion or anger like the gorilla can. Other than gorillas, the only primates in Africa dangerous to humans are baboons and mandrills. The largest male baboons can kill a leopard or tear a man apart with their powerful teeth and strong limbs. Baboons are extremely savage and formidable, but mandrills are worse. Fortunately, baboons and their cousins have a marked fear of humankind and normally leave us alone.'

Marion watched four male gorillas passing fruit and leaves to the females and young, and over the make-believe border with Cameroon baboons were eating a dead antelope and some drills and mandrills were feeding on fruit in the forest. 'You have forgotten hyenas and wild dogs,' she pointed out.

'Hyenas have a terrible reputation as evil, bloodthirsty killers,' Guamo replied. 'So too do African hunting dogs and jackals. But all three species are only dangerous to humans if hungry or threatened. In some areas of Africa, hyenas and hunting dogs are even dominant over lions. Jackals are almost always scavengers and won't threaten a human unless in a pack. But hyenas have severely injured or killed people in a few areas of Africa, taking an arm or a leg in their powerful jaws. The honey badger and the smaller cats of Africa are also formidable adversaries. But the honey badger and such smaller wild cats as the caracal and the serval only show ferocity if cornered.'

Marion witnessed the dreaded hyenas and hunting dogs feeding on two zebra kills, with the jackals waiting to scavenge on the remains, and the stocky honey badger dining in the distance. The caracal was consuming a small antelope whilst the serval was tearing at a bird with his teeth.

'So that's all,' Guamo concluded. 'We've dealt with all the deadly creatures except the snakes, and their lethal reputation is legendary.'

'Well, thanks, Chief,' Marion replied, 'very soon I'll leave Africa and head for Asia. I'm very nervous, but I'll try my best to face up to my fears there and tame the native wild animals.'

'I wish you luck, young lady,' Guamo said warmly. 'But first, rest. You can leave in the morning.'

'Thanks again,' she said evenly, and retreated into the thatched hut.

CHAPTER 4

The hills below the towering Himalayan mountains of Nepal were teaming with forests of giant rhododendrons and exotic trees. The mountain forests of southern Nepal gave way to the rainforests of India just over the border. Marion greeted three Chinese Buddhists who introduced themselves as Chong Lee, Sun Ying and Mao Sing. They were all Shaolin monks who were proficient in the martial arts of kung fu and tai chi. They were wise, profound men, utterly devoted to their faith, and Marion was impressed by their modesty, gentleness and politeness. Such an attitude was lacking in the more modern, get-rich-quick culture of the West. Marion also marvelled at how the younger generation of Chinese and Nepalese respected their elders, and turned to them as a source of mental strength and wisdom. But the East was changing fast as the modern age loomed on the horizon.

'Nepal is such a beautiful country, and the people are lovely,' Marion said, addressing the monks. 'Most people in Africa are the same.'

Chong Lee smiled. 'Your politeness and

intelligence do us proud, my dear. But now we must begin a lesson on the cult worship of Asia's dangerous animals.'

'I'm ready for anything,' Marion said, determined.

'We will begin with the Indian elephant and the Indian rhino,' Mao Sing told Marion. 'The Indian elephant is also called the Asian elephant, as it is found all over the Far East, including China, Nepal and India. Unlike African elephants, Indian elephants are worshipped by Asians for their strength, gentleness, intelligence and wisdom. They are decorated and covered with gold cloth and jewellery for ceremonies in countries like India, Malaysia, Thailand and Indonesia. The Indians and Chinese treat elephants with enormous respect and veneration. In Indian mythology, the all-powerful deity Indra mounted and rode the elephant Airavata to take him on journeys around the world. The people of Thailand turn to the elephant for solutions to their problems or dangers, and whisper their secrets to the elephant. Take a look at these images of elephants as we conjure them.'

Marion watched these spectacles and saw Chinese, Nepalese, Indians, Malays and Thais worshipping elephants as the beasts drank from waterholes. They even held sacred ceremonies where tamed elephants were covered in jewels and gold cloth. Then she saw Indra being transported around Earth by the elephant Airavata, and the

Thai people whispering their own secrets into the ears of their beloved elephants.

'I see it all now,' Marion whispered breathlessly. 'What else is there for me to know about the spiritualism of elephants?'

'In India and south-east Asia,' Chong Lee began, 'elephants are sacred animals — just as sacred as cattle. If you harm or kill an elephant, you will suffer the death penalty or life imprisonment. In India, elephants and cattle are as sacred as human beings.'

'But there is more,' Sun Ying explained. 'In Hindu spiritualism in India, the elephant god Ganesha is the elephant-headed son of Parvati and Shiva. The Hindus worship Ganesha as the wise lord of the demigods who attend Shiva, and he is frequently asked to perform a task because he is thought to get rid of obstacles. Ganesha is also revered, venerated and respected as the patron of businessmen all over Asia.'

Marion watched Ganesha performing tasks and removing awkward obstacles, like rocks and logs, and then the scene changed to show people in India and south-east Asia protecting elephants from huntsmen.

'I'm no longer afraid of elephants,' Marion said, fixated on the scene as it changed again. 'But what is that I see? It looks as if ancient soldiers are mounting elephants and rhinos covered with armour, then riding them into battle.'

'Elephants were frequently used in battle in ancient wars throughout Asia,' Sun Ying said. 'They were terrifying animals for the enemy to confront, and more than a match for cavalry with horses. Elephants were protected by armour, and used like tanks later employed in modern wars of the twentieth century. Indian rhinos were also used in battle; covered in armour and armed with formidable horns, with fearsome teeth and heavy hooves, they were as terrifying as elephants.'

Mao Sing spoke up again. 'But, sadly, times are changing. People used to respect elephants and rhinos, worshipping and revering them. Now they are being hunted almost to extinction, and rhinos are in worse peril than elephants. As was the case in Africa, poaching in Asia began from big game hunting which was started by India's maharajas and British colonists who ruled India from the beginning of the nineteenth century. They rode elephants to hunt and kill wild elephants, as well as hunting rhinos, wild boars and tigers…'

Mao Sing waved his hand and the scene changed yet again. Marion saw British colonists using tamed elephants to corner a wild elephant, a rhino, a wild boar and a tiger. All four beasts fought with terrible ferocity, but they were outnumbered and outmatched. They didn't stand a chance and were shot to death by the huntsmen. Marion was sickened by this mindless carnage.

Sun Ying did not seem to see the sorrow and horror on her face. 'People also hunted tigers and wild boars on horseback,' he explained. 'Tigers were terrifying animals to confront with horses, and wild boars were even more lethal. On many occasions, a rider on horseback would plunge his spear into a wild boar's flank. But the wild boar would then bite through the shaft of the spear and charge the horse, maiming or killing both the horse and the rider in a devastating counter-attack. Many terrible tales have been told of the wild boar's strength, courage and ferocity when cornered or wounded. It is frequently said that the wild boar is the only animal who will boldly make his way between two tigers to drink at a river or waterhole. So, watch these next few scenes.'

Marion was taken aback as she witnessed a savage tiger lunging towards a horse and killing both the horse and hunter, but she was even more amazed at the wild boar slashing through the shaft of a huntsman's spear with his scimitar-like tusks, charging with explosive speed and power, and viciously attacking and killing both the horse and rider. Then she watched a wild boar boldly drinking at a waterhole as he was flanked by two enormous Bengal tigers. She had heard how even tigers had been maimed or killed by wild boars they had tried to hunt and kill. Then the scene changed, and Marion saw wild boars in the jungle and was amazed at how enormous they were.

'These wild pigs are twice as large as the wild pigs we get in Europe,' she said with shock and wonder. 'How much do these brutes weigh?'

'Nearly 600 pounds,' Chong Lee told her. 'In Hindu mythology, Varaha, the wild boar, was one of the three incarnations of Vishnu; the other two incarnations were Kurma, the tortoise, and Narasimha, the lion. But the wild boar was worshipped and venerated more in medieval Europe than in Asia...'

Marion suddenly saw Varaha standing beside Kurma and Narasimha. Then she turned to watch the wild boars in the jungle, and heard the trumpeting of elephants, the bellowing of rhinos and the grunting of water-buffaloes. The elephants and rhinos were drinking at the river alongside the water buffaloes bathing in the cool water, the elephants spraying the water over themselves and their calves with their trunks like giant hoses. The elephants and rhinos were joined by the wild boars, whilst farther downriver three enormous Bengal tigers satisfied their thirst on the cool water.

'Guess what?' Marion said excitedly. 'I see tigers. Three of them.'

'I do too. You know, there is a vast range of spiritualism and worship surrounding tigers,' Chong Lee informed Marion. 'Look at all these temples, dedicated to tigers and lions.' Marion was awestruck by the temples and shrines, and amazed by the statues of these big cats. She admired them silently until Chong Lee's voice cut into her dazed thoughts.

'The tiger is dreaded and respected

throughout Asia,' he told her. 'These temples, shrines and statues exist all over Asia, from Malaysia and Indonesia to as far north as Siberia. Siberian tigers were feared, respected and venerated as much as Bengal tigers are in India and Nepal. And now, look at the paintings of lions and tigers in art and pottery designs.'

Outside the buildings were paintings and pottery with images of lions and tigers, and, seeing this, Marion turned towards the three Buddhist monks. 'I've noticed that as well as tigers there are statues of lions in India and China,' she observed, 'and both big cats appear in the art and pottery designs, but this surprises me. I never knew that there are lions in Asia; I thought they were African animals.'

'Well, there *were* lions in Asia, until humankind wiped them out,' Mao Sing informed her. 'Previously, lions roamed the whole of Asia and rivalled tigers as the monarchs of the jungles and grasslands. Now the only Asian lions left live in the Gir Forest in northern India. Asia has no other lions.'

Another scene appeared, showing the lions of the Gir Forest, and then changed so that Marion could admire the fiery beauty and dignity of tigers in the snowy forests of Siberia, the mountains of China and the jungles of India and Nepal. She gulped in amazement at their beauty and power.

'Were all dangerous animals in Asia

subject to worship and spiritualism?' she asked, after a pause.

'Yes,' Chong Lee replied. 'Not only elephants, rhinos, wild boars, lions and tigers, but also sharks, crocodiles and snakes. They are the most dreaded of all dangerous animals, but the Hindus subject even them to spiritualism. The shark and the crocodile have spirits in them, just as much as you or me. The shark is the king of the Indian Ocean, while the crocodile is lord of the rivers and the tiger is king of the jungle, alongside the elephant and the rhino. And in India, the snakes are sacred, from pythons to venomous cobras, vipers and kraits. Snakes are as sacred to Indians as elephants and cattle, and it is a terrible crime for a man to kill one. But look — can you see the primitive killers?'

Marion watched some sharks in the ocean, and then crocodiles and snakes lurking with amazing stealth in the river as the elephants, rhinos and water buffaloes bathed and drank in the water. These giants harboured no terror of the crocodiles; they would easily fight off these killer reptiles should the predators attack.

'What about the other creatures of the forest?' Marion asked breathlessly.

'Well, another dangerous creature is the Indian water buffalo,' Sun Ying replied.

Marion caught another admiring glance at the water buffaloes drinking among the two herds of elephants and rhinos.

'In south-east Asia,' Sun Ying continued,

'the water buffalo is sacrificed at ceremonies. It is regarded as sacred, much like the cow in India.'

Marion watched the sacrifice happening, and remembered the same ceremonies being performed around buffaloes in Africa. 'This is incredible!' Marion exclaimed.

'In one of India's Hindu myths,' Mao Sing said, 'the warrior goddess, Durga, kills the water buffalo, Mahisha, even though Mahisha tries to transform himself many times to escape from her. Durga is riding a lion, and it is the lion who carries out the execution.'

Marion watched with horror as Mahisha tried to transform himself several times to avoid Durga, but eventually the lion mauled him viciously. Marion gritted her teeth and turned her face away as the lion killed Mahisha with a powerful bite to the neck.

'On a more practical level, water buffaloes are used by humans throughout Asia to pull carts and ploughs and cultivate rice fields,' Chong Lee explained. 'Water buffaloes are as valued for their strength and their powers for heavy manual work as elephants are. As in Africa, tamed elephants in India and south-east Asia round up wild elephants and water buffaloes and herd them into corrals. The wild elephants and buffaloes are then tamed and used for manual labour...'

The visions came to Marion, firstly of wild elephants being herded into corrals, and then of water buffaloes pulling carts and ploughs in India, China and south-east Asia.

'An interesting point,' she said slowly. 'Water buffaloes are also used for heavy labour in Australia, the Philippines, South America, Mexico and even southern Europe, where they were introduced from Asia.'

'That's very true,' Chong Lee agreed.

'So we've dealt with the water buffalo,' Sun Ying said. 'Then there is the yeti — otherwise known as the abominable snowman.'

'The yeti!' Marion exclaimed. 'But the yeti is a myth, it doesn't exist.'

'That is a matter of opinion,' Chong Lee objected. 'We three monks have traveled through Tibet and Nepal, and we have actually seen yetis. They are as big as rhinos and are related to apes. They have dark-brown fur with silvery-grey tips. Their heads are rounded and their mouths are filled with massive teeth, but they have hands with fingernails instead of paws with claws. That's how we know they're of the ape family. But unlike all the other apes of the jungles, yetis are omnivores who sometimes eat prey animals, such as yaks, cattle, sheep, goats and even men. The yeti is extremely ferocious.'

'You're scaring me with this bullshit,' Marion snapped. 'It is bullshit, isn't it? You honestly mean you have seen yetis?' she went on, a little more uncertainly.

'Yes, young lady,' Mao Sing replied, his tone sharp. 'Many Chinese and Tibetans have seen yetis. No animal is large enough or has thumbs on its feet to make the footprints we see in the snow. And no human would walk in the snow without boots to cover his feet. An animal would leave paw or hoof prints, whilst a human would leave shoe or boot prints. They have to be made by a yeti. And if yetis don't exist, how do you explain the disappearance of so many men and yaks in the mountains?'

'I don't know,' Marion admitted.

'Other predators would leave some evidence of human victims, but these men have disappeared without any trace,' Mao Sing said darkly. 'And only three other predators in these mountains are powerful enough to kill yaks: the Asian brown bear, the Himalayan black bear and the snow leopard. All three kill yaks in their own specific ways and leave the carcasses lying around; they do not hide them in caves. But yaks and cattle killed by yetis have been smashed to pieces with one blow and eaten whole — flesh, bones and hide. Himalayan black bears can't do that, nor can snow leopards or the Asian dholes. Only yetis can do that. Yetis have even driven brown bears and black bears from their kills.'

'This yeti sounds like a mean creature,' Marion said, chuckling nervously, still unsure whether to believe the three monks. 'You say he's as big and aggressive as a rhino...'

'Yes,' Chong Lee said, firmly. 'According to an ancient Buddhist tradition, the yeti is a creature through which a human's soul passes after death, and you can see the monks dying and their souls passing through a yeti's body.'

Marion gritted her teeth, tensed her face

and sharpened her eyes as this spectacle was shown to her. She fought back the temptation to faint, reassuring herself that she was well protected by three Shaolin monks, all masters of kung fu. But, then again, what could three kung fu experts do against a giant yeti should he attack them?

'Okay, I believe you,' Marion said shakily. 'I think we've talked enough about the yeti. What other dangerous animals do I need to know about?'

The three monks looked slightly mollified.

'Apart from the tiger and the lion, there are also the leopard and the Asian bears,' Chong Lee replied.

'There are four species of bears in Asia, not including the giant panda in China,' Mao Sing went on. 'Giant pandas are not true bears, but are related more to raccoons. But the true bears are the Asian brown bear, the Himalayan black bear, the sloth bear and the sun bear. These bears also have spirits in them, and of these four species, brown bears are very rarely dangerous to humans. However, Himalayan black bears are notorious for their ferocity and unprovoked attacks on humans, and sloth bears and sun bears are also very savage.'

'The Himalayan black bear is also called the Asian black bear — or the moon bear, because of the white moon-shaped marking on its chest,' Sun Ying explained. 'Black bears, sloth bears and sun bears are all black in colour, but the black bear, or moon bear, has lighter fur cover on their bodies, whilst the sloth bear has thick, shaggy fur and the sun bear has a smooth, glossy pelt and an egg-shaped head. Unlike the black bear, or moon bear, the sun bear has a yellow sun-shaped marking on its chest. They are also the smallest of all bears. The black bear weighs three hundred pounds, the sloth bear two hundred pounds and the sun bear weighs only eighty to a hundred and thirty pounds, and measures only four feet long. But sun bears are stocky and strong, with powerful claws like the black bears and sloth bears, and all three species are deadly when confronted. The sun bear has also been called the honey bear, and in Thailand it's called the dog-bear. Both sloth bears and sun bears eat honey, ants, termites and birds, but, like black bears, they are omnivores who will eat vegetation and livestock.'

'That is fascinating,' Marion said, eyes shining in wonder.

'The superstitions and legends will begin soon,' Mao Sing replied, 'but first watch these three Asian bears feeding.'

Another scene came into Marion's vision: this one showed two Himalayan black bears on a mountain slope chasing a young goat. They caught it and killed it with blows from their powerful claws, and then tore at the body with fearsome teeth. The second scene was of a sloth bear eating honey and termites. The last scene showed a female sun bear with cubs eating a sheep she had slain, and in the tree the male sun bear lazed in the sunshine, having eaten his fill. Marion took note of the sun bear's glossy-black pelt that was thin in texture, and his egg-shaped head, plus his strong, scimitar-like claws and powerful teeth. All these bears seemed gentle, but Marion was well aware that even the Asian bears were capable of making unprovoked attacks on humans.

'I'm going to slowly walk away,' Marion told the Buddhists. 'I treat all bears with respect and caution.'

'That's very wise,' Sun Ying agreed, 'because despite their small size, sloth bears and sun bears are known to be among the most ferocious beasts in Asia's jungles. They injure or kill more humans than leopards, and can severely injure even tigers in self-defence. And Himalayan black bears are even more dangerous; they have a reputation almost as terrifying as grizzly bears and black bears in North America and polar bears in the Arctic. Some people have told me that humans thought to have been killed by yetis may really have been killed by brown bears or black bears. But who knows?'

'In that case, I'll definitely avoid these bears,' Marion said fearfully. 'But Mao Sing told me that the superstitions and legends of dangerous animals are about to begin. I can't wait.'

'Then we will begin,' Chong Lee said with a small smile.

Marion and the three Chinese walked at a

casual pace along the mountain paths of the Himalayas and then down into the rainforests on Nepal's border with India. They witnessed many dangerous animals, including a honey badger, a herd of water buffaloes and two sloth bears. Marion remembered the terrible reputation of sloth bears, but these particular beasts simply consumed the honey in peace. Then, a honey badger tried to steal some from them, and the bears changed in their nature. They began to growl and snarl viciously, and chased off the honey badger.

Unnerved, Marion and the monks advanced along the rugged pathway.

'I see three leopards,' Marion told Chong Lee, pointing to a mountain ledge.

'Those are not normal leopards,' Chong Lee said wisely. 'They are two snow leopards with their cubs — and look, the smaller wild cat in those bushes is a clouded leopard. These animals are named "leopards" and resemble leopards, but I repeat they're *not* normal leopards.'

'Are they as dangerous as normal leopards?' Marion asked, slightly confused.

'Definitely not,' Chong Lee said firmly. 'Not unless you really provoke them, but that applies to all wild cats and all other predators. Snow leopards and clouded leopards have been given a spiritualism of their own by Asians. Are you ready to learn more, Marion?'

'Be my guest,' Marion replied, fascinated by these wild, beautiful creatures.

Chong Lee smiled. 'Mao Sing, you tell

Marion because you're the expert on snow leopards.'

'It will be my pleasure,' Mao Sing replied with modesty and respect. 'The snow leopard has been the subject of profound mystery and folklore for many centuries. In Tibet and Nepal, mountain villagers believe that, instead of eating the flesh of their prey, snow leopards suck the animal's blood. This probably stems from the bite wounds on the victim's neck, inflicted by the snow leopard's fangs. And there's more. Tibet has a Buddhist saint called Milarepa. Legend has it that Milarepa was stranded for six months in the Great Cave of Conquering Demons by a violent and brutal snowstorm. He had gone to this cave to live in solitude and carry out his devotions as a Buddhist. When the storm died and the snow melted, Milarepa's followers went to locate his body, only to find he had been turned into a snow leopard.'

'That's so strange!' Marion said. 'What about the clouded leopard?'

Mao Sing turned to Sun Ying and said, 'You're the expert on clouded leopards, so tell Marion what you know.'

'Well, unlike snow leopards, who live in the mountains and snowy terrain of central and eastern Asia, clouded leopards dwell in the rainforests of China, Nepal and south-east Asia,' Sun Ying began. 'Clouded leopards are half the size of most other big cats, yet they are very strong and, in proportion to their size, have the longest fangs of all the cat tribe. But what about the spiritualism of this big cat? Well, to some people in south-east Asia, the clouded leopard is sacred. However, other people in south-east Asia eat the flesh of clouded leopards, and in some areas clouded leopard meat is a delicacy.'

'I see,' Marion said, feeling sorry for the clouded leopards.

'Look,' said Chong Lee, 'the two snow leopards have retreated into their cave, and the clouded leopard has set off hunting.'

'Yes, but there are two smaller wild cats ahead of us,' Mao Sing whispered. 'It looks like they are fighting an eagle and a hawk. I think they are an Asian golden cat and — yes — a jungle cat.'

The four humans stooped to the ground and witnessed two wild cats hissing and spitting at the eagle and the hawk, causing the two raptors to take flight. Marion remembered her walk with Chief Guamo on the savannas of Rwanda, where they saw the caracal and the serval fighting with an eagle and a hawk, but in that battle the wild cats had killed the two raptors. In this present battle, fought in the rainforests of Nepal, the golden cat and the jungle cat had only repelled the eagle and the hawk; the wild cats' strength, speed and ferocity had deterred the two birds from tangling with them.

Mario watched as the cats began feeding on the carcasses of two water buffalo calves which they had killed. Chong Lee turned slowly towards Marion.

'Four years ago,' he began, 'I went on a pilgrimage to western Africa and, whilst walking in the rainforests, I saw an African golden cat. But he was afraid of me and ran away. The forest cats of Africa are afraid of humans, and they will not show any ferocity, even in self-defence, unlike the Asian golden cat and the jungle cat.'

'How many smaller wild cats are there?' Marion asked.

'There are many,' Mao Sing replied. 'There are some cats who dwell in rainforests in Africa, Asia and South America, such as the African golden cat. Then there is the cheetah of Africa and Asia — that is the fastest land animal. Although cheetahs are very thin in build, they are very powerful and ferocious, and they are capable of killing humans or dogs. They have been known to repel African hunting dogs, dholes and jackals — mostly in fights over food — and have even killed ostriches. However, fortunately, cheetahs are not a real threat to humans and rarely attack us. But four smaller wild cats of Africa and Asia are as dangerous as cheetahs or snow leopards when cornered or protecting food or young: the caracal, found in Africa, the Middle East, India and Nepal; the serval in Africa, which has been known to kill large snakes, eagles and hawks; and then there are the Asian golden cat and the jungle cat in Asia, who are ferocious, but only if cornered.'

'Were these smaller cats worshipped by Asians?' Marion asked.

'No,' Mao Sing replied. 'Only the snow leopard and the clouded leopard are worshipped here.'

'But now, the two smaller wild cats have disappeared into the thickets,' Chong Lee indicated. 'And I must tell Marion about her next challenge.' He turned to Marion. 'I see you're carrying crocodile organs. Do you know why?'

'They can kill an enemy if needed,' Marion replied.

'Exactly. And now I am going to give you some sleeping gas grenades which will render enemies unconscious without killing them,' Chong Lee told her. 'They and the crocodile organs will protect you from dangerous animals. The organs must never be used on animals unnecessarily, but they could be used against evil humans or witches and wizards in self-defence.'

'There are plenty of evil humans, but the only witches I've encountered are the ones I met in Rwanda,' Marion said. 'They used two wereleopards and a pack of five werehyenas to kill two men. Then they tried to kill me and my mentor, Chief Guamo, but two packs of African hunting dogs and jackals saved us.'

'That sounds like quite an ordeal. Mao Sing said, patting Marion's shoulder. 'But be warned — witchcraft and sorcery also exist here, in the mountains and jungles of Asia.'

'Again, hyenas are associated with this witchcraft, and again wild dogs will save us,' Chong Lee added. 'But this time, the hyenas will have a different role, and the leopards and black panthers will be our protectors alongside the lions, tigers and wild dogs. The wild dogs of Asia are the dholes and jackals. Although bloodthirsty, they are also heroes, friends and guardians to many Asian peoples, for they are clever, resourceful and helpful to humans. Some Asians cultures fear dholes, but many more hate and fear hyenas even more. Hyenas have the appearance of wild dogs, but, unlike wild dogs, hyenas are no friends of humans. In Africa, hyenas are regarded as messengers of evil and as carriers of witches and wizards. But in some villages in India, hyenas are evil witches and wizards who have been reincarnated in this form. We're about to encounter four witches from a village across the border in India, and only the powerful magic of crocodile organs will kill them.'

'Oh my God!' Marion said, her face draining of colour. 'You mean we're about to face witches again? Oh no, I'm having no part in this!'

'It's too late, young Marion,' Sun Ying pointed out. 'You are already involved.'

'And when the witches come, the crocodile organs will kill them and destroy their magic,' Chong Lee added reassuringly. 'True, they might then come back to life as four savage hyenas, but fret not; the dholes and jackals will save us.'

'I'm going to regret this,' Marion murmured, and then sighed. Then she heard the evil, malicious giggling of four nearby witches, and the women came into her view from behind the undergrowth. Marion's blood ran cold and her stomach churned as if a stormy ocean were inside her.

'Go on, Marion!' Mao Sing cried out. 'Use the crocodile organs.'

Marion waved the organs at the sneering witches and felt magic flow through the moist jungle air. The witches were dead in a matter of seconds.

Marion simply stood there, shocked by what she had done, but then the corpses transformed into four ferocious, bloodthirsty hyenas, very much alive. Their eyes blazed with a burning hatred and their bone-breaking teeth flashed from the light of the moon. The witch-hyenas growled and began their sadistic bouts of laughter. Foam and saliva spilled from their black lips, and Marion was frozen to the spot as images of the long-ago wolf attack, and the more recent battle between hyenas and jackals in Africa, flashed through her mind.

Marion could feel her chest tightening and darkness closing in at the edges of her vision — but then she heard the savage snarling of dholes and the fierce growling of jackals. She held her breath as the wild dogs closed in on the hyenas, their tawny bodies covered with powerful muscle and their teeth exposed as they barked. The jackals attacked one hyena, mauling its hindquarters, stomach and front legs, and the hyena fled. The dholes ganged up against the other three hyenas and savaged their legs and stomachs. Although hyenas are formidable fighters, these ones were heavily outnumbered; they galloped off into the night with severe injuries. The dholes and jackals turned their amber eyes, now lacking the threat of death in them, towards Marion and the monks, and Marion dared to breathe again. She found she was shivering and sweating.

'It's okay, young Marion,' Chong Lee said, trying to calm her. 'You controlled your fear very well. But these wild dogs mean us no harm.'

'Thank you,' Marion said nervously.

'There is an old Chinese proverb,' the wise priest went on. '"It is only when you know fear that you become truly brave." You see, true courage comes through overcoming your fear. Fear is our guardian angel, in a way, as it keeps us safe, but a wise person learns how to master and control the fear so that it does not control them. You'll get there — I have faith in you.'

'I-I hope you're right,' Marion stammered, her voice not yet recovered from her terror. 'I just need some time to calm down.'

The dholes and jackals cantered off through the blackness of the night, and Marion began to relax, the tightness in her chest slowly disappearing.

CHAPTER 5

The night in the jungle was cool and refreshing, and a mild breeze stroked Marion's bare arms as she and the three Buddhist monks passed through a village. They saw statues and totems of lions and tigers, and on a wall in the left side of the village were paintings of the moon and a tiger chasing a man.

'This is incredible,' Marion exclaimed. 'Everywhere we go, there are statues of lions and tigers.'

'That is because lions and tigers are featured a great deal in Buddhism and Hinduism,' Chong Lee replied. 'That's why so many statues, shrines and totems were built for these big cats. But now, look at those two paintings on the wall.'

'I see them. What do they stand for?' Marion asked.

'One of the paintings shows the crescent shape of the moon,' Sun Ying said. 'The other is a tiger with enormous jaws and teeth chasing a man. In China, the crescent shape of the new moon is thought to be a tiger's jaws and teeth chasing mankind.'

'But we are in Nepal,' said Marion, confused.

'Ah, but Chinese people painted these.'

'Look over there!' Mao Sing cried. 'In the graveyard! Two large Bengal tigers are guarding the tombstones.'

'Jesus Christ!' Marion said.

'Those tigers will not attack us,' Chong Lee said. 'They are only guarding the graveyard against gravediggers and wild animals.'

'I'm sorry,' Marion said, 'but they look so intimidating.'

'In many parts of Asia, tigers are thought to protect souls and guard graves. So these tigers are not only protecting the graves, but also the souls of the dead people in them. Another creature who protects souls is the yeti.'

'The yeti?!'

'Yetis are the guardian spirits of the Buddhist god of mercy, Chen-re-zi,' Chong Lee said. 'See the two yetis over there, protecting Chen-re-zi.' Marion watched as Chong Lee cast a spell and a couple of yetis appeared, guarding the god, and she was afraid. But both the yetis and tigers fell asleep over the graves.

'Now, have you heard of weretigers?' Sun Ying asked, fixing his gaze on Marion.

'No, but it wouldn't surprise me if they exist,' Marion replied. 'In Europe, there are myths and legends about werewolves, and in Africa, there are legends about wereleopards. The leopards the witches used to kill the two men were really wereleopards. So, is the same thing true of weretigers and wereleopards in Asia?'

'That is right, young lady,' Chong Lee confirmed. 'In Asia, in this dreamworld, we believe in weretigers and wereleopards and werelions. And in South America, there are the same beliefs about werejaguars — humans who become jaguars at night.'

'But do they really exist?' Marion queried.

'That depends on your opinion,' Mao Sing told Marion. 'Many people do not believe in yetis, but we wise men of the Far East do. So the same thing applies to werebeasts.'

'But let's reach the point,' Chong Lee suggested. 'In parts of India, the human victims of man-eating tigers are thought to be the work of wicked sadhus, puritan holy men corrupted into eating human flesh. Look over there, to the south.'

Marion's apprehension and fear increased as she watched the conjured sadhus turning into tigers and then killing men and women in the villages in India. She gulped to get rid of her fear and turned back to Chong Lee.

'There are many beliefs in the Far East that associate tigers with weretigers and reincarnation,' he said. 'It is said that dead people who have been slain by tigers have their spirits passed on to the tigers, and other people simply become weretigers. However, we do not know how werelions and wereleopards were caused.'

'It is only a few minutes past midnight — still very early in the morning,' Mao Sing suddenly announced to the others. 'We are about to encounter a war between two armies of large predators.' He turned to Marion again. 'You saw the battle between those four hyenas on one side and the dholes and jackals on the other. Well, that battle was only a skirmish in a much greater war being fought across the jungle, even as we speak. On one side, hyenas are allied to an army of crocodiles and of Komodo dragons introduced into Nepal from Indonesia. On the other side are lions, tigers, leopards, black panthers and wild dogs.'

'Really?' Marion asked. She was fascinated by all this new information, and was determined to take it all in.

'Yes,' Chong Lee continued. 'But it has been said that the war will be settled once and for all by a battle between a tiger and a dragon. In some forms of Buddhism, the tiger stands for yin, or evil, whilst the dragon stands for yang, or good. But in our form of Buddhism, and in many other forms in China, it is the other way around. We personally hope that the tiger will defeat the dragon. Then we believe a disciple of Buddha will ride a tiger to demonstrate his supernatural powers and his ability to overcome evil.'

Sun Ying nodded gravely, and added, 'So, three events will conclude the war: a battle between Komodo dragons and crocodiles; a battle between crocodiles and leopards; and a battle between a dragon and a tiger. I foresee that when we have diffused a violent situation between the Komodo dragons and crocodiles, four large crocodiles will escape and continue to pose a threat to humans in China. Now, in China there are as many beliefs about leopards and black panthers as there are about tigers. They symbolise aggression, cunning and warlike behaviour; they are leaders when they want to be. So, the leopard and the black panther will lead the snow leopard and the clouded leopard against these crocodiles. These wild cats will kill the four crocodiles who escape, and the battle between the tiger and the dragon will commence. The disciple of Buddha will ride a tiger in the end.'

'That sounds incredibly exciting,' Marion said, her eyes lit up with emotion. 'And I guess the dragon is in fact a Komodo dragon? But Komodo dragons only live in Indonesia, not China or Nepal. If my guess is correct, how did these creatures come over here?'

'They were introduced here in this dreamworld, not in the real world,' Chong Lee explained. 'However, in the real world there may originally have been Komodo dragons throughout China, Nepal and south-east Asia until humankind reduced their population to a few islands in Indonesia. We have no way of knowing. But people in China have very strong beliefs about dragons; in fact, one year in the Chinese calendar is the year of the dragon. And, more importantly, I believe you are right — the Komodo dragons are the ones predicted to battle the tigers.'

Marion nodded, her face flushed in excitement and nervous anticipation.

'Friends, we must hurry if we are to intervene with the devastating battle between the crocodiles and the Komodo dragons,' Sun Ying said worriedly. 'We will need the sleeping gas grenades to knock the reptiles out and destroy their evil spirits. Did we mention that Komodo dragons, crocodiles and hyenas are possessed by evil spirits, whereas big cats and wild dogs are possessed by good spirits? The sleeping gas in the grenades will destroy the evil spirits so that the ferocious reptiles and hyenas will never fight the big cats and wild dogs again. Let us proceed on our mission.'

'This is going to be terrifying,' Marion muttered, strain apparent in her voice. She dismissed her fears; she had to trust the three monks.

She followed them into the jungle again, but it was only a matter of time before they were confronted by two large armies closing in on them: the Komodo dragons emerged from the south while the crocodiles climbed out of the river to the west in a vast hoard. There was also a clan of seventeen ravenous hyenas galloping towards them from due east, and then they halted. Marion's petrified gaze fixed on the crocodiles, and anxiety grated at her mind as her blood seemed to stop flowing in her veins.

Fighting hard to suppress her terror, Marion reached for two grenades, and the three Shaolin monks caressed the grenades in their robes. The hyenas' striped bodies were thick and powerful, with hard muscle.

Their serrated teeth were fully exposed and their eyes blazed like infernos. They laughed with insane fury, but the hissing, snarling and roaring of the crocodiles and Komodo dragons was far worse. Their fierce chorus of hatred and rage made Marion's eyes widen as adrenalin caused her to tremble. Her mind darted back to the crocodiles in Rwanda who had invaded Guamo's village, and she felt bile rise in her throat.

The Komodo dragons were enormous, primitive, grey beasts, and their thrashing tails were powerful enough to break a man's arms, legs or ribs with one blow. They flashed their teeth and claws as they hissed and snarled with savage rage, and the crocodiles also flailed their powerful tails and opened their gaping mouths to expose their dreaded teeth. The eyes of the Komodo dragons and crocodiles were cold and cruel, conveying a brutal killer instinct.

Suddenly, the hostile chorus was countered by the roaring of the lions and tigers, the cries of the leopards and black panthers, the snarling of the snow leopard, the growling of the honey badger and the vicious barking of the dholes and jackals. These fearsome killers were converging towards the reptiles and hyenas from the jungles and mountains to the north. As the monks kept an eye on the Komodo dragons and crocodiles, Marion swung round to face the approaching beasts, trembling even though the big cats and wild dogs were possessed by good spirits.

'H-how did I get myself into this?' Marion muttered through gritted teeth. This was her worst nightmare. Her shaking hands brushed against the sleeping gas grenades, but she did not pull them from her pocket.

The lions were enormous masses of muscle with thick legs and giant paws. Their eyes gleamed amber in the darkness. However, the tigers were bigger, heavier, stronger and faster than the lions, and much more savage. The leopards and black panthers also swelled with sinuous muscles, their teeth flashing in the darkness and their glowing eyes blazing with vicious fury and hatred.

Only the lions and some of the tigers were powerful enough to attack the Komodo dragons, and so they charged. The leopards, black panthers and five remaining tigers confronted the crocodiles. At the same time, the dholes, the jackals, the honey badger, the snow leopard and the clouded leopard had to face the seventeen hyenas coming from the east. Overcome by indignation and rage towards the jungle cat's violent death, the snow leopard, the clouded leopard and a honey badger prepared to defend themselves against three hyenas, whilst a caracal and an Asian golden cat fought against two hyenas.

The fifteen dholes and twenty jackals stood up to the remaining twelve hyenas, and Marion and the Shaolin monks were caught in the middle of what was to be a ferocious battle. The various beasts were bellowing, roaring and snarling again with far greater ferocity than a monsoon.

'Get ready to throw the sleeping gas grenades,' Mao Sing commanded above the racket.

They all sent a hail of grenades flying towards the massive reptiles who were immediately clouded in gas; it knocked them unconscious and killed their evil spirits. Marion had one grenade left, and she flung it towards the wild dogs and smaller predators. It landed amongst the seventeen hyenas, knocking them out and destroying their evil spirits. The battle had successfully been stopped in its tracks, but Marion noticed that the big cats and wild dogs were refraining from killing the unconscious reptiles and hyenas. She turned towards Chong Lee.

'Now that the reptiles and hyenas are unconscious, why are the predators with good spirits hesitating to kill them?' she asked. 'They all harbour a vicious hatred of crocodiles and hyenas, and are powerful enough to kill them — especially now they are unconscious.'

'Because most predators will not touch animals who appear to be dead,' the monk explained. 'This is because the animals may have died of poisoning or disease. That's why many animals like the opossum escape predators by playing dead, and humans have survived predator attacks in the past by playing dead. But there is a more important reason. Did you notice that the sleeping gas from the grenades gives off a very unpleasant smell?'

'I did notice,' Marion said, screwing up her face again at the recent memory.

'That is precisely to stop humans or other animals killing unconscious animals knocked out by the sleeping gas,' Chong Lee told Marion. 'The gas contains a concoction of harmless chemicals and herbs which cause this smell, tranquillise the animal and kill the evil spirit within. Buddhists and Hindus of the Far East and the Indians of North America respect all forms of life, and once an animal has been knocked out it is unnecessary, cruel and cowardly to kill the animal. So, due to the smell, the dholes, jackals and smaller predators can't kill the hyenas, and the big cats can't kill the reptiles. We monks believe in using only necessary force to bring down an enemy, without inflicting unnecessary injury or death.'

'I see,' Marion said, and chuckled. Then she spotted four crocodiles swimming away along the river. They must have escaped the gas clouds by diving underwater; they got away, just like the monks had predicted!

'Those four crocodiles you told me about!' Marion said frantically. 'They have escaped upstream! They'll prey on other humans because their evil spirits have not been destroyed!'

'That is where the two leopards, the snow leopard and the clouded leopard come into play,' Mao Sing told Marion. 'We told you earlier that in China, the leopard symbolises aggression and warlike behaviour, and can be a great leader. Well, these two leopards, a spotted leopard and a black panther, will now lead the snow leopard and the clouded leopard into a commando-style attack to kill the four crocodiles.'

* * *

Marion was overpowered by disbelief to witness Nepal's border with China merge and the big cats cross it easily. In fact, the very concept of solitary big cats, operating in armies of tigers, leopards and black panthers transforming themselves into weretigers and wereleopards — and werelions, which did not exist in any spiritualism in the real world — was overwhelming. Marion knew that these amazing things could only occur in a dream, and she reminded herself that she was trapped in the world of fantasy until she awoke. But the war between the big cats and killer reptiles was by no means over, as the lions and tigers glared into China and watched the tiger and the dragon preparing to do battle, the tiger standing for yang, good, and the dragon standing for yin, evil. The leopards, black panthers, dholes and jackals also watched, flanked by the honey badger, the caracal and the Asian golden cat. The female jungle cat came up behind them and hissed her thanks to these smaller killers and the wild dogs for avenging the death of her mate. Marion marvelled at the beauty of the creatures, then turned her gaze towards the biggest tiger and the fiercest-looking Komodo dragon, as they prepared to fight a battle that would settle the war. She also spotted the yang spirit hanging over the tiger and the yin spirit hovering over the dragon. The hyenas came to and fled through the jungle whilst the Komodo dragons and crocodiles also recovered and formed an uneasy peace with the four armies of big cats. The only battle now would be between the vicious tiger and the bloodthirsty dragon. They lunged towards each other and fought a titanic battle with extreme ferocity.

The tiger's roar resonated through the mountain atmosphere, mingling with the hissing of the dragon. Razor-sharp claws ripped through muscle. A Komodo dragon is large, powerful and savage enough to kill a fully grown elephant, and this dragon was a giant who dwarfed the tiger in size and strength. Although enormous, powerful and swift, the tiger was getting severely slashed and torn by the dragon's rapier claws and bone-breaking teeth. Both beasts were locked in savage combat, teeth tearing at each other's shoulders and necks, talons ripping flesh to the bone, the dragon's legs crushing the tiger to his chest in a bear-hug as his claws raked down the striped shoulders and back. The tiger clawed at his chest in retaliation.

Marion was shocked and traumatised by this violent aggression and ruthless savagery, and she turned away, her hands covering her eyes. Chong Lee embraced her.

The dragon was far stronger than the tiger, but the tiger wrenched and twisted like a snake, his rippling muscles and strong legs fighting against the dragon's awesome strength. The dragon snarled and hissed, his eyes red with rage, whilst the tiger growled with vicious aggression and hatred that would put a lion to shame, and then his hind legs were free as the dragon rolled on top of him. The tiger kicked upwards towards the dragon's groin and stomach, shredding the beast's genital region and opening the flesh of his belly to the intestines so the dragon was disemboweled.

The dragon roared in agony and recoiled onto his back, all four legs covering his stomach and groin. But the agony only drove him further in his quest to finish his opponent, the pain feeding his rage, and he snapped at the tiger's face.

The tiger leapt out of the way, raced behind the dragon and lunged, hurling his huge, powerful body onto the killer reptile's back. It clawed at the dragon's back and shoulders with all four sets of talons whilst his bone-crushing teeth fastened onto the side of the dragon's neck. Coiling like a snake, the tiger worked his way towards the vulnerable jugular vein to deal a killing bite. The dragon fought and flailed around, but the tiger's fangs finally ruptured its jugular, and the huge reptile lay in a lifeless heap, its eyes dilated with death.

The tiger leapt off the dead dragon and stood over the beast, roaring his victory with majestic pride. Marion turned from Chong Lee's embrace, knowing that good had triumphed over evil, and she grinned and blushed with relief, tears of joy flowing down her face.

The Komodo dragons and crocodiles, free of their evil spirits, retreated into the jungle and the river, and the lions, leopards, dholes, jackals and other tigers joined in with the vocal celebration.

Marion and the Shaolin monks yelled with joy, and then Chong Lee cast a spell that changed the scene entirely.

* * *

They were in a forest in China, and the escaped crocodiles, still full of evil spirits, were tearing at the carcass of a giant panda which they had killed. Stalking the four killer reptiles were the leopard, the black panther, the snow leopard and the clouded leopard. Marion was overcome by worry, for these crocodiles were massive giants measuring eight to twelve feet long, and they could kill even a leopard with one crushing bite.

The four big cats depended on the element of surprise.

The spotted leopard led the other wild cats into a swift, savage attack like a renowned bandit leading their men. All their sinuous power and speed was concentrated into the attack. The leopard and the black panther screamed with savage aggression as they hurled themselves towards the two largest crocodiles and landed on their backs with sickening impact. Their hind and front claws penetrated the armoured flesh of the killer reptiles and worked to shred it, and their dagger-like fangs reached for their jugular veins.

The snow leopard and the clouded leopard repeated this ruthless, savage attack against the two smaller crocodiles, the snow leopard blasting the atmosphere with his vicious cry whilst the clouded leopard hissed in a deadly fashion. The snow leopard's attack was exactly the same as the ferocious attack by the two larger leopards, and he finished the third crocodile in thirteen seconds. The clouded leopard's smaller size was an advantage, as he was swifter and more agile than the fourth crocodile, and he ripped the crocodile's armour and shredded his flesh. However, the crocodile's violent thrashing and turning nearly threw him off; the clouded leopard could not quite fasten his long, powerful fangs into the crocodile's jugular, but, as the reptile's head lurched to the right, the clouded leopard's left paw slashed at the left side of the crocodile's neck and ripped through flesh and arteries. The crocodile died in that next instant, and the four big cats announced their victory with the same pride as the tiger who had vanquished the giant Komodo dragon.

'Thank God,' Marion said breathlessly, feeling exhausted just by witnessing the war;

she could not imagine how tired the fighters were.

Then, as the leopard, the black panther, the snow leopard and the clouded leopard rejoined the tiger, the disciple of Buddha seemed to appear. He mounted and rode another tiger in order to convey his ability to conquer evil. The tiger was roaring, and then both tigers pawed each other, signalling friendship.

Marion and the three Chinese headed back through the rainforest and the Himalayan mountains, trundling over rocky ground and passing giant rhododendrons and other exotic trees along the way. Marion was deep in thought, for she had noticed that the snow leopard and the clouded leopard had attacked, fought and killed two of the crocodiles with as much deadly violence as the leopard and the black panther, despite their smaller size.

'Even though they're not true leopards,' Marion told the Chinese, 'the snow leopard and the clouded leopard were just as savage as the leopard and the black panther.'

'You've seen how savage they are,' Chong Lee agreed. 'I assume you've been told how leopards and black panthers are the most ferocious of all the great cats, more so even than tigers? Well, snow leopards and clouded leopards are just as ferocious, and can outclass lions and tigers in savagery and cunning.'

'The snow leopard is a shy cat, but is well capable of deadly violence in some circumstances,' Mao Sing added. 'It normally preys on wild sheep and goats, deer, birds and rodents, but it is capable of killing yaks many times its size and weight. Also, I saw one snow leopard viciously attack a wild boar by leaping onto its back and raking its claws across the wild boar's neck, killing it. I have even seen a snow leopard driving two wolves from a sheep kill, and yet another snow leopard fighting a terrible battle against an enormous bull eight times its weight. When we witnessed the battle, the snow leopard's speed and ferocity against the brute strength of the bull was incredible. Then there's the clouded leopard, of which Sun Ying knows a great deal.'

'The clouded leopard is extremely fierce and cunning,' Sun Ying said, nodding gravely. 'It is also extremely powerful, with jaws and teeth that can bite with incredible force. It has the longest fangs of all wild cats, relative to its size. The clouded leopard is shy, like any true leopard, and normally preys on deer, cattle and monkeys. But I've seen how savage a clouded leopard can be; one killed a twenty-foot python, and another killed an adult water buffalo. They are even powerful enough to kill an eight-foot crocodile, as we have seen.'

'I see,' Marion said. 'It is fortunate that snow leopards and clouded leopards never eat humans, then!'

'That's true,' Chong Lee agreed. 'But they will attack a human if cornered, which, fortunately, has never been known to happen.'

Marion and the monks finally reached the

Shaolin temple, Marion's temporary home. They heard the trumpets blasting through the mountain atmosphere and the gongs being struck by the other Shaolin monks. These sounds rang out through the mountains and forests.

After entering the temple, Marion sat in a room with Chong Lee. 'Why are we here?' she asked.

'Because we have reached the next stage of your training,' the old man replied. 'You need to understand how we use certain dangerous animals for food, clothes and medicines. On these plates are five different forms of cooked meat: elephant, rhino, water buffalo, crocodile and tiger. We were given these different meats by the Tharus, an ancient tribe in Nepal. They eat tiger meat and we view it as a delicacy. The tiger meat is far superior to all these other meats. Do you want to try some?'

'It would be my pleasure,' Marion enthused; she was starving. It was the work of fifteen minutes for her to demolish all five meats, and then she moved on to some eggs and vegetables.

'Amongst a great many people in the Far East, the tiger has medicinal properties,' Chong Lee told her. 'But we Buddhists do not condone this superstition. This tiger was killed by the Tharus because it had killed several humans. Had they not killed it, the tiger would have continued its rampage. That is the reason we have tiger meat today — not for its supposed medicinal properties. We also do not believe in the Chinese superstition that rhino horn is an aphrodisiac or some form of medicine. It is because of these beliefs that thousands of tigers in India, south-east Asia and Siberia — along with African and Asian rhinos — have been killed to feed. People buy rhino horns and tiger bones, powder them, and either rub them into injuries or eat the powdered substances with water.'

'I was given powdered rhino horn in Rwanda,' Marion said. 'This superstition exists in Africa as well as Asia. They also gave me gorilla hands to enhance my strength and courage, and powdered gorilla fingers which I rubbed into grass scratches on my arms and face. These superstitions still seem very strong, even now.'

'Yes, but we Buddhists, among others, have campaigned for years to educate people and tell them that man-made medicines are more effective,' Chong Lee explained. 'We try to teach them that there is no need to buy rhino horns or tiger bones, and we have put pressure on the Chinese, Nepalese and Indian authorities to curb the trade in these products. But still it continues.' He looked sad for a moment. 'The tiger is extinct from most of China, except Manchuria, and tigers in other areas are quickly dying out — especially in India, where a growing population are pushing the tigers out of their forests through deforestation, and poverty is a major incentive for people to poach tigers and other animals. In many parts of India and south-east Asia, elephants compete with farmers for land, and both the cutting down of the forests and ivory poaching have drastically reduced the elephant herds. It is very sad.'

'Surely if we use money raised for wildlife protection we can set more land aside for elephants, rhinos and tigers, so there is still a chance of a future for them,' Marion said. 'Then again, I suppose some of the money for wildlife protection has to go into anti-poaching patrols, and some must go into meeting the needs of poor people who compete with wild animals for space. You cannot effectively protect wildlife and their habitats unless you meet the needs of the poor farmers and villagers, and compensate them for crops destroyed or livestock killed by wild animals. If you reduce poverty, you reduce the incentive for people to poach wildlife and cut down the forests for wood or land.'

'That's very true,' Chong Lee agreed. 'But some of the money for wildlife protection also has to go into educating the next generation that rhino horns and tiger bones are not medicines, and that there are alternative medicines. If you get rid of the demand for wildlife products by educating people, the evil dealers at the top have no reason to supply them and they will be put out of business.'

'But we have a long way to go before these animals are properly protected and poverty in Africa and Asia is defeated,' Marion stated. 'And we must put a stop to the destruction of the tropical rainforests.'

'You're right,' Chong Lee replied. 'But now, I have given you an education as to how Asia's dangerous animals were exploited for human needs. The next stage is to train you in how we calm aggressive animals. In Africa, I believe you were trained in how to pacify or diffuse animals with food. In the Far East, we are trained in animal whispering and meditation. Very few people in the world have the skill to calm down a dangerous animal, but we Shaolin monks have honed this skill over centuries.'

'I've heard of animal whispering, but I don't really know that much about meditation,' Marion said. 'Who invented animal whispering?'

'The Buddhists in Asia and the Native Americans,' Chong Lee told her. 'Now, I will train you not only to calm down an angry horse and a furious bull, but also a vicious lion and a savage tiger.'

Marion's terror returned and she bit her lip, hard. 'You're scaring me,' she whispered. 'Are you serious?'

'I am serious,' he replied. 'In time you will acquire the necessary skills. Fear not.'

'How do I start?' Marion asked in a small voice.

'You start with deep breathing exercises to calm your nerves. Then you will try relaxation exercises derived from kung fu and tai chi. This will involve tensing your muscles and then relaxing. Then you will pray and allow positive energy to flow through you.'

'I don't believe in prayer.'

'But your faith will guide you. If you pray, the energy of the Shaolin temple will flow through you and make the animals respect you. Animal whispering and meditation are similar to martial arts: it's a matter of mind over body. Your mind is far more powerful than your body, and if you have faith, confidence and an indomitable spirit, you can do anything. You know the old saying I'm referring to?'

'Yes,' Marion replied. 'Faith can move mountains.'

'In Nepal, there was a real-life example of this where a Buddhist monk was confronted by a Himalayan black bear. He prayed, and this diffused the bear's aggression and it left him alone. People have been known to calm elephants, water buffaloes and even tigers by talking calmly and showing no fear. And we Shaolin monks have done the same thing. This calming technique can also be used with dogs, horses, donkeys and mules, and it really works. The only thing you have to remember is that you should not look the animal straight in the eyes, or try to dominate or intimidate it. You should only stroke the energy field in the animal's body.'

'The energy field?' Marion said, her eyebrows raised slightly.

'Every human or animal has an energy field which feeds energy into their body,' Chong Lee explained. 'There are pressure points in the neck and shoulders of the body, and by rubbing them you can calm the animal. It helps if you have faith to guide you, but if you do not, the power of your mind and soul and your lack of fear will be sufficient. Animals are drawn to attack you by your fear, so if you master your fear you have won half the battle. You must walk towards the animal relaxed and confident.

'People who have been threatened by sharks or barracudas in the sea have often discouraged the beasts from attacking them by staying still and showing no fear; in most cases, the shark swam away. People have also managed to calm aggressive dogs, but meditation will not work against extremely savage, primitive animals like crocodiles, alligators or Komodo dragons. It is most effective on intelligent animals. You must act submissive and not look them directly in the eyes. This applies to all animals, from elephants down to house cats.

'Now, animals which lack intelligence, like bison, buffaloes, oxen and bulls, can be put to sleep by waving your hands across their faces. This confuses and disorientates them, and because they are stupid animals they will eventually collapse and fall asleep. But although this works on bulls, oxen, buffaloes and bison, there are some stupid animals which this will not work on because they are too large and savage, like hippos and rhinos, and it won't work on wild pigs. So, there are three skills we aim to teach you: animal whispering, meditation and the sleep technique. Do you follow, Marion?'

'I follow,' Marion replied. 'I'll give it my best shot.'

* * *

Marion spent five days practising deep breathing and relaxation exercises, involving tensing her muscles and then relaxing completely. Then, on the sixth day, she felt a strange energy flowing through her body; she had no idea whether it was the power of God, the Shaolin temple or simply the mental power of her mind and soul. Because she harboured no real belief in God, she felt it was most likely a combination of powers from the Shaolin temple and her mind and soul.

Next, she practised waving her hands across the eyes of humans, confusing and disorientating them. After this, she tried the technique with bulls, oxen and water buffaloes. She also tried meditation techniques with vicious dogs, and animal whispering techniques with six restless horses, a flighty donkey and a stubborn mule. She was amazed at what powers she had gained, but her journey wasn't over yet.

Her next challenge was to use these calming powers on an aggressive horse, a vicious bull, a lion and, finally, an enraged Bengal tiger from Nepal's rainforests.

Marion approached the arena of an ancient circus, originally built by a maharajah, where criminals and political prisoners used to be thrown to the tigers to be devoured, rather like lions and tigers were used in the arenas of ancient Rome. Now this arena had a more peaceful purpose: it was used as an area in which to subdue tigers and other animals, rather than to exploit their aggression. Marion was very nervous, but Chong Lee put a comforting arm around her shoulders.

'I see you are still scared,' he said softly. 'Don't be; I have confidence in your abilities. Now, in order to pacify an aggressive animal, we start by diverting its ferocity towards another beast that is just as large, powerful and vicious. Both animals will be too wary of each other to attack the human. For example, you may have noticed in the past that circuses will sometimes mix lions and tigers in the same arena, so that the fear and wariness the big cats feel towards each other will prevent them from attacking the lion-tamer. However, you must remember that this will not work on herbivores, which are generally at peace with each other; it only works on predators who have a natural hatred of each other. Although herbivores are not enemies of each other, the horse and the bull are actually two powerful herbivores which hate each other more than they hate humans or predators. So you will be fine with them both in the arena with you, and with the lion and tiger in there too.'

'Thanks for the comforting words,' Marion replied, her shaky voice betraying her lingering nerves despite her attempts to seem brave. 'I'll do my best.'

Mao Sing and Sun Ying opened the gate

and Marion entered the arena, as nervous as ever. But she refused to back out now. Two cage doors opened in the arena and a bulging black bull charged out, along with an aggravated brown mare.

The bull blundered across the stony ground, and his enormous black body rippled with muscle from shoulders to rump. His head was huge, topped by fearsome horns as large as a water buffalo's. His furious eyes were bloodshot and filled with rage. Marion instinctively knew that this bull was the more dangerous of the two herbivores. She swiftly dodged its oncoming assault, and felt the warm rush of air as the bull raced past.

The horse then began to leap about with impressive power, agility and speed, her body bristling with hard muscle, her hooves capable of delivering a kick powerful enough to kill a human with one or two blows. Her eyes were wild and rolling, almost as evil as the bull's. Marion slowly retreated, and then mustered the courage to charge in between the two hostile animals, diverting their attention, and then jump out of the way. She knew that even a one-second delay in leaping out of the way would prove fatal.

Shoving her doubts deep inside her, she threw caution to the wind and ran towards the wild beasts.

The bull almost plunged his formidable horns into her, but she leapt aside at the last second. The bull snorted, grunted and then bellowed in furious frustration. The horse screamed, enraged by the commotion.

Marion came between the two beasts and flung her cape over the bull's head in the fashion of a matador. The bull reared up onto his hind legs and kicked the cape with his front hooves, narrowly missing Marion's head, then struggled to free his vision, his horns ripping the cape apart. The horse began to kick repeatedly at the bull, but Marion wrenched the horse away by pulling on its reins and shouting, 'Stop it! Enough fighting!'

Luckily for her, the horse was surprised by Marion's dominant display and retreated to the other side of the arena. Encouraged, Marion grabbed the bull's horns and waved her hands across the beast's eyes. She did this for five minutes until the bull became dumb and confused, and then its huge, musclebound body crashed to the ground as he succumbed to sleep.

Suddenly, the horse began to race around the arena, bucking and stamping the ground. Its eyes black with hatred, it reared and flailed its lethal front hooves. Marion dodged the onslaught and retreated swiftly, but then she once again gathered her wits and walked towards the horse with confidence and courage. She reached towards the energy field around the horse's neck and shoulders, and spoke softly yet firmly to the horse. The horse was caught off guard again, and its hooves thrashed the air with less force. The horse eventually calmed down and retreated towards the gate of the arena.

Mao Sing and Sun Ying appeared and opened the gate, releasing the mare into the forest where she could roam free. They then placed one of their capes over the bull's head and, as he awoke, they guided him outside the arena to begin a new life on a farm where he would be treated with kindness and respect, not ill-treated or killed; devout Buddhists like these Shaolin monks harboured a profound respect and veneration for all animals and their welfare.

Marion then sweated and trembled, for she knew she would have to confront a lion and a tiger next. However, she drew a tiny bit of comfort in the fact that the predators should be too wary of each other to attack her. She knew that giving in to her terror was the worst thing she could do, so she gritted her teeth and prepared herself.

Two other enclosures opened their gates. A lion and a tiger padded out into the arena.

The lion let out a roar which charged the atmosphere with as much savagery as the lions Marion had encountered in Rwanda. His voice rumbled like an avalanche, and the tiger soon joined in, snarling with deadly ferocity. The tiger was more savage and bloodthirsty than the lion, as well as being faster and more agile, but the lion's thick, bushy mane would protect his neck and shoulders from the tiger's lethal fangs and claws. Both cats were massive beasts, weighing in at around 500 pounds, and their enormous bodies rippled with hard, solid muscle. They roared again in unison and Marion clenched her eyes shut, muttering, 'Oh my God!'

However, her fighting spirit kicked in, and she slowly made her way between the big cats. She adopted a submissive body posture, just as Chong Lee had advised, and forced herself to smile at the big cats with confidence. The nausea in her throat was tormenting and her nerves were shredded, but she hid her terror extremely well. The big cats approached her slowly, stalking her, their eyes blazing — but then they hesitated.

This human was not attacking them.

It was not afraid.

Doubt dimmed the fire in their eyes. Lions and tigers generally hate the taste of human flesh, much preferring the flesh of wild animals, and these two cats were not man-eaters.

Marion approached the tiger slowly, disciplining her mind and silently praying as she did so. Power flowed through her wiry body and put her mind and soul at peace, the power from the Shaolin temple combined with her mental powers. The meditation appeared to be very effective against the tiger, which was so appeased by Marion's confidence and courage that it turned and trotted back towards its enclosure.

Marion repeated the meditation technique with the lion, talking softly, stroking the energy field in his neck, shoulders and back, parting his thick mane with her hands and caressing his huge head. The lion responded calmly to this and then bounded back towards his enclosure. Both the lion and the tiger were now as placid as sheep. Marion took some deep breaths and relaxed as Chong Lee opened the arena gate and invited her outside into the forest.

'You did well, Marion,' he said, beaming with pride. 'I told you that you could do it. Three cheers for Marion!'

Several other Shaolin monks had come out to cheer for Marion, and she beamed at them, proud and relieved.

Marion had completed her tests with the three calming methods, and was told she now had to leave Nepal for South America. But first she had some questions that needed answering.

'Chong Lee,' she began. 'Just before I left Africa, Chief Guamo told me about his country's most dangerous animals. Asia has many dangerous animals too, including venomous snakes and pythons. Apart from snakes, what do you feel are the most dangerous animals here?'

'Oh, lots,' Chong Lee replied. 'But we'll start with the herbivores. As is the case in Africa, Asia's elephants and rhinos can be extremely dangerous. Elephants are mostly dangerous when they go through the mating period. The males become very aggressive and will trample crops, attack villages and even kill people. Elephants which have been tamed by humans lose their fear of humankind, and this makes them dangerous. A placid, tamed elephant can turn lethal in a matter of seconds. They will kill people if provoked or injured, or if the females are protecting calves. In the whole of Asia, elephants kill three times as many people as tigers do — an average of a hundred and fifty to two hundred people a year. However, millions more people die in road accidents, floods or monsoons. Most elephants are placid and friendly if you treat them with respect, and the same thing is true of rhinos.

'Asia's three species of rhinos, especially the Indian rhino, are more aggressive than elephants, but very few cases have occurred in Asia where people have been attacked by rhinos. As you know, all five species of rhinos in Africa and Asia are endangered, and they have more to fear from people than people have to fear from rhinos. Rhinos will avoid humans, generally, but it is still not wise to approach one — especially a female with young. I'm convinced that rhinos have only become aggressive towards humankind because they have themselves been persecuted for centuries, and no species has suffered more from humankind's aggression than rhinos.'

'I understand that water buffaloes and wild boars can be dangerous,' Marion said. 'Wild boars in India are twice as large and aggressive as wild boars in Europe.'

'You're quite right,' Sun Ying said. 'Water buffaloes are more placid and friendly than the buffaloes in Africa, but when threatened by tigers or armed men they are just as savage and deadly. They may appear cumbersome, but they can move much faster than a human and their horns are lethal weapons. Plenty of people in Asia have been injured or killed by water buffaloes, but not as many as by elephants. The water buffalo is normally an inoffensive animal until roused, but the wild boar is far more dangerous. Wild boars have been given an unjustified reputation for savagery, but they are only savage when attacked, cornered or wounded. In that situation, or when a sow defends her young, a wild boar is just as lethal as a rhino and its tusks can even kill the tiger. Some people in India have been maimed or killed by wild boars, as has happened in Europe, but you are more likely to be run over by a car or killed in a monsoon than be attacked by a wild boar.'

Marion watched the scene change slightly, and gaped at the majestic power and beauty of a herd of elephants and rhinos drinking at the river, and then the water buffaloes drinking downstream alongside a herd of enormous wild boars. She knew that all demanded respect as mighty and formidable beasts.

'What other animals are there that I must be wary of?' Marion enquired.

'Crocodiles and tigers,' Mao Sing replied. 'The Indian marsh crocodiles and the saltwater crocodiles on India's coastline are not as dangerous as the Nile crocodiles of Africa, but have still been known to attack people unprovoked. All crocodiles must be treated with extreme caution, which means not swimming in the river or leaning over the riverbank or the edge of a boat. The same thing applies to sharks, barracudas and Komodo dragons. People swimming in the Indian and Pacific Oceans off southern and eastern Asia and Australia have been attacked by sharks, and sharks and barracudas are even more terrifying and deadly than crocodiles and Komodo dragons when they want to be. As for Komodo dragons, they are found only in a few islands of Indonesia, but, as you have discovered, in this dreamworld some have been introduced into India and Nepal. Like crocodiles, they have no fear of humankind and will kill people without provocation. They are so strong, fast and well armed that they can kill wild boars, water buffaloes and even elephants. They are extremely savage and must always be avoided.'

'We've dealt with crocodiles and Komodo dragons,' Marion said. 'But tigers are the really lethal animals, I feel.'

'In Asia, it is true that tigers kill more people than crocodiles, even tigers which are not man-eaters,' Chong Lee said, nodding. 'You see, tigers are the most dangerous man-killers of all the big cats. Like lions, tigers only become man-eaters through being injured by gunshot wounds or porcupine quills, or by disease. In the Sundarbans National Park in north-eastern India, tigers are extremely aggressive, but the reason for this might be because unnatural salts in the rivers and marshes caused by river pollution have upset the tigers' stomachs after they've drunk the river water. Another possible reason is that they have lost their fear of humans. There have been many cases of man-killing by tigers all over Asia. In Siberia and Manchuria, the Siberian tiger is the largest of all big cats, at 700 to 800 pounds, and has been known to kill people, but the Bengal tiger of India and Nepal has the worst record for man-eating. Over many centuries, millions of people have been killed or maimed by tigers all over Asia, as well as in zoos throughout the world, and not only by man-eaters but also tigers defending themselves or their young, their prey or their territories from human intruders. However, it is possible to walk in jungles full of tigers for many years without ever being attacked, but tigers must always be treated with caution, and the same thing applies to lions. But throughout the world, crocodiles and alligators kill more humans than sharks, which attack an average of eighty to a hundred people every year. But only half that number of shark victims die. On average, tigers kill between fifty and a hundred people every year, whereas crocodiles and alligators kill over a hundred and fifty to two hundred humans every year. However, the real menace to humans are, as you mentioned, venomous snakes, who kill more humans even than crocodiles and alligators.'

'I understand that crocodiles are dangerous

and tigers have the worst reputation of all big cats,' Marion replied, 'but what about leopards?'

'Leopards in Asia very rarely attack people, but once a leopard turns to man-eating, it is more cunning and deadly than a lion or even a tiger,' Mao Sing explained. 'Man-eating leopards have been credited at killing over a hundred to two hundred people per leopard, including men, women and children. They hunt in darkness, are not afraid of entering buildings to kill a man, child or dog, and they are far harder to hunt down and kill because of their cunning. Leopards and black panthers stalk men, women or children in darkness, and are almost impossible to track down, as they know of the presence of humans long before the humans can reach the big cats. They are also extremely powerful for their modest size, so strong that they can kill large crocodiles and pythons.'

Marion watched as the scene changed swiftly; she saw a few crocodiles eating a water buffalo, a couple of Komodo dragons tearing at an elephant in Indonesia and some lions nurturing their cubs in India's Gir Forest, all in quick succession. The Siberian tiger dined on a deer in Manchuria just as two Bengal tigers consumed a nilgai antelope in Nepal, and not far from the Bengal tigers were a leopard and a black panther lazing in the trees. The leopards ignored each other and avoided the tigers.

'Is that all the dangerous animals there

are?' Marion asked, turning back to the monks.

'No, there are thirteen more,' Sun Ying told her. 'Four have been known to attack humans whilst the other nine have the potential to attack if cornered or protecting young.'

'Which are they?' Marion asked.

'The yeti is the worst,' Sun Ying said.

'Oh, the yeti again,' Marion moaned.

'Okay, we will avoid talking of the yeti again,' Sun Ying replied, looking hurt. 'Let's move on to the Asian bears, of which only three are dangerous,' Chong Lee told Marion. 'They are the Himalayan black bear, the sloth bear and the sun bear. Attacks by the Asian bears are more often defensive rather than aggressive, but these bears have been tarnished with a fearsome reputation which they do not deserve. Travellers and wood-collectors in the Himalayas have been severely attacked by black bears, whilst people travelling in the jungles of India and south-east Asia have been charged and mauled by sloth bears and sun bears, but these attacks are only defensive. Although they are the smallest of all bears, sun bears can be extremely aggressive, whilst black bears have a reputation almost as terrifying as yetis. In many areas of the Far East, including China, eastern Russia and even Japan, black bears have savaged people, inflicting severe injuries with their teeth and claws. However, Asian bears will generally leave men alone if unprovoked, and most attacks happen when humans venture into a bear's territory or go near its cubs. So, of these last thirteen deadly beasts, only yetis and bears are a threat to humans.'

'Which are the other nine?' Marion enquired curiously.

'The first three are hyenas, dholes and jackals,' Mao Sing answered. 'In Africa, hyenas and hunting dogs have a dreaded reputation, and have been known to injure or kill people, but striped hyenas in India have never injured people. The same thing is true of jackals and the Asian wild dogs called dholes. Like jackals in Africa, Indian jackals are too cowardly to attack a man, but they will fight back if cornered and can be very fierce. Dholes are worse than hyenas or jackals, and have a fierce reputation. Packs of dholes roam the jungles and mountains, and are dreaded by all animals, including humans. However, like African hunting dogs, they have never attacked humans and their vicious reputation has been blown out of proportion.'

'I was terrified of the dholes and jackals who saved us from those four werehyenas, for they were as mean as guard dogs,' Marion said. 'Luckily, they were our friends.'

'Indeed,' Chong Lee said. 'Now, the last six predators are the honey badger, the snow leopard and four smaller wild cats — the clouded leopard, the caracal, the jungle cat and the Asian golden cat. None of those cats are that dangerous to humankind —

although they are capable of terrible ferocity if cornered.'

Marion watched all the killers of the mountains and jungles, first the enormous yeti roaming the mountains and the Himalayan black bear eating a sheep, then the sloth bear consuming termites and the sun bear dining on some honey. Three hyenas had killed a sambar deer, only to lose their kill to about twenty dholes, whilst fifteen jackals were feeding on a chital deer. The snow leopard was camouflaged against the snow and the clouded leopard obscured in the foliage of a tree. The jungle cat and the Asian golden cat tended to their mates and young.

The honey badger and the caracal fed together on a python the honey badger had killed, the honey badger having the lion's share of the kill. Marion marvelled at the richness and diversity of these jungles and mountains with all their deadly creatures, from giant elephants down to the diminutive jackals. She was reluctant to leave this beautiful green land for the rainforests of South America. She turned again to Chong Lee.

'Why am I leaving for South America?' she asked, trying to keep the disappointment out of her voice.

'To overcome your terror of the jaguar, the largest cat in the Americas,' Chong Lee replied. 'It is also one of the most savage big cats alongside the tiger and the puma, and its strength and killing power are awesome. Relative to its size, it is more powerful than the lion or the tiger, and its jaws and teeth can bite through an animal's skull with incredible brute force equal to the tiger's jaws. The tiger, the jaguar and the puma are the most ferocious of all wild cats, alongside the leopard, the snow leopard and the clouded leopard, and all six great cats outclass the lion in cunning and ferocity. What about the jaguar? Jaguars are stockier than leopards and can weigh over two hundred pounds, although their normal weight is a hundred and fifty pounds. The jaguar's sheer savagery is equal to that of the tiger and the leopard, but fortunately very few jaguars have become man-eaters. Out of tigers, lions, leopards, pumas and jaguars, jaguars kill the least humans, and pumas kill fewer humans still. Even so, throughout South and Central America, Indians and even white men are terrified of jaguars. They are so terrified that the jaguar has been called the South American tiger. In some regions of South America, the locals prefer to call them tigers because of their strength, cunning and ferocity, but where you're going, Peru, jaguars are called jaguars. And there is much spiritualism and worship surrounding the jaguar, including the existence of werejaguars.'

'They sound terrifying. Overcoming my fear of these beasts is going to be a real challenge,' Marion said nervously.

'I don't mean to scare you, but that's not all you will be facing. Before you reach your destination you will need to travel across the Pacific and face your fear of sharks,' Mao Sing said. 'We wish you luck, Marion.'

Marion gulped down her fear and forced a smile. 'Thank you for everything,' she said. 'I'll give it my best shot.'

'You can do this,' Chong Lee said encouragingly.

The three Shaolin monks bowed to Marion as a gesture of respect, and Marion bowed back. Then the monks cast a spell to transport Marion to a harbour near Shanghai on the Pacific coast of China. Marion prepared for the long voyage across the Pacific, the largest ocean in the world.

CHAPTER 6

Marion was being taken across the Pacific Ocean in the hunting ship navigated by a hundred rainforest natives led by Chiaguar.

'How many dangerous sea creatures are there in the oceans apart from sharks, Chiaguar?' she asked.

'There are very many,' Chiaguar replied. 'But they are generally only dangerous to other sea creatures, not to humans. However, all of them are lethal when humans intrude on their domain. The most dreaded are sharks, but despite their reputation for extreme ferocity and bloodlust, sharks very rarely attack people. Every year, one hundred people on average get attacked by sharks, but only about forty or fifty die from these attacks, and even fewer are eaten. Compared to a shark's natural prey of whales, walruses, seals and fish, humans are too bony to satisfy a shark's appetite. Besides, sharks do not like the taste of human flesh which means that they often spit any human victims out. Also, even though a hundred shark victims every year seems like a frightening figure, it is a very small number of people compared to the millions of people who swim in the world's oceans every year. Most attacks on humans occur in oceans near South Africa, Australia, New Zealand, Hawaii, South America, Florida and California, but even they are rare occurrences. Even so, being attacked by a shark is a terrifying experience that one never forgets.'

Chiaguar paused and stared into the surrounding waters, apparently deep in thought, before continuing. 'Most species of shark are not normally dangerous to humans, and the two largest species, the whale shark and the basking shark, have never attacked humans. The species most dreaded by humans is the great white shark, which is extremely savage and lethal. Their enormous jaws and teeth can bite with awesome power, and are capable of tearing off a human's limb, or crushing all their bones or breaking their ribs and spine, but even so the great white sharks do not particularly like human flesh. Four other species that have been known to attack and kill humans are the tiger shark, the bull shark, the blue shark and the hammerhead shark. All five species have recently made a few attacks on people swimming off the coast of Peru. In the last five years, seventeen of my people have been maimed or killed by great white sharks and eleven by tiger sharks. Only four of my people were attacked by bull sharks, but blue sharks and hammerheads have proved to be more deadly; in the last two years, nine people I have known have been savaged by blue sharks and fourteen by hammerhead sharks.'

'I'm more petrified of sharks than of most other dangerous animals,' Marion said, her voice weak.

'Most people are,' Chiaguar replied. 'As soon as they see a shark's fin in the water, people panic and race towards the shore. There are many horror stories about sharks that have been exaggerated and blown out of proportion by humans.'

'Like the film *Jaws*,' Marion said.

'Like *Jaws*,' Chiaguar agreed. 'Sharks are often turned into sea monsters. There is truth in the idea that sharks are drawn to blood; they can smell it from half a mile away. When sharks smell blood, they lose control and will attack the source of the blood without mercy, often killing humans in the process. With this in mind, sharks can be more lethal and ferocious than crocodiles, alligators or tigers. From early history, sharks have given rise to myths, legends and even true-life stories of man-eating sea monsters. Have you heard of the story in the Bible of Jonah being swallowed by a whale?'

'I have,' Marion said. 'But it could never have happened because the gullet in a whale's throat is too narrow to swallow a human. And in real life, Jonah would have died in the attack.'

'But the sea animal which swallowed Jonah may not have been a whale, but rather a shark,' Chiaguar pointed out. 'And because sharks really hate the taste of humans, the shark spat him out. That's *if* the story of Jonah is true. But most of the Bible is open to interpretation and is not borne by fact.'

'To be honest, I don't believe in the Bible,' Marion admitted. 'But what other superstitions, legends and spiritualism exist surrounding sharks?'

'A great deal,' Chiaguar replied. 'Many sailors have attributed sharks with supernatural abilities, like their ability to smell blood from great distances — but I've already told you that there is much truth in this belief. Ancient tribal peoples of the Pacific and Indian Oceans, also the Caribbean, Florida and the Atlantic coast of eastern South America, are less petrified of sharks because they understand them far better than the modern societies of Europe, North America and Australia. But they still call on supernatural powers from God for their own protection in case sharks do attack them. In Sri Lanka, Brahman priests set off magical spells to pacify and disorientate sharks so that pearl divers can search for pearls and other treasures in safety.'

'I like the sound of that idea, if the spells worked!' Marion said.

Chiaguar nodded. 'Sharks have given rise to many gods, you know. In India, the Hindu god Vishnu sometimes comes out of the shark's mouth. In Shinto Buddhism in Japan, the storm god is a warrior who shows off his great strength by swimming with a shark under each arm. Many tribal societies in the

Indian and Pacific Oceans revered sharks, and the beasts were worshipped as mighty, powerful spirits who could change their shape frequently. In New Guinea, young men and boys prove their manhood by sailing alone in canoes to catch a shark — but that process is too complex to describe to you now.'

Marion nodded.

Chiaguar gestured and said, 'But now take a look at all these scenes of sharks from eastern and Pacific tribal spiritualism.'

Marion saw the charm reveal a dramatic scene of some Brahman priests in Sri Lanka casting magical spells to pacify sharks in the sea so that the pearl divers could reach the treasures of the ocean without being attacked. The next scene was of India's Hindu god Vishnu emerging from the shark's jaws. Then Marion saw the situation of the Japanese storm god demonstrating his enormous might and brawn by making his way through the ocean with two sharks underneath his arms. The scene changed again to show tribal societies on Indian Ocean and Pacific Ocean islands worshipping and respecting sharks as mighty spirits who changed their appearances in the sea. And lastly, she watched teenagers from New Guinea's ancient tribes calling into the ocean and then spearing any sharks that came to the surface.

'That's all very fascinating,' Marion said, her eyes wide. 'What else can you tell me?'

'In the Polynesian islands, the shark is regarded as a god by tribal societies,' Chiaguar told her. 'They are worshipped and revered as gods throughout the Pacific, and in the waters of Hawaii fishermen and tribesmen approach tiger sharks and come to no harm. In savagery and bloodlust, tiger sharks are thought to be more lethal even than great white sharks, but these tiger sharks do not attack the men walking through the sea. Probably because the sharks know that these men are humans, and most sharks have no interest in attacking or killing humans. Other than the Indian and Pacific Oceans, there is shark worship among the native tribes of the Americas. The indigenous peoples of South America, and even North America, as far north as Canada and Alaska, respect sharks. In Alaska, there is a belief that the first humans came out of the mouth of a shark-god. Although sharks very rarely attack humans, relative to the millions of humans who swim in the oceans every year, it must be remembered that they are still wild animals; they are unpredictable and lethal killing machines, and they are not to be trusted or underestimated by humans. They are potentially dangerous killers.' He paused. 'And now, I'll conjure another spell… Look.'

Marion watched, and witnessed tribal societies in the Polynesian islands worshipping a god in the form of a shark. She was in awe. She watched many tribal societies across the oceans worshipping shark-gods, and then saw that in the sea off the coast of Hawaii tribesmen and fishermen waded through shallow water towards a group of tiger sharks, and the sharks swam around the men with no expression of hostility or violence. She saw the first man coming out of the jaws of a shark-god, and shuddered at the grotesque sight. Lastly, she witnessed with utter horror people swimming with sharks and then being viciously attacked. Her old terror of sharks returned, and she knew she would never forget that they were vicious wild animals that had to be fierce and bloodthirsty to survive in the hostile world of the oceans. They were unpredictable, and were more savage and deadly than even lions and tigers.

Marion turned towards Chiaguar again. 'Apart from sharks, I've heard that barracudas and sawfish are incredibly dangerous.'

'Oh yes,' Chiaguar said, nodding. 'I'll start with barracudas which are extremely ferocious. Like sharks, they are hunted for their meat in the Caribbean Sea or the Gulf of Mexico, and throughout the Pacific and Indian Oceans. Most tribal societies are petrified of barracudas. Throughout the Pacific Ocean, where most island tribes regard the shark as a god, people view the barracuda as a devil or an evil spirit. This is especially the case in the Polynesian islands.'

He stopped and gazed into the distance for a while until Marion prompted him to continue by saying, 'Please, do go on.'

'Ah yes, sorry!' Chiaguar said. 'Where was I? Ah yes... Although the barracuda's savagery rivals the shark's, barracudas attack and kill fewer people than sharks. Even so, it is perfectly understandable why people dread barracudas as much as, or even more than, they fear sharks. The largest barracudas can reach nine or ten feet in length, and they have long fangs that bite with an enormous amount of power. Like sharks, barracudas are not to be trusted.' He paused again briefly. 'Now, sawfish are even larger than sharks and barracudas, and are just as ferocious. They can reach fifteen to twenty feet in length and weigh up to two tonnes, and, as their name suggests, they have a double-edged saw-like rostrum. With this fearsome weapon, sawfish can rip into their prey very easily. They have been known to attack walruses, whales and even sharks.'

'That is terrifying!' Marion cried, fear showing in her eyes and mouth.

'That's not all,' Chiaguar went on grimly. 'The sawfish is as ferocious and bloodthirsty as the sharks and the barracuda, and in some oceans they have attacked and killed humans in the past. My people dread sawfish more than we do sharks. However, moray eels are also lethal predators despite being much smaller. Their bodies are as thick as a human's arm, their flesh is poisonous and their teeth can tear the flesh from the arms, legs or body of a human or a prey animal. They can even kill humans. Their bites are also poisonous because they often eat venomous fish or ones with poisonous flesh, and the venoms or poisons collect onto their teeth as they eat the fish. Bites from moray eels then leave festering wounds on humans, and these wounds have to be treated in hospital immediately otherwise the victim will die. As well as the Pacific Ocean, moray eels roam the Caribbean Sea, especially off Florida, alongside barracudas, sawfish and conger eels. All of these predators are as dreaded by people in Florida as sharks and alligators. After the moray eels, other dangerous sea creatures are conger eels and stingrays. The stingrays have poisonous stings on their barbed tails which emit poisons powerful enough to kill humans. The sharp tails of stingrays can easily tear through a flipper or a swimsuit and leave a horrible injury in a human's flesh. Conger eels are bigger than stingrays. They are known by fishermen for their strength, speed and ferocity, and they have deadly sharp teeth. Even so, it is very rare for people to get attacked by conger eels or stingrays. Then there are giant squids and octopuses, which are invertebrates — animals without backbones.'

'They must be terrifying!' Marion exclaimed.

'They look terrifying, but again they seldom attack humans,' Chiaguar said evenly. 'The largest octopuses can reach twelve feet in length and width from the first tentacle to the last tentacle, but the biggest giant squids can reach fifty feet in length. Octopuses have eight tentacles on their bodies which are longer than those of a giant squid. Giant squids have eight short tentacles and two longer tentacles which they use to catch prey. On the tentacles of both beasts there are suckers that are used for sucking, holding and pulling apart their prey. On the tentacles of a giant squid, the suckers are reinforced by horny rims that can cut through the flesh of a victim, pulling them apart. As with sharks, seamen have told many horror stories of shipwrecked sailors being attacked and torn apart or mutilated by octopuses and giant squids, also of giant squids even attacking ships and boats and dragging the vessels underwater. Although the former case is the truth, the latter case is definitely exaggerated myth and fantasy; even fifty-foot giant squids cannot drag huge ships underwater. This is a physical impossibility.'

Marion nodded and thought for a moment, slightly comforted by the fact that no tentacle beast would drag them in their ship down to the depths that day. 'You have forgotten cuttlefish, manta rays and pike,' she finally told him.

'Okay, let's deal with cuttlefish first,' he suggested. 'Cuttlefish are relatives of giant squids and octopuses. Like giant squids, cuttlefish have tentacles consisting of sharp, horny rims, and these lethal weapons can kill people. As for manta rays, they are relatives of stingrays, and are also known as "devil rays" or "devilfish". They are the largest of the ray family. Although they do not really deserve their fearsome reputation, their sharp tails and teeth can severely injure humans. They normally feed on plankton, and like stingrays they fall prey to sharks and killer whales.'

'Fascinating...' Marion said breathlessly. 'I've heard a dangerous fish in the rivers and lakes of Europe and North America is the pike. They reach five feet in length and can seriously injure any animal up to the size of a dog, or even a fully-grown man. Their teeth are deadly. When I was twenty-one I saw a dog in France being attacked by a pike...' Marion's memory flashed back to 1997 when she had watched her mother's Labrador swimming in the Seine in northern France. She relived the horror when an enormous pike attacked the dog with a level of ferocity almost equal to a shark's. The big fish, with large, deadly teeth, then abandoned his attack and swam off when people swimming in the water raced to the Labrador's rescue. The dog suffered a broken leg and torn rump. Marion shuddered as she saw the mutilated muscle again in her mind's eye.

Chiaguar spoke again and she returned to the present.

'There are several dangerous fish and invertebrates in the world's oceans and rivers capable of attacking humans,' he said. 'Let me ask you a question. Are you scared of snakes?'

'I'm not scared of snakes, spiders or scorpions,' she replied, a hint of pride in her voice.

'Interesting... You know, you have more reason to be scared of snakes than anything else,' Chiaguar told her. 'Snakes kill more people every year than all the man-eating predators. Venomous snakes which kill people include mambas, cobras, kraits, vipers and rattlesnakes, and constricting snakes, like pythons, anacondas and boa constrictors also claim many victims. It is ironic that you're not scared of snakes.'

Marion looked uneasy. 'Why have you gone from the subject of dangerous ocean killers to dangerous snakes?' she asked the chief.

'Well, in the same way that people have more to fear from snakes than from man-eating predators, there are many creatures of the ocean depths which you have more reason to be terrified of than man-eating sharks,' Chiaguar explained evenly. 'Your terror of sharks and other big predators of the oceans and rivers greatly magnifies the true dangers from these killers. I'll go down the list of smaller ocean killers, some of whom use lethal venoms or poisons, or sharp claws or teeth. The sea wasp, a type of box jellyfish, and the Portuguese man o' war contain lethally poisonous stings on their bodies, and they injure almost as many humans every year as sharks. The sea urchin and the pufferfish can sting you very badly if you step on them, either on the beach or in the sea. Four other deadly sea creatures with poisonous spines are the scorpionfish, the stonefish, the lionfish and the weever fish, and they also kill and injure many humans every year. Predatory fish, like lampreys, are parasites on other large fish, such as sharks, but they have also been known to attack humans, usually to suck a person's blood. Much more harmless are crabs and lobsters, but even they can take a man's fingers off with their powerful pincers. Yet you would think nothing of venturing near them.'

'You're right, Chiaguar,' Marion said. 'Very often, we have more to fear from the smaller creatures than the larger ones. However, I'm still most afraid of sharks, barracudas, sawfish, moray eels, conger eels, stingrays, octopuses and giant squids. And in the colder oceans, such as near Antarctica and the Arctic, killer whales and walruses roam wild and they can also be dangerous.'

'Again, your terror is exaggerated,' Chiaguar told Marion. 'Killer whales and walruses are not dangerous to humans. It is true that killer whales will kill other sea animals — even large whales — and walruses will defend themselves against smaller sharks and polar bears. But few humans have been attacked by walruses and no humans have ever been killed by wild killer whales. Like the sharks, killer whales have been given a bad reputation that they do not deserve.'

'To be honest, I would rather swim with a killer whale or walrus than with a shark,' Marion said, letting out a nervous chuckle.

'Fortunately, you will not have to experience the terror of swimming with a killer whale, walrus or shark,' Chiaguar told her, smiling. 'But remember that the dangers of the ocean must never be underestimated. People must always exercise caution when swimming in the sea and respect all the creatures that live there. Now you'll see if the jaguar in South America is dangerous compared to the shark.'

'I'll have to take my chances,' Marion said, trying to keep her voice light. However, deep down, she was scared and found it an effort to control her fear of these creatures.

Chiaguar left her as another vision began.

In the distance, Marion saw a young blue whale carcass being eaten by a great white shark. When the shark had eaten its fill, two groups of cuttlefish and manta rays began picking at the carcass. They were soon joined by an octopus, a giant squid and three stingrays. Further ahead was the bloodied carcass of a large female blue whale — presumably the young whale's mother. Tearing chunks from her carcass were great white sharks, tiger sharks, bull sharks, blue sharks and hammerhead sharks. The ocean churned with blood as the sharks savagely ripped at the whale's flesh and blubber in a feeding frenzy. Marion fought against a chill of horror that ran through her blood, down her spine and into her stomach. She felt relatively safe in the hunting ship, but remembered her nightmare at the beginning of her coma, where a great white shark and a tiger shark launched a savage attack on her, their huge teeth wrecking the boat and causing her to fall into the water before her nightmare ended. The great white shark and the tiger shark were about to deal a dreadful death to Marion, and through her horror she remembered seeing a blue shark, a bull shark and a hammerhead shark approaching, ready to share in the spoils. It was true that the boat on which Marion now travelled was made of thicker wood, and she had a hundred warriors to protect her should the bloodthirsty sharks decide to attack, but this failed to give Marion much reassurance; men armed with spears and arrows were no match against such fearsome opponents.

The great whites and the tiger sharks gorged themselves on the flesh, fat and blood, whilst the blue sharks and hammerhead sharks used their serrated teeth on the carcass with a stomach-churning ferocity and power. Then the sharks abandoned the whale carcass, and the barracudas closed in on the spoils. Marion watched them as they mauled the bloated carcass. Strangely, her terror of both sharks and barracudas began to diminish until she felt relatively safe. She remembered what Chiaguar had said — that they very rarely attacked humans, and attacks by barracudas were even less frequent. What was more, she remembered reading somewhere that sixty percent of human shark victims survived each year, for humans were too bony to feed a shark properly, and this applied with equal truth to barracudas. Marion now looked beyond her terror and admired the power, speed and grace with which the great whites and tiger sharks moved through the blue sea. She developed an admiration and respect for sharks and, to a lesser extent, barracudas.

Suddenly, the sharks and barracudas

pursued the boat, ready to devour any who fell overboard. Marion stayed well away from the edge, paling slightly as the sharks and barracudas were joined by the other lethal killers Chiaguar had told her about. According to the book on dangerous sea creatures that Marion had read, conger eels and sawfish were dreaded for their savagery and bloodlust as much as sharks and barracudas. Marion gulped as she watched the conger eels and sawfish pushing their way in among the great whites and tiger sharks. After these sawfish and conger eels came the moray eels, and Marion knew they were deadly killers who could leave festering wounds on humans with their fearsome teeth. What Marion had read about these creatures terrified her, but she lowered herself into a sitting position on the deck whilst glancing through the gaps between the wooden bars, making it impossible for her to fall overboard. The moray eels were much smaller than the other ocean killers and remained at the rear of this savage army. The stingrays also remained in the rear, and she knew that their poisonous stings could stun or kill a human. In addition, their sharp, barbed tails could easily tear through a swimsuit — though they usually only attacked humans in self-defence. Lastly, there came the octopuses and giant squids, both species of invertebrates carrying a terrible reputation for killing humans. Marion's mind immediately flashed back to the monstrous giant squid in the film *Twenty Thousand Leagues Under the*

Sea. These giant squids ranged from thirty feet to fifty feet from tentacle to tentacle, and they had a cold glare in their eyes that made them look sinister, and the huge octopuses with their vicious eyes and powerful tentacles also came across as evil. Marion had to remind herself that these creatures did not deserve their bad reputation.

The five groups of sharks surrounded the massive hunting ship, with the barracudas, conger eels and sawfish pushing their way in, whilst the moray eels and stingrays stayed in the rear. The giant squids and octopuses flanked the sharks, barracudas and sawfish, the giant squids using their tentacles to deter any moray eels and stingrays who tried to push their way in among them and the octopuses. The natives were prepared to fight with their spears, but then Chiaguar sent the ship through a time warp by casting one of his spells. This shortened the journey across the largest ocean in the world by ten days, and then the ship sailed into a river on the Pacific coast of Peru.

Nearby was the imaginary border between the Andean Mountains of Peru and the tropical rainforests of Brazil, the dream having reduced the land area of Peru so that the border with Brazil was much closer than it would have been in the real world. In the river Marion saw giant electric eels. She had read how the largest electric eels could pack enough voltage to stun a horse. The electric eels then fled from a shoal of piranhas, and rightly so; Marion had heard many terrifying tales of the bloodthirsty reputation of piranhas. In reality, piranhas virtually never attacked humans, but a shoal of piranhas would strip a large prey animal to the bones in a matter of seconds. Marion glanced into the river below and shuddered as she saw that each of the piranhas was armed with powerful, razor-edged teeth that could easily cut chunks of flesh from their victims. Their reputation for ferocity and bloodlust rivalled that of sharks, barracudas and sawfish, and she could see why. Lunging from the banks into the river were caimans, the crocodiles of South America. Some of the natives shouted a warning; they dreaded caimans as much as crocodiles and alligators were feared in Africa, India, Nepal and Florida.

At last, the boat reached the village and everybody disembarked from the vessel.

'We're home,' Chiaguar said as he approached Marion.

'I'm glad to be here,' Marion replied. The two of them vacated the vessel with the other warriors, and as they did so Marion caught sight of the caimans in the distance glaring at her with sinister eyes.

She hurried towards the village with Chiaguar as the caimans retreated, and the rainforest exploded with thunderous roars from jaguars and pumas.

Night soon fell, and Marion finally got some much-needed rest.

* * *

Marion had lunch with Chief Chiaguar the next day: monkey meat and fish served with a side of vegetables. She ate the food with relish and then turned towards the chief. 'That was a delicious meal,' she enthused. 'But I have a question, Chief.'

'Ask away,' Chiaguar replied.

'How many dangerous animals in the jungle will I have to be wary of when I hunt for a jaguar?'

'Well, in South America, people have been killed by jaguars and pumas, and these are the top predators on the continent,' Chiaguar told her. 'Some people are killed by caimans or man-eating fish in the rivers, but such cases are rare. Caimans are more dangerous, but not as dangerous as the alligators in Florida. Many constricting and venomous snakes kill people, like the anaconda, the boa constrictor and the venomous bushmaster, a species of viper.' He paused to take a bite of the monkey flesh. 'People have apparently been attacked by the harpy eagle, but only if they were stupid enough to go near the eagle's nest. Giant anteaters will attack people if defending themselves, and so too will llamas, alpacas, guanacos and vicuñas, which are related to camels. From time to time, people get injured or killed by horses, donkeys, mules, bulls or oxen, but the wild pigs called peccaries are amongst the most dangerous animals in South America. They kill more humans than even jaguars and caimans!'

Marion gasped. 'I'd never have guessed

that! Is that all the dangerous animals there are?'

'No. As you already know, moray eels are very dangerous. They have injured and occasionally killed people off the coast of Peru. None of the people in this village have died from being attacked by moray eels, but stingrays stung and killed four people I knew. As if that weren't enough, eight people in a village north of here were killed by giant squids. As I said on our voyage, sharks are the greatest menace in the ocean.' He paused and, upon seeing the unease on Marion's face, added, 'But, overall, the mountains and jungles of South America and the oceans surrounding us here are very safe. Wild pigs are the biggest man-killers, but jaguars, pumas and caimans kill very few people. Even so, all three predators are greatly feared and respected by the tribespeople, and the most dreaded of them all are jaguars.'

'Tell me more about the jaguar,' Marion said, controlling the hint of fear in her voice.

'They are extremely cunning and savage creatures, and violently strong. One or two blows from its powerful paws can kill a man. Its jaws and teeth can bite through an animal's skull with crushing power equal to the jaws of a lion or a tiger, and that is how jaguars kill their prey. Lions, tigers, leopards and pumas kill animals or humans with a crushing bite to the nape of the neck or the throat. But jaguars go for the head and only very rarely the throat.'

'That's terrifying,' Marion said, her eyes

wide. 'And I'm about to face a jaguar and try to calm it! *How*?'

'Praying to a jaguar or puma god has worked for me and my people when we've faced jaguars or pumas, so if your faith is strong then it will work for you,' Chiaguar said. 'But if it does not work, then you have the powerful magic of a crocodile's organs to bring death to any beast that attacks you.'

'I hope I'll never have to use them,' Marion said, with a slight shudder. 'However, on our way into this thatched hut, I saw the bodies of many dead men with crushed skulls. I guess they must've been killed by jaguars.'

'They were indeed killed by jaguars, and the jaguars were too cunning for us to catch and kill,' Chiaguar explained. 'But I know for a fact that they killed the men in self-defence — although there is one jaguar in the forest who is a notorious man-eater. He is the one you will face. Let me take you outside and show you some of the spiritualism we have surrounding the jaguar.' Marion and Chiaguar got up from the floor and headed out of the thatched hut, into the village itself, and people were crying over the bodies of hunters and warriors killed by jaguars. But her guide, whose name was Chico, gave her some sort of meat.

'What meat is this?' she asked.

'Jaguar,' Chico replied. 'We hunt and eat the jaguar to make us strong and brave. If you eat jaguar meat, you will be as strong and brave as the jaguar. It will help you to conquer your fear when you face that man-eating jaguar in the forest.'

'Okay, I'll have some,' Marion said reluctantly. She took the chunk of cooked meat and chewed on it. The meat was very tough but, after ten minutes, she had eaten it all. 'That was delicious,' she said.

'There is other spiritualism and worship,' Chiaguar informed the young woman. 'We associate jaguars with rainfall and fertility — just like leopards and black panthers represent rainfall and fertility in Africa.'

'I see…'

'There is the same belief associating jaguars with fertility and rainfall amongst some tribes in Mexico, but here in South America we have a ritual to guarantee these two events,' Chiaguar explained further. 'Blood has to be shed in the jaguar's honour, so two warriors will fight each other dressed in jaguar costumes. Watch...'

Marion turned around and witnessed two men, dressed in jaguar skins, boxing bare-fisted, like prizefighters. One man suffered a severely cut mouth and the other sustained a bloody nose and a black eye. Then both men withdrew from the fight.

Marion and the others heard jaguars bellowing and roaring in the jungle like thunder, and then real thunder exploded across the sky and rain began to fall.

'Let's go inside until the rain stops,' Chiaguar suggested. The three of them made their way back inside the hut.

The rains stopped after three hours, and

they then emerged from the hut and saw the vegetable and fruit crops growing bigger and healthier. Marion grinned with glee. 'The crops are fertile!' she said.

'Do you want me to cook some vegetables to honour this occasion?' Chico asked.

'No thanks,' Marion replied. 'I've already eaten plenty.'

'I see,' Chiaguar said, smiling. 'Now, you must know that the jaguar is the spirit friend of shamans who turn into jaguars. They set off into the forest to carry out their deeds. There are evil shamans and good shamans. The evil ones bring sickness, death and bad luck, whilst the good ones fend off these bad things. Let's go outside the village so I can show you the bodies of some evil shamans who were killed in a battle with good shamans.'

Marion followed the two men towards the village entrance and then outside the village to see the mutilated bodies of evil shamans who had died in the battle.

'There were more good shamans than evil shamans, but eight out of twenty-one good shamans died alongside nine evil shamans,' Chiaguar informed her as she gazed around in awe. 'When shamans die, their spirits become real jaguars...'

The seventeen dead shamans were transformed into real jaguars, which then glared at Marion before bounding off into the forest.

'This is how werejaguars are created,' Chiaguar added. 'Men who turn into jaguars.

The whole belief in werejaguars came from the Aztec rain gods in Ancient Mexico. The Aztecs ruled southern and central Mexico until the sixteenth century, and, like us, they believed the jaguar controlled the rains that fertilize crops. But because of its size, strength, cunning and ferocity, the jaguar is called the "Lord of Animals" and the "Master of Spirits". In the Andean Mountains running through Ecuador, Peru and into Chile, pumas are the dominant big cats, and the Incas regarded their nation as a puma mounting and riding the Andes. But even here, the jaguar was treated as the father of all wild cats, and this was due partly to the fact that puma cubs have spotted skins like jaguars. But the spots go and the pumas' pelts become tawny-brown when they grow up.'

'In Asia, tigers are associated with Eastern medicine and aphrodisiacs,' Marion told Chiaguar. 'Are jaguars in South America associated with medicines?'

'Yes, they are,' Chiaguar told her. 'In the rainforests, healers make contact with powerful spirits derived from jaguars to assist them in curing sick patients. Because jaguars are powerful and savage, it is believed that their spirits scare off or destroy the evil shades of darkness that cause illness, sickness and disease. To you Europeans, all this spiritualism may seem like ancient tribal nonsense, but the ancient tribes of the world take these things very seriously — including us Peruvian tribes.'

'I don't think it's nonsense,' Marion

reassured him. 'When I began this dream in Africa, a Rwandan tribal chief called Guamo introduced me to some of the spiritualism, worship and superstitions in African tribal societies, and they all made sense. Their medicines also made sense. I've learned a great deal about ancient tribal beliefs since I left Rwanda.'

'But now, it is time for you to search for that man-eating jaguar in order to calm it,' the chief suggested.

'Which I seriously aim to do,' Marion said. 'And I'll keep this crocodile liver and intestines with me as self-defence weapons just in case my attempt to appease it fails.'

Chico walked beside Marion as they bade farewell to Chiaguar and headed off into the forest.

As they trundled through the thick, dense forest of hardwood trees, vines and lianas, Chico told Marion how jaguars and pumas in both South America and North America stood for life, death and the underworld, as well as rainfall and fertility.

Then the jungle exploded again to the blood-curdling roars of a jaguar and the screams of a puma.

Marion and Chico were terrified; they presumed this jaguar to be the man-eating beast that had killed a number of tribespeople. Fighting the temptation to run back towards the village, they sprinted through the undergrowth and came to a river. Confronting each other over the carcass of a tapir were the two killers. Marion and Chico were awestruck by these two big cats, but Marion immediately remembered what Chong Lee had taught her in Nepal with the bull, the horse, the lion and the tiger: jaguars and pumas in South America are deadly adversaries, and Marion's only chance of pacifying the jaguar was to exploit his fear and wariness of the puma.

Marion hesitated. The jaguar was a churning mass of muscle with blazing eyes and black lips that were curled in a snarl that exposed its hideous fangs. The puma was also very muscular, with ears flattened to its skull, fiery eyes ignited with hatred. Then the big cats bellowed again, charging the atmosphere in the jungle like thunder or a monsoon. The jaguar's roars were combined with the puma's blood-chilling screams, tearing Marion's nerves. The big cats circled each other as they prepared to do battle over the tapir carcass — but then ten massive caimans emerged from the river, closing in on them. Marion could see that these fearsome reptiles were the same caimans who had stared at her and Chiaguar as both of them left the boat and made their way to the village.

The caimans' eyes were cold and sinister, and their gaping mouths were lined with bone-crushing teeth as they hissed with blood-curdling savagery, their tails swiping at the big cats. With both powerful beasts surrounded and outnumbered by these savage crocodiles, the bellowing jaguar and the screaming puma lunged and swiped at the dreaded reptiles.

Chico held back, but Marion raced into the situation armed with the liver and intestines Chief Guamo had given her in Rwanda. Marion despised herself for what she was about to do — killing crocodiles with a crocodile's organs — but if she held back from using the powerful magic of these organs, then the jaguar and the puma would be torn apart by the caimans. Overpowered by guilt, Marion nevertheless chanted like an African witch-doctor and waved the liver and intestines, casting a spell that carried through the moist, murky jungle atmosphere towards eight of the caimans. The caimans rolled about in agony and then died. The jaguar and the puma sprang towards the last two caimans, fastened their rapier claws into the reptiles' scaly hides and drove their fearsome fangs into their necks.

The battle was over.

Marion came between the jaguar and the puma as they abandoned the ten dead caimans and circled her. She lowered the organs as a spasm of conscience tormented her mind at how she had killed the caimans. By acting submissively, avoiding eye-contact with the big cats and praying to the jaguar and puma gods, she diffused the blazing ferocity of the formidable killers. They read her lack of fear and were too wary of attack from each other to even think about attacking her. The puma slunk away into the undergrowth, and the jaguar ripped at the tapir carcass with its rapier talons and gleaming white fangs and chewed on the tough flesh.

Marion kept her distance as Chico came up behind her. They watched the massive beast. Its chest was deep and shoulders broad as its hard muscles rippled down its body and its huge head was buried in the carcass. Then Marion saw the head of an arrow embedded in its shoulder and a gaping wound. That must be why the jaguar had been transformed into a vicious man-eater; it had obviously suffered this wound in a violent encounter with a local tribe. Later on, the shaft of the arrow must have broken off, leaving only the arrowhead.

Marion slowly crawled towards the jaguar and touched the injury with her hand. The jaguar spun round towards her, growling and snarling with venomous fury. Marion acted submissively again.

'It's okay, sweet cat,' she murmured. 'I'm not going to hurt you. I only want to cure your wound.' Her voice was soft and gentle, and even the most ferocious beasts would respond to such a loving, compassionate voice. The jaguar lowered itself onto its side, and Marion took hold of the arrowhead, twisted it gently and, with a firm tug, pulled it out of the big cat's shoulder.

Chico passed a large leaf to her so she could apply the leaf to the bleeding wound and stem the flow of blood. Now that a human had cured its injury and pacified it with her faith in pagan jaguar gods, this jaguar's man-eating days were over.

What's more, Marion guessed that the tapir must have been an old, sickly animal for this wounded jaguar to kill it so easily. This had proven the jaguar's enormous brute strength and extreme ferocity, because this big cat, despite being hindered by a painful injury, had conquered the largest of all South America's mammals. The jaguar would presumably go back to killing its natural prey as soon as its injury was properly treated.

Marion and Chico led the jaguar into the village and into Chiaguar's thatched house. She showed the chief the jaguar's wound, and told him that as soon as this injury had some form of antiseptic applied to it and was properly cured, the jaguar would no longer regard it as necessary to kill and eat humans. Chiaguar strolled outside the house to gather the village doctors. And once her task of treating this jaguar was fulfilled, Marion was prepared for her trip to Alberta in Canada in order to overcome her fear of North America's dangerous wild beasts and learn meditation from the natives.

CHAPTER 7

As soon as she had arrived in Alberta, Canada, Marion was introduced to five native warriors who were experts in the art of meditation and horse whispering. Meditation allowed them to pacify aggressive animals. The five warriors on the reservation near Banff National Park were named Nacoma, Ten Bears, Talking Crow, Talking Arrow and Yellow Knife. Nacoma was also the chief of this reservation. It seemed that the Native American reservations scattered across the United States and Canada housed the mere remnants of what was formerly a vast population of natives roaming the entire continent before the Europeans arrived.

Nacoma addressed Marion as he raised his hand to greet her. 'So you are the young woman who has come here to learn from us…' Nacoma stated. 'You wish to overcome your fear of Canada's deadliest creatures by learning native meditation and horse whispering. Well, welcome to our reservation, young European.'

Marion chuckled. 'My name is Marion,' she said, 'and I need to ask you a question.

How many dangerous animals exist in North America?'

'Oh, there are many,' Nacoma replied. 'In Florida, there are alligators, for example. They are the most dangerous of all America's man-killers. In Canada and the rest of America, there are bears, pumas, bison and moose. They are the top killers of humans. We will be dealing with them first, and then deal with the smaller creatures.'

'Tell me about bears,' Marion said eagerly. 'There are brown bears in Europe, but they do not usually attack humans. In Asia, there are Himalayan black bears, sloth bears and sun bears, and they are extremely dangerous. But the Shaolin priests in Nepal told me that these bears are more defensive than aggressive. Is this the same with the North American bears?'

'It is the same,' Nacoma told her. 'Apart from polar bears in the Arctic regions of Alaska and Canada, North America has three species of bear: the Kodiak bear, the grizzly bear and the black bear. The Kodiak bear and the grizzly bear are larger sub-species of the brown bear which lives in Europe and Asia. The Kodiak bear of Alaska is the largest land carnivore, weighing in at nearly 2,000 pounds, but the grizzly is far more ferocious and dangerous. It is very rare that Kodiak bears attack humans, but grizzlies and black bears are unpredictable and must always be treated with caution.'

'When do bears attack people?' Marion asked nervously.

'When people threaten or surprise them, or

go near their food or cubs,' Nacoma replied. 'Or, in the case of black bears, when people feed them and then the food supply stops. This makes the black bears aggressive. Now, although people fear grizzlies, they generally do not fear black bears, who appear to be more cuddly and cumbersome. But both grizzlies and black bears are enormously strong and can move much faster than humans. Grizzlies have been known to move at a speed of thirty miles per hour! Black bears are almost as fast as grizzlies and very agile when climbing trees. So, the last thing you should do when threatened by a bear of any species is to run away. Whether you should climb a tree or not depends on whether the bear attacking you is a grizzly or a black bear. The grizzly bear is too large and heavy to climb trees, but the black bear can climb trees faster than a man. Also, when faced by an enraged grizzly, you must not fight back or scream. Apart from climbing a tree, the best thing you can do is pretend to be dead. The grizzly, then, will most likely sniff you for signs of life and leave you. However, playing dead will not work against a furious black bear, for this species will eat the corpses of dead or presumably dead humans. When you're attacked by a black bear, you have to fight back, with some kind of weapon if possible.'

'I see,' said Marion thoughtfully.

'To avoid being attacked by bears, you must never leave food or garbage lying around. The smell of food attracts bears. Also, when hiking through mountains or forests you must make plenty of noise or blow whistles or wear bells so that bears know there are humans nearby. This is because bears are not really out looking for trouble, but taken by surprise bears will attack humans. I'll describe the bears of North America so you'll recognise which is which. A Kodiak bear is over a quarter of the size of an elephant and weighs between 1,600 and 2,000 pounds. Their fur is light brown. A polar bear weighs 1,000 to 1,500 pounds and is unmistakable with his creamy-white coat. A grizzly bear weighs 600 to 900 pounds. And the black bear weighs 400 to 550. Now, it is easy to confuse grizzlies with black bears and black bears with grizzlies. Both bears can be brown, black, cinnamon, grey or white. I've seen grizzlies that are black, for example, but as a general rule grizzlies are brown with silvery-grey tips to their fur whilst black bears are obviously mostly black. Other than that, the grizzly has a pushed-in face and a broad head, and the black bear has a longer head with a sloping face. You must remember that most attacks by grizzlies and black bears are defensive rather than aggressive. You don't have to live in fear of bears, you just have to treat all of them with respect and caution. If bears know there are humans nearby, in nine cases out of ten they will retreat.'

'I see! So, what about pumas?' Marion asked.

'They are also called cougars or mountain

lions,' Nicoma told her. 'They are extremely powerful, savage and lethal, and can easily kill a man. However, attacks on humans by pumas are rare, and we have never heard of attacks on humans by wolves or coyotes, even though wolves are sometimes dreaded as much as grizzlies, black bears and pumas.'

'That's reassuring to hear!' Marion said, her expression becoming slightly more relaxed. 'Then there are bison and moose — how dangerous are they?'

'American bison and moose are more dangerous than grizzlies because they lack intelligence,' Nacoma answered wisely. 'All bears are extremely intelligent, but not bison or moose. These herbivores are very territorial and stupid, and will often charge humans for no reason. Bison and moose have been known to attack cars and trucks, but sometimes people are even more stupid. People violate the space of these massive herbivores, often to take photographs, and this provokes the animals. The bison and the moose are the largest and heaviest of all North America's wild animals, but they can also run three times faster than a human. They can kill a grizzly with their horns, antlers or hooves and are extremely dangerous when roused. But the only bison herds now live in Yellowstone National Park, overlapping Wyoming, Montana and Idaho, plus a few areas of western Canada. Moose are more common than bison.'

'Thanks. I'll be sure to bear all that in mind,' Marion replied.

'But there is more,' Nacoma told her, smiling. You see, our spells will take us all over Canada and America in order for us to encounter the spiritualism and worship of these wild animals by different tribes.'

'And what is the next stage of my training now that I have overcome my fear of sea predators and jaguars?' Marion asked, surprised at how calm she was.

'The next stage is cult worship,' Nacoma told her. 'And the first scene of our cult worship will take you to the prairies of Texas to explore the relationship between the Mandan people and the bison herds.'

Nacoma performed the spell, and the five natives and Marion found themselves on the frontier between Texas, Colorado and New Mexico. They saw the Mandan people, who were very short of food, it seemed. A group of between fifteen and twenty warriors wore bison masks and did a dance that would change the direction of the bison herds. Nacoma explained all this to Marion, and then told her how these twenty men wore their bows and arrows and carried out this dance in front of the Great Medicine Lodge. The dance lasted for four hours, during which the dancers would copy the strength, speed and endurance of these bison. Some of the men fell out of the dance with fatigue, muscle-pain and exhaustion, but others replaced them and the dance continued for another ten minutes.

Eventually, the bison herds advanced past the reservation in enormous numbers and the Mandans set off in hot pursuit.

After an hour, the warriors returned to the reservation with a dead bison carcass. They cut out the most delicious parts of the bison and placed them in front of the Great Medicine Lodge.

'What are they doing?' Marion whispered to Nacoma.

'Offering the most delicious parts of the bison to the Great Spirit,' Nacoma explained. 'All tribes of America and Canada believe in the Great Spirit, which is like a god to them. And now, we're about to travel to North Dakota to meet the Sioux people. The bison is the supreme being for this tribe and plays a big role in ceremonies of certain tribes who perform the sun dance.'

'What is the sun dance?' Marion asked.

'It is a ritualised ceremony where the natives torment themselves with a ritual of pain, strength and endurance in order to bring over the bison herds, but also to wish them good luck in their hunt for the bison. Now, let's set off for North Dakota.' With another spell, Nacoma transported Marion and his five-strong band to North Dakota, where the prairies of grass, corn and maize gave way to the Rocky Mountains to the west. Marion and the others watched the Sioux tribes perform the sun dance.

* * *

After three hours of the sun dance and then the hunting, killing and eating of a bison, Marion and Nacoma's group were transported towards British Colombia's north-western border with the Yukon Territory and Alaska, where Marion witnessed the worship of bears. Nacoma turned towards Marion who fixed her gaze on the elderly chief and smiled.

'All over Alaska, Canada and the United States, the native tribes hunt grizzlies, black bears and moose as proof of strength, manhood and bravado,' Nacoma explained, 'and throughout the Rocky Mountains and prairies of North America from Alaska to Texas, the tribes worship, revere and respect the grizzly bear. There are countless tales of the grizzly bear's strength, wisdom, cunning and ferocity. The natives of Alaska have the same tales about the giant Kodiak bear, but there were no legends in Canada or America about the strength, wisdom and ferocity of the black bear. Like Kodiak bears and grizzlies, black bears are seen as strong, intelligent and wise, but not as cunning or savage because they feed mostly on fish, honey and vegetation — not other animals.'

'I understand,' Marion said.

'There is a superstition amongst some tribes of North America that all bears were descended from the Daughter of the Great Spirit,' Nacoma told her. 'And all three species of bear are as important as the chiefs and leaders of game animals because they resemble mankind by walking on two legs, not just four. Now watch these two spectacles...'

Marion witnessed Kodiak bears, grizzlies and black bears giving thanks to the Daughter of the Great Spirit, their ancestor. Then she watched as the bears led deer, mountain goats, bighorn sheep, bison and moose across their territory. Marion was filled with awe, wonder and amazement, but deep inside her lurked a great terror of all bears. Nacoma turned to her again.

'Now we will head back to Alberta,' he announced. 'There, we will watch the Canadian and American tribes conduct a ceremony to show thanks to two dead bears for the resources they provide. The dead bears' spirits will then return to within the bodies of a grizzly bear and a black bear.'

* * *

By another spell, Nacoma, Marion and the others were transported to southern Alberta, close to the border between Canada and America. They watched the natives from both sides of the Canadian-American frontier bringing in a grizzly bear killed in Canada and a black bear killed in America. The men carried out their ritualised ceremony to thank the creatures. Then Marion saw the spirits of the two bears leave their bodies and hover through the atmosphere, out of the reservation towards two live bears, again a grizzly bear and a black bear. The grizzly and the black bear felt the spirits pass into them and knew that the natives would hunt them again. The bears fled into the thick, dense forest, joining other grizzly bears and black bears.

Nacoma addressed Marion. 'The North Americans from British Colombia and the Yukon Territory down to as far south as Mexico also worshipped pumas, not only bison, grizzlies and black bears,' he said slowly. 'The puma was a feared and respected deity, and was also called the Ghost of the Rockies. Watch the ghosts of pumas — over there...'

Marion witnessed the ghosts of dead pumas wandering through the tree-covered mountains and then entering the bodies of live pumas. Marion remembered similar reincarnation acts in Africa where the souls of tribal chiefs entered the bodies of lions and became real lions, as this had happened to Chief Jomo in Rwanda. Similar reincarnation and soul-transfer occurred with tigers, leopards and black panthers in Asia, with crocodiles and hyenas in both Africa and Asia, with jaguars in South America, and just now with dead grizzlies and black bears in Canada and the United States. Now this reincarnation and transfer of spirits was being repeated with pumas in the Rockies. Then she watched the tribes worship and respect puma deities, and the statues of these pumas glared down as they performed their worship.

Marion nudged Nacoma. 'Is this the end of the cult worship?' she wanted to know.

'Yes,' the old man answered. 'Our next stage will be superstitions and legends.

For this, we will have to meet America's Blackfoot and Navajo tribes. The Blackfoot make powerful medicine during a bear dance. But we'll encounter Navajo spiritualism first. The Navajos believe bears and humans are represented by two-legged deities. This stems from the fact that bears sometimes walk on their two hind legs, like humans. We must travel to the mountains on the border between Colorado and New Mexico to meet the grizzlies and black bears worshipping these deities alongside the Navajo people. Are you ready?'

'I'm ready,' was Marion's fearful answer. She was nervous at the prospect of encountering an army of grizzlies and black bears, the most dreaded and lethal predators in North America. Her terror of dangerous animals returned, but she knew she must fight this fear and not allow it to conquer her.

She knew what it was like to encounter brown bears back in Europe — in the Apennine Mountains of Italy, the Balkans of Yugoslavia, Romania and Bulgaria, and the forests of Russia and Poland — even though it never came to the point where she met these bears face-on. This fear of brown bears was bad enough, but encountering grizzlies and black bears was to be far more unnerving and petrifying. Marion set off with Nacoma's group towards the meeting place of the Navajo tribes, the bears and the deities.

* * *

The six of them were transported towards the border between Colorado and New Mexico, and they were positioned a mile from the meeting place of the bears and deities. The natives were absent from this meeting point, for today's Navajo people were crammed into reservations and denied their traditional right to worship.

Marion and her new friends walked at a leisurely pace through the mountain forests of Colorado, and saw the animals were coming out to feed. Deer, mountain goats and raccoons fed on the vegetation as porcupines and chipmunks gnawed trees and nuts, and the ducks floated along the river. A herd of moose dined alongside the deer, chewing leaves and twigs, and were forever vigilant of wolves on the prowl. Marion heard the wolves in the valleys, and then saw a bobcat eating a wapiti it had slaughtered. The wapiti was many times bigger than the bobcat, which proved the feline predator had great strength and ferocity. Marion was wary of walking near the beast. In the mountains and forests of the United States and Canada bobcats mind their own business and generally avoid fighting, but they are known to be capable of facing even a man or a dog when cornered.

Marion watched the river meandering and churning against the rocks, white foam against bluey-green water. Twenty large geese were fighting off a coyote, but then the bold waterfowl fled when the five other coyotes appeared.

Further downstream, three wolves tore at a white-tailed deer they had slain, but the wolves were then attacked and repelled by two pumas. The wolves growled and snarled viciously at the pumas, but the pumas screamed and swiped at the wolves with their slashing claws and the wolves retreated from the river. With the wolves fleeing, the pumas started feeding, and the coyotes and the bobcat watched the big cats from a safe distance.

Marion's group headed away from the river and through the forest when she caught a glimpse of a very big, reddish-brown fox dining on a fawn he it killed. Watching the fox from the sky was a golden eagle, hovering like a helicopter, along with a feral cat lurking in the thickets and an American badger emerging from his sett.

Nacoma turned towards Marion and said, 'My people and I worship the eagle, the wolf, the coyote and the fox. But we'll tell you more about their spiritualism later.'

'Do you worship the dog and the cat, like that cat over there in the bushes?' Marion asked, pointing to some nearby shrubs.

'We worship the dog, but not the cat,' Nacoma replied. 'The cat was introduced into North America by the Europeans, and some domesticated cats escaped from humans and became feral. That cat is a feral cat. But we've had the dog for many centuries. We made good use of domesticated dogs, as we did of wolves and coyotes, but not foxes.'

They then stopped to witness the feral cat stalking the fox in order to repel it from the deer kill and scavenge a meal. The cat's back and shoulders were hunched, its ears set back and its eyes sinister. It charged from the bushes and through the grass at great speed and attacked the fox, hurling itself onto the fox, clawing ruthlessly at its back and shoulders and dealing severe injuries.

The fox fled rather than fight. Although much bigger, the fox seemed to want to avoid fighting the fearsome feline. As the cat fed on the corpse, an eagle awaited its turn to scavenge its share of the carcass.

Half a kilometre away to the north, the fearsome howling of the wolves and coyotes, together with the barking and growling of feral dogs, numbed Marion's nerves and caused her blood to curdle and freeze. She walked with the others at a casual pace down the mountain slope, and they were slightly intimidated by the bellowing roar of the bears rumbling through the forest, far more unnerving than the howling or barking of wolves, coyotes or dogs.

'I can't wait to encounter those bears,' Marion told Nacoma bravely. 'This is my chance to stare fear in the face and conquer it.'

Eventually, they found themselves in a snow-covered canyon devoid of trees, and they lay down on the ground to stay hidden from the bears.

'This is where the bears will meet,' Nacoma told Marion. 'Now all we have to do is be patient. Do you still want to encounter these bears?'

'I've come this far, I can't give up now,' Marion replied boldly. 'But no sudden movements.'

'Your common sense is taking over,' Nacoma said proudly. 'But how did you know about not making any sudden movements?'

'My husband Klaus once told me when we were searching for brown bears in Poland, Yugoslavia and Romania,' Marion replied. 'It was very unnerving to hunt bears, but Klaus told me that sudden movements would startle the creatures and could provoke an attack.'

'The same thing is true with grizzlies and black bears in America and Canada,' Nacoma informed her. 'So you must stay still so that the bears become accustomed to you. Win their respect and trust.'

* * *

The army of grizzlies and black bears finally came from the west, and they saw the two-legged deities emerge out of thin air. The bears raised their heads and roared, grunted and growled to the deities to convey their respect. Marion sat shivering in the lotus position and fought her temptation to panic and scream. The grizzlies and black bears approached her and she clenched her fists, feeling slightly faint. However, she need not have worried, as the bears pawed and licked her, and after four minutes she became accustomed to this treatment. She very quickly awoke to the fact that the North American bears did not entirely deserve their reputation for savagery and blood-lust because they demonstrated no ferocity at all. For all their enormous size and strength and crushing power, these bears were apparently gentle giants!

The grizzlies vacated the area and separated, but the black bears stayed with Marion. These black bears lived up to their image of being cuddly, gentle and loveable, and with their black bodies, creamy-white muzzles and gentle eyes, they reminded Marion of Baloo the bear in the Walt Disney cartoon *The Jungle Book*. Marion stroked the bears and petted their heads. Nacoma's group came up to her and watched in awe as Marion interacted with the black bear.

* * *

Eventually, after about an hour of wandering, Marion's group reached an ancient village belonging to the Blackfoot tribe. Marion was impressed by the huge wigwams that were their homes.

'Now you are about to see a shaman of a grizzly bear making powerful medicine during a bear dance,' Nacoma told Marion. 'In the dance, the shaman will wear a grizzly bear skin and imitate the bear's noises and movements. He will dangle his spear and the bear's claws in front of him, growl and grunt like a grizzly bear and then sing to the spirits.

The Blackfoot people will bring out a patient who is sick, and the shaman will then push and roll the patient on the ground and paw at him to scare his illness away. Now, watch the healing ceremony…'

Marion still found this hard to believe, but she disciplined herself to accept this tribal superstition. All six of them were among the other men and women of the reservation as they watched the shaman appear from a wigwam, dressed in a grizzly bear hide. He waved his spear around, along with the terrible claws of the grizzly, before growling and grunting at the crowd. Marion watched the shaman singing to the spirits, and this singing rang through her ears. Then two men led a sick patient out of their wigwam towards the shaman and laid him on the ground. The shaman pushed and pulled the patient about like a real grizzly bear tearing a human to pieces, and he pawed and clawed the patient to frighten off the illness. Marion knew that this had some similarity to faith-healing, the shaman's faith in his healing powers curing the patient, and this worked very effectively. The patient got up smiling, his illness having gone, and he made his way back towards the wigwam whilst the shaman raised his hand and retreated towards another wigwam.

Marion thought this was too good to be true, but she already knew about witchdoctors in Africa and faith-healers who existed throughout the world. She grinned at Nacoma. 'That's incredible!' she exclaimed.

Marion, Nacoma and their four warrior companions travelled slowly back to their village in Alberta where Nacoma taught the young woman more about spiritualism.

'You already know how the puma was worshipped, feared and respected as a deity, and there are also tales of the puma's strength, cunning and savagery as there are of the bears,' he said. 'But in some tribes of America and Canada the puma rules the watery underworld under the ground, and in the skies and rivers, and he controls storms. There is about to be a violent storm, but a puma in the sky will calm it. You watch very carefully.'

Marion saw a violent storm converge on the village. She was amazed to see a puma in the watery underworld of the sky screaming and using his claws and fangs to seemingly control the storm. Eventually, the storm calmed down and faded into nothing, and Marion followed the others into a nearby wigwam to sleep.

* * *

In the morning, Marion rose from her slumber, climbed out of bed and slowly approached Nacoma. The chief was making use of different parts of the carcasses of an enormous male bison and a massive bull moose. He glanced up at Marion.

'The next stage of your training is how North America's dangerous animals were exploited for food, clothes and medicines,' he said. 'Are you interested?'

'I am,' she said. 'Please educate me, Nacoma.'

'These two carcasses are the carcasses of a bison and a moose — both bulls,' he explained. 'First the bison, or buffalo. There were once bison throughout the prairies and Rocky Mountains of America and Canada, from the boundary of the Appalachian Mountains in eastern America to the mountain forests of British Colombia and the Yukon Territory. The vast bison herds numbered over 60,000,000, and the plains were black with this overwhelming army of herbivores. The buffaloes outnumbered the entire population of Native North Americans, and to us they were a limitless supply of meat. The bison was a vital resource which provided the tribespeople with its hide, meat, bones, fat, tendons and horns. The natives used every part of the bison carcass so that not a single part of it was wasted. They never over-hunted the herds of bison, for they lived in harmony and balance with all North America's creatures, from enormous bison down to tiny mice.

'Then, at the beginning of the nineteenth century, the white men colonised the prairies, travelling from eastern America behind the Appalachian Mountains and from California. What followed were ruthless wholesale massacres of the bison herds, where these bison were callously slaughtered and their bodies mostly wasted. The white men massacred whole herds of buffalo, only to cut out the stomachs for buffalo beef to feed the colonists, pioneers and soldiers who built the railroads. Millions of buffalo carcasses were left to rot in the sun and to feed the grizzlies, pumas, wolves and coyotes. In the space of a hundred years, the white men exterminated the bison herds and the natives, and a vast population of 60,000,000 bison in Canada and America was reduced to only 500 animals. The bison and the native tribes were doomed. Fortunately, American conservationists realised that extinction would take the American bison as it had taken the Dodo, and they persuaded the American Government to conserve and protect the last bison herds in Yellowstone National Park which spans Wyoming, Montana and Idaho. The bison were saved just in time, and now there are over 40,000 bison in Yellowstone National Park, plus thousands more in the prairies and Rockies of Canada, as far west as British Colombia. We natives were also saved from extinction, but only just. Our culture, language and traditions are still in danger of dying out.' Nicoma sighed, and Marion could see clearly the sorrow in his eyes.

'I'm sorry, Nacoma,' Marion said quietly, placing a hand on the chief's shoulder. 'We Caucasians have a great deal to answer for, as we are responsible for some truly terrible things that have happened in the world. But I hope that times are changing for the better.'

'You must hang onto that hope,' Nacoma

said. 'And now I'll tell you about this moose carcass. Like the bison, the moose also provided food, clothes and medicines for us Native Americans. There is the superstition that eating the meat of a moose will make you very strong, as, apparently, the moose's strength and power gets transferred to you through its flesh or muscles. Have some moose meat that I've cooked.'

'Okay.' Marion ate the moose meat with gusto. 'That was delicious — it tastes a bit like venison.'

'Other parts of the moose are also valuable,' Nacoma told her. 'The bones from the moose's antlers are supposed to cure headaches, and part of an antler can be powdered and given as a cure for snakebite. The moose's hooves, when powdered, will cure over 500 diseases.'

'That's fascinating,' Marion replied in amazement.

'Now let me show you some animal skins and paintings in the wigwam opposite mine,' Nacoma said.

The two of them ventured outside and crossed the reservation into a giant wigwam. Marion was astounded by what she saw, the paintings of the bison, of the tribes stalking the bison herds, also paintings of moose, grizzlies, wolves and coyotes. Scattered across the walls and floor were the hides of grizzlies, black bears, moose and wolves, all of which provided clothes for the natives. In the next room were the hides of some bison. Marion smiled in admiration at the ingenuity of the native cultures of North America. But behind her smile was sadness that these Native American cultures, with their languages and customs, were fast dying out.

Nacoma and Marion vacated the wigwam, and he took her to witness another healing ritual similar to the shaman's bear dance. But, this time, the ritual involved parts of the puma. The wise, old chief took Marion by the arm and informed her of what this healing ritual involved.

'About twenty years ago in Florida,' he began, 'a Seminole tribesman was arrested, tried and sent to prison for killing a puma. His defence was that the puma was part of a healing ritual for curing sick patients, and parts of the puma had ceremonial and medicinal purposes. However, the white American state government of Florida saw the puma as an endangered and protected species. This is an example of how conservation can come into conflict with tribal interests in a country or state.'

'Talking about the puma being used for medicinal purposes,' Marion said, 'this is also done with the tiger in parts of Asia and the jaguar in South America. And tigers are being wiped out by poaching for their body parts and bones that are thought to have medicinal powers. So if the Americans want to be in a moral position to educate the countries of Asia not to kill tigers because of ancient tribal or cultural beliefs in these medicines, then they have to set an example to the world not to allow tribal beliefs in America to become an excuse to kill endangered wild animals. Like pumas in Florida. I know it sounds harsh to you, as you did not cause the wildlife of America and Canada to become endangered, but if America is to set a moral or ethical example to the world regarding conservation, then the Americans have to practise what they preach.'

'That is a very valid point,' Nacoma said, nodding. 'And we now realise that, in order to live in a changing country, like America or Canada, we have to adapt or die out. So, now we do not kill pumas for our healing rituals; we wait for some pumas to die of old age or natural causes. And what you're about to see is another patient being cured by the ritual.'

Nacoma and Marion watched the ritual as the patient was lying on the ground, and eventually he was cured. After seeing the bear dance in the Blackfoot village, it failed to surprise Marion that this superstition turned out to have some truth in it. Then she witnessed parts of the dead puma being used for ceremony and medicine.

Nacoma took Marion into a clearing in the nearby forest and showed her an incredible sight. They witnessed five feral herbivores — a bull, an ox, a horse, a donkey and a mule — confronting five bison. These bison, plus the bull and the ox, raked their hooves against the snow and tossed their huge heads about with their great horns, whilst the horse, the donkey and the mule reared up onto their hind legs and screamed, brayed and flailed their front hooves. The bull was the largest of the feral beasts, with the horse and the mule being almost as big.

'Why are these ten herbivores about to fight?' Marion asked Nacoma.

'The fight is symbolic,' Nacoma replied. 'But all they will do for the first twenty minutes is intimidate each other. The five feral herbivores are invading the forest belonging to the five buffaloes. These bison are defending their territory, and that's why there will be a battle. This symbolises domesticated or feral herbivores, or cats and dogs, invading the wilderness and competing with the wild animals for food, as has happened recently in Europe, America and Canada — in fact, all over the world. It also symbolises the white men invading the lands which belonged to the Native Americans long before the twentieth century and competing with them. But the battle between these feral herbivores and the bison will be resolved in the end, proving that feral animals and wild animals can live in balance with each other, and the white people and the Native Americans and Canadians can live in peace. The wars between the Europeans and the Native Americans eventually ended with the tribes being defeated, but now the white people and the natives are apparently at peace with each other. And we pray that, one day, the whole world will be at peace. But when a race or nation invades another nation, there will be war. That's why the feral herbivores are now fighting the five bison.'

'I see,' Marion said slowly. 'Shall we head back to the reservation? I don't want to see animals fighting, even if it is symbolic.'

The two of them made their way back through the forest.

Marion had lunch with Nacoma and the other four warriors. The lunch consisted of venison stew with vegetables, and she took great pleasure in consuming this delicious meal. She remembered eating the venison of red deer, roe deer and fallow deer when dining in restaurants back in Germany. This venison from a black-tailed deer and a white-tailed deer, mixed with vegetables in a stew, was even more delicious, and Marion had gained the strength and courage of a moose after having eaten that moose meat. When she had finished her meal, she confronted Nacoma with another question.

'The stage of my training involving Canada's wild animals being used for food, clothes and medicines must now be over,' she said. 'What is the next stage?'

'The next stage will be to introduce you to the spiritualism of the less dangerous animals of North America, like the wolf, the coyote and the fox, and the wolverine, the lynx and the bobcat,' Nacoma explained. 'First, I'll take you through the nearby forest and introduce you to North America's lethal killers. Come with us when you're ready.'

Marion and her friends ambled along a pathway running through the forest. The air smelled of champagne and perfume, as deciduous and evergreen trees were intermingled with coniferous trees, thickets and wildflowers.

'I know that bears and cougars can be dangerous, and bison and moose are also potential man-killers,' Marion began, 'but which other animals in North America are a threat to humans?'

'There are many animals that have the capacity to be highly dangerous but are, on the whole, not that dangerous at all,' Nacoma told her. 'The most serious threat to humans is alligators, but they live only in the south-eastern United States, mostly in Florida. Sharks are also a danger, but Chiaguar already told you that most victims of shark attacks survive.'

'Yes... I remember learning about them!' Marion said, shuddering. 'So which other wild animals do we have to stay clear of?'

'Another animal similar to the yeti of Asia is the Bigfoot creature,' Nacoma replied. 'It is similar partly because we don't know if it really exists, and partly because, if it does exist, it is related to the apes. Many Native Americans and white men in all fifty states in America, as well as in western Canada, claim to have seen Bigfoot creatures, and my people have legends of worship of these creatures going back many centuries. A few people have apparently been injured or killed by Bigfoot creatures, but normally they are gentle animals, and such attacks which were blamed on Bigfoot creatures may have actually been committed by grizzlies or black bears. But we believe that the Bigfoot really exists.'

Nacoma conjured another vision that exposed the forests of north-western America, and Marion and the other five caught the vision of brown, ape-like creatures larger than gorillas. Although they were enormous, intimidating and fierce, the Bigfoot creatures were not hostile to humans. Other apes, such as yetis and gorillas, had a terrifying reputation for ferocity, and so too did baboons, drills and mandrills, but although they were capable of matching yetis and gorillas in savagery, Bigfoot creatures lacked a reputation for being vicious man-killers. Marion was overwhelmed by the awesome size and strength of these creatures, and admired how gentle and peace-loving they appeared.

Then Nacoma gently led Marion away and informed her of a few other deadly foes. 'Three small predators who are extremely ferocious are the wolverine, the lynx and the bobcat,' he said. 'On our way to visiting those bears who worshipped the Navajo deities in Colorado, you and I saw a bobcat eating a wapiti it had killed. Well, there are bobcats in Mexico, the United States and Canada, but lynxes and wolverines are found only in Canada and Alaska, as well as in Europe and Russia. Lynxes and bobcats are savage, formidable and cunning, but wolverines are even more lethal. The wolverine is a giant weasel that resembles a cross between a small bear and a badger. They are usually brown in colour with a black or brown stripe running across their face. The wolverine is the largest killer in the weasel family, and they are so powerful, cunning and savage that they can kill an adult moose. The lynx and the bobcat can kill a large deer many times their size, and both smaller wild cats are as savage as the puma. But although the wolverine is by far the largest and most dreaded of the weasel or mustelid tribe, and the lynx and the bobcat are miniature tigers, none of these three killers has ever been known to attack humans. If a human corners a wolverine, lynx or bobcat, then these killers will attack and can kill the human, but left to themselves they never really attack humans. Now, watch these killers in another of my spells.'

The magic exposed an evergreen forest with tundra to the north, and Marion watched the wolverine lying in wait for prey in a pine tree, the lynx silently stalking across the tundra and the bobcat sneaking through the forest grass.

The wolverine roared and bellowed with psychotic savagery, causing Marion's blood to curdle and her bones to freeze, and then the two wild cats uttered their venomous hissing screams and snarls.

'Then there are three other large predators who are cunning and ferocious: the wolf, the coyote and the fox,' Nacoma went on. 'Wolves have by far the worst reputation of all predators in North America, and also in Europe. They have been labelled as vicious, bloodthirsty man-eaters, roaming the countryside in large armies, attacking livestock and humans with no provocation, and ravaging towns and villages. There are many tales in Europe of the Big Bad Wolf — tales that have been repeated in North America. But people on both continents are now more educated to the fact that wolves are not man-eaters and normally mind their own business.'

'Back when I was fifteen,' Marion said, 'I was walking in Germany's Bavarian Forest when a female wolf viciously attacked me as she protected her pups. The strength and ferocity of this wolf was incredible. Although I know it was my fault, ever since that terrifying attack I have been more petrified of wolves than of any other animals. I labelled wolves as savage, bloodthirsty man-killers, hungry for human flesh and blood, but now I'm learning that wolves do not normally attack humans.'

'You were very unlucky and also ignorant,' Nacoma said, as gently as he could. 'You should never have touched the wolf's pups, and as a consequence of such stupidity you have spent your whole life being petrified of all the deadly creatures on this Earth. A few people in Europe have been attacked or killed by wolves, but there have been no wolf attacks on humans in the whole of North America. Wolves will only attack humans in self-defence.'

'And coyotes and foxes never attack humans?' Marion enquired.

'Never,' Nacoma replied firmly. 'Let's start with foxes. In North America and Europe there are two types of red foxes: the lowland foxes and the mountain foxes. The mountain fox is much larger, longer in the legs and fiercer than the lowland fox, and is strong and vicious enough to kill a small deer or a dog smaller than a Doberman — hence the five mountain foxes in the Bavarian Forest were able to kill your two terriers. But even the largest foxes will always run away and will only bite a man or a dog in self-defence, and coyotes are the same. The coyote is as fierce and cunning as the wolf, and slightly larger than the mountain fox. Even so, the wolf, the coyote and the fox are not a threat to humans, but they will bite you if you corner them.'

Nacoma cast another spell in the forest which exposed the deciduous forests of birch, aspen and maple trees, and all six humans watched the wolf, the coyote and the fox hunting rabbits, hares or deer. The wolf snarled savagely, the coyote growled fiercely and the fox barked like a dog. Marion shook slightly as her mind travelled back to that ferocious wolf attack in the Bavarian Forest that drastically effected the rest of her life, then seeing her two terriers at the vet's after they had been savaged.

'Other dangerous animals have been introduced into America and Canada by Europeans and have turned feral,' Nacoma continued. 'Feral animals are domesticated or farm animals that have escaped and turned wild, like the horse, the dog and the cat. The most dangerous feral animals are dogs. Dogs attack more people in America and Canada than any other animals. Feral dogs roam the cities, towns and countryside, becoming as wild and untamable as the wolf and the coyote. Dogs have been tamed by humankind — but they still retains their wild, vicious instinct.'

He paused for effect.

'Now,' he continued suddenly, 'bulls and oxen in North America are more wild and savage than any in Europe. With their sheer size, weight, strength, speed and formidable horns they can kill even a grizzly bear. Bulls are as ruthless as American bison, which they are related to, and bulls in rodeos and bull-fights can move with awesome power and speed. Many cowboys and matadors have been killed by bulls or oxen. Then there are horses, mules and donkeys. The two most dangerous horses are mustangs and rodeo horses, and they too are very strong, agile and fast. The feral horse is usually a placid beast, as is the mustang, but if you corner, lasso or ride the horse it will leap about to throw you off and then kick you to death with its hooves. A horse usually has to be abused or frightened before it turns hostile and attacks a human. The donkey and the mule can also violently kick and bite people.'

'So we've dealt with six feral animals,' Marion said, her mind racing. 'What about billy-goats and rams?'

'Goats and rams are generally not

dangerous — although they can deal a man or a dog a nasty battering with their horns and hooves if attacked themselves,' Nacoma told her. 'Even feral pigs and feral cats will defend themselves if cornered. But these four beasts will normally flee from trouble. Only the really large animals are seriously dangerous, such as alligators, bison, moose, bears and pumas. The smaller herbivores and predators will normally run away.'

Marion felt somewhat reassured, knowing that even the creatures with the worst reputations would never attack her unless they felt that they or their young were threatened.

Nacoma decided that his group and Marion must return to the reservation.

CHAPTER 8

The next stage of Marion's training began — the spiritualism of the less dangerous wild animals of North America. And having been overwhelmed by different spiritualism surrounding the world's lethal creatures, Marion was dying to hear more spiritualism before carrying out her training in native meditation.

'Which animal will we begin with amongst the less dangerous?' she asked Nacoma, as both of them sat outside his wigwam.

'Well, you already know about the Bigfoot creature,' the old man said.

'Yes. You know, before I went through the dreamworld, I did not believe in the yeti or the Bigfoot creature,' Marion replied thoughtfully. 'I still don't, because this dreamworld is different from the real world. But I'm more open-minded now, and anything is possible.'

'Quite. Then there is worship of the wolf and the coyote,' Nacoma told Marion. 'Firstly the wolf. White people in Europe were terrified of wolves and brought their fear of wolves to North America, but as you know we Native Americans have always worshipped, venerated and respected the wolf. The first domesticated dogs were reared by ancient peoples in North America, Europe, Asia and Africa who captured wolves, coyotes or jackals and tamed them. The domesticated dog is descended from wolves, coyotes and jackals. Dogs, wolves and coyotes were treated by the North Americans as guardians and companions of humans, for they are intelligent, clever and useful to us.'

'The Africans had the same attitude towards African hunting dogs and jackals,' Marion said excitedly. 'In Rwanda, two packs of hunting dogs and jackals saved me and Chief Guamo from witches, werehyenas and wereleopards. The Asians regarded dholes and jackals as heroes, and these wild dogs rescued me and the three Shaolin priests from four hyenas in Nepal, who were actually witches who had transformed themselves into hyenas after they died. This hero-worship of wild dogs is repeated with wolves and coyotes in the Rockies and prairies of Alaska, Canada and the United States.'

'That is right,' Nacoma said approvingly. 'And dogs were given the same hero-worship as wolves, coyotes, hunting dogs, dholes and jackals. And, as with all wild beasts in Canada and America, the coyote has been the subject of worship and spiritualism. For example, the coyote is a protective guardian of the Navajo healing ceremony called "Coyoteway". This curing ritual is carried out in order to treat those men who have fallen ill of a disease called "coyote sickness". This disease attacks any man who disrupts the Navajo tribe's peaceful relationship with the divinity — for example, by injuring or killing a coyote. In the ceremony, an individual in the tribe takes on the identity of the coyote and assists in bringing back the state of harmony and curing the illness. So the Navajos use the coyote for healing purposes in the same way that the Blackfoot tribe uses the grizzly bear in their bear dance, and other Native American tribes, like the Seminoles in Florida, use the puma. In Europe, there are many tales recounting the cunning of the wolf and the fox, and the natives have as many tales about the coyote in North America. In particular, the plains tribes regarded the coyote and the fox as sly tricksters.'

'So I know you worship the wolf and the coyote,' Marion said, 'but what other animals feature strongly in your spiritualism?'

'The eagle,' Nacoma said. 'Throughout North America, it is believed that eagles fight with the spirits of the underworld and cause storms and earthquakes. In some tribes, a clan shows the eagle on their totem poles, as the bird of prey stands for the founder of the clan... Other predatory birds are also represented by our spiritualism. We believe that every living thing has a life and a spirit and demands great respect. Every animal, bird, insect, fish, plant, tree or rock — and even the soil. Take a look at the birds of prey in the sky, all just as noble and brave as the eagle...'

Marion followed Nacoma's gaze and glanced up towards the sky. Circling above, she could see a raven, a hawk, a falcon and an owl.

Nacoma continued. 'These four predatory birds have spirits in them. The raven is a trickster and a hero, much like the coyote, and he brings fire and daylight. We have many tales of the raven's adventures as a cunning trickster — similar to coyotes and foxes. But what about the owl? Well, in Europe and most of North America, the owl was a bird of ill-omen and death, but out on the American prairies it was a protector and guardian.'

'You obviously treat birds of prey and predators with more value and respect than modern humans do in Europe,' Marion told Nacoma.

'We do,' Nacoma agreed. 'Because every predator and bird of prey has its place in the food web. The eagle preys on the hawk, the hawk and the owl prey on the falcon, and all four birds of prey eat small animals and birds, such as crows and ravens. Every bird has its place in the pecking order, with the eagle, the hawk and the owl at the top, just as every animal has its place in the animal pecking order with the bears at the top.'

'But, like all predators,' Marion cut in, 'birds of prey can be dangerous to humans if people does not exercise caution when approaching their nests. I know that a few people in Europe have lost an eye to the talons of an owl or a hawk. The eagle is the most formidable bird, and even the falcon can take your eye out, but they say that the owl is the worst.'

'But it's extremely rare in North America and even in Europe that people get injured by birds of prey,' Nacoma countered. 'I've only known of two cases where owls have injured warriors, and only three where three warriors had their eyes ripped out by an eagle, a hawk and a falcon. All five cases were caused by the birds defending their nests and young. But all predators will fight a human in self-defence. The rattlesnakes are the most dangerous small predators in America and Mexico, for their venom is lethal. The feral cat and the American badger will claw and bite you if you try to handle them. The weasel and the stoat can almost sever a man's finger with their powerful, razor-sharp teeth, and so too can the mink and the fisher marten. It is not only the larger predators who can be dangerous, and rattlesnakes and vipers have a reputation as terrible as alligators, sharks and barracudas.'

'Okay,' Marion said. 'Going back to the spiritualism… We know that the wolf, the coyote and the fox are the subject of profound spiritualism, and we know there are legends of the Bigfoot creature going back centuries. Do you cast spiritualism around the predators white people tend to dread most? I'm talking about alligators, sharks and barracudas.'

'Yes, we do, Marion,' Nacoma told her. 'What is generally ruthless and evil to Europeans tends to be a noble animal to us Native Americans. The wolverine has a spirit in him, and so too do the lynx and the bobcat, among many others. Every creature is part of the chain of life, and the most dangerous creature is not the shark or the alligator. It is humankind. We lived in peace and harmony with the land and its wildlife until people came over from Europe, massacred our tribes, destroyed the land and herded us into reservations, treating us as second-class citizens in our own country. They called us savages and uncivilised, but we were not. It was the white men who were uncivilised.'

'But hopefully we live in better times,' Marion said.

They stared up at the clear blue sky, and it began to rain lightly. 'And now that the spiritualism of North America's less dangerous animals is over, I'm dying to learn native meditation. I'm petrified of facing dangerous animals, like bears and pumas, but I've already learned other types of meditation in Nepal.'

'The native meditation is similar to the kind you have learned,' Nacoma informed her. 'But first you will have to repeat the relaxation and deep breathing exercises you learned in Rwanda and Nepal. You must practise these for eight days. Then we'll train you further in horse whispering and meditation.'

'I'm dying to begin,' Marion enthused. 'I've grown in confidence. I'll begin the relaxation tomorrow.'

Nacoma began his explanation of meditation as soon as the eight days were over, and his smile conveyed a calm and confident attitude which bordered on arrogance.

'First of all, you will face four feral animals

that we captured — a bull, a horse, a goat and a ram,' he told Marion. 'Rather than retreating, face them by moving towards them, but in a submissive posture. Remember: they are herd animals who rule by dominance, as do bison and moose. But don't be intimidated or unnerved by their level of aggression or ferocity. Relax and allow the energy of the Great Spirit to flow through you. But bear in mind that each herbivore requires a different calming method depending on its level of intelligence or its degree of aggression. The bull and the ox are massive and powerful, but also quite stupid. Bull-fighters in Spain, southern France and Mexico can curtail a bull's attack by waving their capes in front of the charging bulls and redirecting their attacks.

'The Japanese martial arts of judo and aikido work on the same principal. But we natives use yet another method similar to what the Buddhists and Hindus use in Asia and the Aboriginals use in Australia. This is the fingers-to-eyes technique. Because of the beast's lack of intelligence or cunning, we can knock the bull or the ox unconscious by waving two fingers across the beast's eyes. This confuses and disorientates the beast, pacifying his brain and making him dizzy. After five or six minutes, the bull or ox will collapse. This will also work on bison, buffaloes, moose and elks, who also lack intelligence, but it will never work against bears or pumas who are more intelligent and cunning. It certainly won't work on crocodiles, alligators or sharks underwater because, for all their lack of intelligence, these predators are extremely savage and cunning. The horse, the goat and the ram require a different calming method from the bull and the ox, and this is called horse whispering.'

'I've done horse whispering,' Marion interrupted proudly. 'I was trained in horse whispering in Nepal by the three Shaolin priests.'

'But our method of horse whispering is more advanced,' Nacoma explained patiently. 'The mustangs and rodeo horses we have in North America are far more wild, savage and dangerous than the horses in Asia. Again, we adopt a submissive body posture. Horses, donkeys, mules, goats and rams are herd animals who rule by dominance, and the same thing is true of pack animals, like dogs and wolves. In fact, with all herbivores and predators you must act submissively and not look the animal straight in the eyes. All animals, especially dogs, wolves and coyotes, will mistake this for aggression and will respond with aggression. Never shout at or try to dominate the animal. All animals are stronger and better-armed than humans, and if it ever came to a fight the human would come off worse. Avoid eye-contact with the horse and try to find the energy field in its body — this is most accessible in the neck, back and shoulders. Then stroke its energy field, for this has a calming effect. Talk to the horse softly, without raising your voice. Avoid its legs because they can pack a kick powerful enough to maim or even kill a human. This will also work with aggressive billy-goats and rams, which normally will only attack a human if they themselves are threatened. Donkeys and mules are the same, though it is easier to pacify a donkey, a mule, a goat or a ram than it is to pacify a bull, an ox or a horse. Have you got all that?'

Marion nodded slowly.

'Then let's begin your training.'

* * *

Marion made her way into the farm enclosure. Suddenly, an enormous brown bull charged from the doorway opposite. He was almost as big as a bison, measuring a metre from shoulder to shoulder and tipping the scales at 1,000 pounds. His massive horns were lowered like the horns of a buffalo, his body was packed thickly with solid muscle and his eyes were bloodshot and savage. The bull was so fast that Marion only just managed to dodge out of the way, and she knew she had to repeat this dodging until the beast tired. Feral bulls, buffaloes and bison cannot suddenly turn aside or change direction when their charge is focused towards the target, and any human who dodges at the last second could avoid injury or death just in time.

This also works against elephants, hippos and rhinos, but not horses, moose or elks, who are more agile. Marion was cornered against the wall of the enclosure, and the bull roared, coughed and grunted with rage. He charged again with awesome power and speed, but Marion swiftly dodged him and the bull's horns crashed into the wall, smashing a hole in the wood. This was too much for the enraged beast, incapacitated by the aching pain to his head. The bull retreated, and Marion stood directly in front of the brute, her body relaxed, passive and submissive and her face turned aside to avoid eye-contact. She stroked the bull's head to diffuse his savagery, and then waved two fingers across the bull's eyes. Marion had also seen this technique used on a water buffalo in *Crocodile Dundee,* and she remembered calming down the bull in the arena in Nepal, therefore, she persevered with appeasing this bull in Canada.

The bull became dizzy and confused, and he retreated and plummeted onto his side, unconscious from exhaustion. Marion sighed with relief, and gained more confidence.

'Now for the horse!' Nacoma called.

The horse charged, snorting and grunting, into the enclosure, and Marion leapt aside as the horse's hooves flailed at her with deadly strength and speed. It was a black rodeo horse, but Marion was passive, gentle and submissive again, and she found the area of the horse's energy field where its shoulders joined its neck. The horse's eyes were black with fury, fear and hatred, but Marion caressed the energy field and gently pressed the pressure point in its shoulder. She spoke to the horse softly and with love, saying, 'It's okay, boy. I'm not going to hurt you. You're a good boy now.' The horse knew that Marion meant it no harm and soon calmed down. The horse retreated and Marion sighed a second time.

'Very good! Now for the goat and the ram!' Nacoma cried.

Charging into the enclosure were a large black billy-goat and a big white ram, both very capable of injuring Marion, and she dodged both beasts before fleeing frantically into a corner. A human could dodge a heavy, cumbersome bull, but not a more agile goat or ram, especially when two beasts attack the human from either side. Marion was cornered, and the goat sprang with incredible speed from the right whilst the ram lunged with equal speed and agility from the left. When they were both a metre from her, Marion jumped five feet into the air, like an athlete, somersaulted and then landed feet-first behind the two beasts. The goat and the ram crashed and they were dizzy. Marion then spoke to them softly and worked her hands into their energy fields, her right hand stroking the goat's shoulder and back and her left hand caressing the ram's neck, shoulder and back, both hands fondling the pressure points. They were easier to pacify than the horse, and both beasts withdrew and then ambled outside the enclosure.

Marion also headed for the entrance, and Nacoma and his warriors faced her.

'So, what's next?' Marion asked, a smile

spreading across her face and brightening her sharp eyes.

'You have to diffuse the savagery of a dog, a wolf and a coyote,' Nacoma said, smiling back at her. 'But do you know why I've chosen all three to confront you at the same time? And why I did not choose three dogs, three wolves or three coyotes, but rather one of each?'

'No, I don't,' Marion replied.

'Because all three species are enemies of each other. The dog defends the sheep flock against the wolf, the wolf preys on the dog, and both will eat the coyote. In the wild, coyotes and foxes always avoid wolves and dogs. The dog, the wolf and the coyote are so wary of being attacked by one another that they will not attack you.'

Then one of the other warriors butted in. 'I once fed some meat to two packs of wolves and coyotes,' he said. 'The coyotes attacked me, but then the wolves attacked and killed the coyotes. Most predators would rather eat the flesh of other predators than of humans, and all predators hate each other.'

'I see what you mean,' Marion said, and chuckled. 'When I was in Nepal, I had to appease a lion and a tiger, and both big cats were so hostile towards each other that they did not even consider attacking me. If the lion had attacked me, the tiger would have attacked the lion — and vice versa.'

'We will give you other examples of how the natural hatred between predators has been exploited by humans,' Ten Bears insisted, 'after you have pacified the dog, the wolf and the coyote. Concentrate on the dog and the wolf first, as they are more vicious than the coyote. Again, remember they are pack animals. Act passively and submissively, avoid eye-contact, talk to them softly and caress their energy fields.'

'I'm ready for anything,' Marion answered, though fear was coming out in her voice. However, she was determined to put on a brave face.

The dog, the wolf and the coyote charged from three directions, all three muscular beasts exploding with their psychotic snarling and growling, and the dog was a vicious Doberman as black as the wolf. But when all three encountered each other, they growled and snarled savagely towards each other. Marion was shaking with terror, her dread chilling the cold streams of sweat that turned to ice on her face as the cold breeze whistled against her head. But she knew wild dogs could smell fear, so she must control emotions. She gulped, smiled and then caressed the energy fields on the wolf and the dog, stroking the pressure points where their backs joined the napes of their necks and their broad shoulders. She slowly gained confidence, stroking the energy fields until both the dog and the wolf withdrew and ambled away. Marion then caressed the energy field between the coyote's shoulders using both her hands — like jackals, coyotes were too cowardly to attack humans. A pack of coyotes would easily kill a man or a dog, but one coyote lacked the confidence to attack Marion. He too cantered away. Marion breathed deeply and then relaxed.

'You see, it worked!' Nacoma explained. 'I saw how scared you were, but you fought your fear very well.'

'Any more of this and I'll have a heart attack,' Marion said seriously.

'We haven't finished with you yet,' Nacoma replied lightly. 'Now we'll exploit the natural hatred of predators that are much larger and more ferocious.'

Marion frowned. 'But I'm petrified enough as it is.'

'Bury your terror,' Nacoma said firmly. 'Bury it deep inside you. Take a positive mental attitude. You can do this!'

'I'll try,' Marion replied, her voice nervous.

'Don't try — *do it*,' Nacoma insisted. 'Fight your terror. A white American once told me of how circus trainers mixed lions and tigers, exploiting the hatred between both big cats so they would be too wary of each other to attack their trainers. One circus trainer was named Clyde Beatty. And when a tiger attacked Beatty, he was saved by one of the lions which attacked the tiger. Do you remember that lion and that tiger you pacified in the arena in Nepal?'

'Yes I do,' Marion retorted, her terror increasing.

'Lions and tigers are too wary of each other, and are more partial to lion or tiger flesh than human flesh to even think about attacking a human,' Nacoma said. 'This tactic is not only used on lions and tigers, but also on bears, leopards, black panthers, jaguars and pumas. If they lived in the same continent, leopards would be wary of jaguars and pumas, and both jaguars and pumas are wary of each other. Another example from your experience, Marion, is how you saved a jaguar and a puma from ten caimans in South America, and they hated each other too much to attack you. That's how you used the power of God to appease their aggression.'

'I see it all now,' Marion said, slightly more reassured. 'So which predators am I about to face this time?'

'Bears, tigers and pumas. The Kodiak bear, two grizzlies and the black bear will charge towards you from the forest, and the Siberian tiger, two Bengal tigers and two pumas will charge from the three cages over there. Your husband, Klaus, introduced the three tigers into Canada from Nepal, with help from the three Shaolin priests. And Mao Sing, Sun Ying and Chong Lee will stand beside you in case things go badly wrong.'

'My husband is here?!' Marion cried.

Nacoma nodded and Klaus appeared.

'Klaus!' Marion enthused as she saw the bearded German standing alongside the Shaolin priests. She ran towards him and they embraced each other. 'I've missed you!'

'I've missed you too,' Klaus said joyfully. 'And the three priests here have told me what progress you've made.'

'That's small reassurance,' Marion complained, but then she beamed up at him and the Shaolin priests. They too greeted her, and then the four men stood beside her to face the tigers whilst the five warriors would confront the bears and pumas. The cage doors of the tigers and pumas were opened. Marion trembled and her teeth chattered, but Mao Sing rubbed her shoulder reassuringly and Marion, again, suppressed her terror.

With a violent chill in her guts, Marion watched the big cats hissing, snarling and growling, their fearsome fangs exposed and their powerful bodies rippling with hard muscle and sinew. Then Marion watched the four enormous bears hurtling through the forest towards her and the others, their ears flattened, heads lowered and eyes blazing with ferocity. All bears sweep back their ears and lower their heads when about to attack. The explosive power and sheer speed of the bears was incredible, their backs and shoulders churning with thick muscle, their tremendous claws black and deadly, and their gleaming fangs letting off jets of foam and the blood of animals they had killed. The Kodiak bear was nearly half the size of an elephant, whilst the two grizzlies were twice the size of tigers and the black bear was two-thirds as big as the grizzlies. The tigers and pumas sprinted with lightning speed and lethal power from the cages, and the tigers too were impressive beasts. The Siberian tiger was almost as enormous as a grizzly, with churning muscles swelling through its powerful body, and the two Bengal tigers were also massive and packed thickly with iron-hard muscles. The pumas, too, were large and powerfully-muscled; two pumas would easily kill the black bear or severely injure one of the grizzlies by leaping onto its back and clawing it, in the manner of a house cat defending itself against an aggressive dog.

The bears bellowed, roared, coughed and snarled with unrestrained savagery whilst the tigers screamed and the pumas snarled. The nine deadly predators were determined to slaughter the humans, but hesitated from attacking their prey when they encountered each other. The bears reared up onto their hind legs, whilst the tigers and pumas circled the Shaolin priests and Marion threateningly. The pumas were wary of the Bengal tigers, just as the Bengal tigers were enemies of the Siberian tiger, the grizzlies feared the Kodiak bear, and the black bear was terrified of falling prey either to the Kodiak bear, the grizzlies or the pumas. The bone-chilling bellowing of the bears and the blood-curdling roaring of the tigers exploded again with the pumas' aggressive screaming, but Marion battled to hide her terror, closing her eyes and clenching her hands together. The tigers and bears circled each other, whilst the black bear lunged towards the pumas, voicing its hissing snarls and growling grunts, and the pumas swiped at the black bear with their scimitar-like claws.

'Now sit down in the lotus position and pray to the Great Spirit,' Nacoma told everybody. Marion and the five others descended into the lotus positions with their legs crossed, followed by the Shaolin priests. In the lotus position, a human could easily and quickly roll up into a ball if a predator attacked, but more importantly this position was passive, submissive and unthreatening to the animal. Everybody closed their hands in front of their chests and faces, their arms protecting their ribs, and they prayed to the Great Spirit.

'Marion, repeat after us…' Nacoma began. 'May the power, might and goodness of the Great Spirit be with us in our time of peril. Please put good intentions into these nine predators. Don't allow them to attack us. We have done them no harm. Thank you, oh Great Spirit.'

Marion repeated what everybody said, forcing confidence and calmness into her mind and heart.

The predators hesitated from their vicious intent to attack each other. Wild animals would always shy away from fighting, for fighting would result in severe injuries and hamper their ability to hunt prey. Solitary big cats, including even tigers, will not commit themselves to a full-scale battle if they can avoid it. Bears will also avoid fighting, especially if a Kodiak bear or a grizzly has met its match in the tiger or a black bear is out-classed by one or two pumas. The predators were pacified by Marion and the eight men praying to the Great Spirit and showing no fear or aggression. The tigers and pumas loped back towards their cages with lightning speed, whilst the bears lumbered towards the forest, all three bear species avoiding each other. For the big cats there were three large cages: one for the Siberian tiger, the second for the two Bengal tigers and the last cage accommodating the two pumas.

Marion was shaking and fighting back tears. 'I nearly wet my trousers,' she said.

Klaus came over and comforted her, embracing her. 'You'll be fine, my love,' he murmured. 'You need more time to conquer your fear and perfect the calming methods. You'll get there. Don't despair.' He caressed her head, and her crying began to stop.

The Integrity Test would begin tomorrow, and Marion knew she had to summon all her mental strength, intelligence and courage to make it through the test.

'You have completed your training,' Nacoma told her. 'And tomorrow, the Integrity Test will begin.'

'Why is it called the Integrity Test?' Marion asked, wiping away the remnants of a tear from her cheek.

'Because it will prove your integrity and good nature, as well as your ability to conquer your fear and to survive,' Nacoma replied. 'In order to uphold your good nature, you must never kill, injure or even slightly hurt any of the animals you will face. I repeat: no animals are to be harmed whilst you're performing the test. But you must control your terror and perform all the calming methods you have learned, and this will take all your mental powers and courage. Nobody before you has ever survived the Integrity Test. Many of our students carried out the test and were killed by the animals they faced. Because their terror of these animals took over and clouded their judgement. There are no shortcuts. You'll have to be very proficient with the calming methods and also very lucky to survive. Then your last destination will be the Arctic in Canada to overcome your fear of the polar bear, before you embark on three final tests which will also push your courage to the very limit.'

'And then what?' Marion asked him.

'Then you will come out of your coma alive,' Nacoma said. 'But this dreamworld and all your experiences will have enabled you to conquer your terror of dangerous animals. Get plenty of rest first, for you will have a long day tomorrow.'

Klaus hugged her tightly. 'Don't worry, darling,' he said softly. 'I'll give you all the encouragement you'll need. You can do it. I know you can. Give it your best shot.'

'I intend to,' Marion replied.

'One last vision before you sleep...' Nacoma said.

They saw the ending of the battle in the forest clearing between the bull, ox, horse, donkey and mule against the five bison. The bull and the donkey were dead in the snow. The ox, the horse and the mule stood over their bodies and made peace with the bison.

'The ox, the horse and the mule are now at peace with these bison,' Nacoma indicated. 'Their battle symbolised war between feral animals and wild animals, and also between the white men and the Native Americans, which ended in peace afterwards. The bull and the donkey symbolised the casualties of war. But the ox, the horse, the mule and the five bison symbolised the survivors of war, and also that deadly enemies can bury the hatchet.'

'I see...' Marion answered. 'The ox, the horse and the mule are very impressive animals. So are the bison. Fascinating stuff!'

'Yes, but we had better get some rest,' Klaus insisted.

CHAPTER 9

'Okay,' the old chief began, 'the Integrity Test is in five stages. In the first stage you will have to save other people who are in danger from wild animals. In this stage are four situations, and the first situation will involve you saving me and the other Native Americans from a prison cell. We will be imprisoned in this cell by the American bison and several other feral herbivores. You will have to calm down these aggressive animals with horse whispering, the fingers-to-eyes technique and native meditation. You will be equipped with a sleep-gun in your holster tied around your waist just in case the odds against you are too great. Now — begin!'

Marion left Klaus in bed and walked slowly along the path into the next time zone whilst the tribespeople made their way along a different pathway into the prison cell. They were risking their lives and placing them in the hands of Marion, whose task was to save them. Some of the tribespeople might not make it out of this situation alive.

* * *

Marion still found herself in Alberta, positioned on a farm between the warehouse and a massive prison where her friends were being held captive and guarded by nine fierce beasts, seven of them feral animals. In the prison, a bison, a bull moose, a bull and an ox were leading a horse, a donkey, a mule, a billy-goat and a ram, and they were about to kill the five warriors. Marion had to act fast, and the farm warehouse south of her caught her attention. She would lure the beasts into the farm building and try to neutralise them with the three calming methods. To decoy them away from the natives, she had to yell for their attention.

'Hey, you!' she called. 'I'm over here!'

When the animals' attention was distracted, Marion sprinted away from the prison and headed for the farm warehouse, and the nine beasts pursued her with great speed. Unless she reached the building fast, she would never outrun them, but she just made it as the bison and the moose were only ten yards behind her and she slammed shut the building's oak door. The beasts were ramming the door and finally smashed it open. The bison and the moose waited outside with the ox, the donkey and the mule to cut off Marion's escape in case she tried to get out of a window, whilst the other four beasts charged inside and split up. The horse and the bull made their way into the furthest room just as the goat and the ram entered the nearest room.

The bull spotted Marion immediately, hiding

behind a big, wooden pillar. In her blind terror, she ran across the warehouse and up a fairly steep ramp, knowing that such enormous, heavy beasts could never pursue her. But she knew that the goat and the ram would easily scale the ramp, being smaller and lighter. Marion ran up the ramp like a greyhound, with the bull leaping up and narrowly missing her with his formidable horns. The horse leapt up like a rodeo horse, biting and kicking at Marion, but he too missed his target. The horse was screaming and flailing with his front hooves, just as the bull grunted with fiery rage and then roared like a jaguar at bay.

The ram and the goat came darting round from the other room, then leapt up the ramp with the same ease that they would leap up steep mountain slopes and over ledges. Sheep and goats were evolved by nature especially for life in mountain country, where they would have to assail steep and rocky slopes. Marion saw a shoot leading from the second floor down to a cell on the ground floor, but the ram and the goat were now on the second floor and they glared with evil fury in their normally placid faces. As Marion adopted a combative stance, they charged with horns lowered, ready to rupture her stomach. Marion leapt into the air in a rolling somersault and landed behind the charging beasts, and they rammed their heads and horns into the wall with a sickening thud that rendered them dizzy. Before they could recover, Marion made her way to the front of the beasts and stroked their energy fields, fondling the pressure points in the goat's neck and shoulders with her right hand and caressing the ram's back and shoulders with her left. Avoiding eye contact, as she had been taught, she spoke to them softly and rubbed their heads, and the goat and the ram retreated in a passive manner. Then Marion leapt and landed inside the warehouse's cell. Landing on her feet, she had no time to think or plan as the horse and the bull came charging into the room and towards the cell, the horse screaming and the bull roaring violently. The bull was the more powerful and lethal of the two beasts, so Marion decided she would have to neutralise him first.

Dodging to the right of the bull, she allowed the massive beast to crash into the cell's wall so that he was dizzy and incapacitated for a few minutes. Marion had to pacify the horse in that short space of time.

The horse flailed his sledgehammer hooves, but Marion avoided eye contact, stood to the side of the horse's legs and talked to him softly and with love in her voice. The horse screamed savagely, his eyes cold and vicious and his muscles rippling through his powerful body as his legs kicked. But Marion was not deterred. She felt for the horse's energy field in his neck, back and shoulders and told him, 'You're a good boy now. Don't be afraid. I'm not going to hurt you.' In exactly three minutes, she had pacified the horse, and the bull was recovering from being disorientated by the impact of his head and horns ploughing savagely into the cell wall. Marion took the initiative and grabbed the bull's horns, using the full weight and strength of her body to keep the bull's head down to the ground. Although a bull was far superior to a diminutive human in his enormous size, strength and crushing power, his head was lighter and weaker than the full weight and strength of the human body, and Marion locked her arms around the bull's horns. Then, as her left arm snaked round to hold his left horn, the fingers of her right hand were flexed in a V-shape in front of the bull's eyes. She waved her fingers across his eyes a few times but then the bull suddenly retreated from Marion, yanking his horns out from her grip. She persevered with the fingers-to-eyes technique, walking towards the bull and covering up her terror, and for three more minutes she waved her fingers across his face.

The bull was dizzy and confused, his brain pacified, and he collapsed, plummeting towards the ground with sickening impact. But in the next minute, the ox, the donkey and the mule came charging into the room, all three of them large, muscular and just as vicious as the horse and the bull. The ox bellowed and roared like a tiger, and lowered his huge head and fearsome horns. Meanwhile, the mule and the donkey screamed and grunted fiercely, like rodeo horses or mustangs, and as they reared up onto their hind legs, their murderous front hooves flailed at the young woman with lightning speed. Not succumbing to her paralysing terror, Marion reached for the sleep-gun in her holster, sprayed the ox in the face with a jet of gas and then did the same to the donkey and the mule. All three beasts collapsed into heaps on the floor.

Marion experienced guilt and remorse for using sleeping gas and knocking animals unconscious, even if the gas was not powerful enough to kill them. The gun was meant to only ever be used as a very last resort, but the odds against Marion had been three powerful beasts against one puny woman, and she would in no way succeed in pacifying the three beasts at the same time. Glossing over her guilt as the calm horse stood beside the bull, with the ox, the donkey and the mule lying out cold on the floor, Marion left the cell and headed with caution down the corridor of the warehouse, before she discovered another ramp leading up towards the second floor. And she made it just in time, for the moose and the bison were at the end of the corridor and they charged with awesome power and speed, both beasts roaring and bellowing with greater rage and ferocity than the bull and the ox.

They lowered their heads as their broad muscles rippled through their enormous bodies, the bison's bushy mane standing up on end, his solid head and long horns ready to gore Marion whilst the moose would stab and kick Marion with both his formidable antlers and hooves. Marion sped up the ramp and assailed the obstacle in five seconds, but this time the ramp was not so steep, and it was strong enough to take a 2,000-pound bison and a 1,500-pound moose, both beasts one and a half times the size and weight of any ox.

She was on the second floor again, and she stood rooted to the spot against a wall. The bison and the moose charged up the ramp with explosive power and speed, and cornered Marion. She was overpowered with a crippling fear from seeing their enormous size and weight packed with awesome muscles, their crushing strength and power, their cold, evil eyes and their fearsome weaponry of horns, antlers and hooves.

They closed in on Marion, but at the last split second she swiftly dodged the bison and rolled on the ground into a corner. The bison and the moose ploughed with lethal impact into the wall in the same manner as the bull, smashing holes in the wood so that the impact rendered them dizzy and disorientated. The bison was sprawled on the ground as it struggled vainly to get up, but the moose had suffered less pain because its large antlers had protected its head from the worst of the impact. Marion ascended to her feet and grabbed hold of the moose's antlers, before using meditation to appease the moose. Avoiding eye contact again, she stroked the pressure points in the moose's neck and shoulders and sang to calm it down.

The moose retreated, but the bison had recovered from its punishment and was on its feet again. Rather than retreating, Marion approached the bison and carried out the fingers-to-eyes technique. Flexing her two fingers again in a V-shape, she waved her fingers across the bison's eyes, and because the bison lacked intelligence or cunning, it was struck dumb and confused by this technique. After a few minutes it crashed to the ground. Marion gulped and her stomach churned as the bison was unconscious on the wooden floor.

Marion released the five tribesmen from their prison, and then the nine powerful beasts came out of the farm warehouse, now as placid as docile sheep. Marion and her new friends stroked all of them before two herds of bison and moose came over to investigate. But these enormous giants were friendly and gentle. The bison, the moose and the seven feral beasts joined the two herds, and Marion and her friends had to prepare for their next task. This, again, would involve using native meditation.

Marion and the others found themselves on a pathway on the imaginary border between Alaska, Canada and Europe. They spotted three Canadian cowboys and a Polish gamekeeper being charged by four massive bears: a giant Kodiak bear from Alaska, a grizzly bear and a black bear from Canada, and a brown bear from Poland. All four bears were terrifying beasts with unrestrained ferocity, charging with hulking brute power and deadly speed, their ears swept back and heads lowered with aggression.

Marion made a mental note of the bears and their levels of aggressiveness as she and the tribesmen charged in to help the four white men, her stomach churning and heart thumping as she tried to ignore her terror. The Kodiak and the grizzly were by far the most savage and terrifying of the four bears. Their bellows shook the forest like an avalanche; their great fangs flashed and their eyes blazed with fury. The black bear was nearly as aggressive and vicious, its fiery eyes focused on its prey, its gleaming white teeth and lethal black claws exposed and its coughing, grunting and hissing escalating into a deadly roaring and snarling. The brown bear from Poland which attacked the gamekeeper was not as aggressive as the grizzly bear and the black bear, and other European predators, like the wolf, the wolverine and the lynx, out-classed the brown bear in ferocity and cunning, but even this enormous beast became as fearsome and ruthless as any grizzly.

Of all bears, only polar bears were more terrifying than these four killers, and Marion's experience with facing those bears, tigers and pumas just before the Integrity Test had brought it home to her how horrific bear attacks are. The white men screamed as the bears savaged them, their giant teeth and lethal claws ripping the men to pieces as they were mauled on the ground, but Marion and the natives reached them in the nick of time. All four bears were enemies of each other, and the six humans exploited this weakness. The

Kodiak bear and the grizzly bear bellowed at the black bear and the brown bear, and both smaller bears snarled at each other and the grizzly with vicious fury and hatred. The bears swiftly abandoned their attacks on the men.

The bears lowered their heads again, but Marion and Nacoma stood to the side of the grizzly just as another two warriors decoyed the Kodiak bear: one diverted the black bear and the last stood to the side of the brown bear. Making no sudden movements, all six of them gently raised their arms and then sat down in the lotus position to face an animal's attack. The injured white men crawled away towards some thickets, covered with wounds inflicted by the bears' claws and fangs. Marion and Nacoma were petrified of the grizzly, the worst of the four bears. As the grizzly roared again, foam spilled from its lips, and its fiery eyes filled the two humans with fear.

Marion and Nacoma turned their heads to the side and raised their arms above their heads in prayer, Marion forcing confidence and cool-headedness into her mind. She said, 'Oh Lord Grizzly, we mean you no harm. You don't want to harm us. Please leave us alone.' Her voice was soft and gentle, and her lotus position diffused the sheer aggression of the giant grizzly. The Kodiak bear and the black bear were also losing interest in attacking three tribesmen. This made sense, as Klaus had once told her that the vast majority of bear attacks were bluff and warning, not a ruthless attempt to kill and eat humans. And she had learned on this dreamworld journey that bears which did attack and injure or kill humans were being defensive rather than aggressive.

The grizzly bear turned tail and lumbered back into the forest with explosive power and speed, its back and shoulder muscles rippling through its enormous body. The Kodiak bear retreated, encouraged by the grizzly's retreat, and then the black bear followed suit. Only the brown bear was remaining, and it too removed itself from the situation, ambling towards the forest in Poland.

Marion forced out a sigh of relief, her lungs fighting for air as her heart thumped like a drum. The five Native Americans were assisting the four white men, who were in shock and covered in claw and bite wounds. However, they managed to get up and make their way to the nearest village. Here, they would be treated for their injuries by skilled healers.

'Can't we help them?' Marion asked Nacoma.

'Our healers will cure them,' Nacoma told her.

Klaus approached them suddenly.

'Ah, here's your husband!' Nacoma said. 'But here is where you and I separate — though Klaus can stay here. You, Marion, are destined to save some men in the ocean from sharks and other ocean predators whilst my men and I protect some sheep from predators. It's been quite an adventure. Farewell!'

'It was lovely meeting you! Goodbye,'

Marion replied. She kissed Klaus goodbye for now.

Nacoma raised a hand in farewell, and then he and his men, and Klaus, sprinted to the ranch to intercept the predators.

* * *

Marion was on a large boat in the Pacific Ocean twenty miles from California, and nearby was another big boat which had been sunk in a violent storm; eight men were stranded in the waves now that the storm had died, but the sea was still rough. To the west, another large boat had sunk, and fourteen men from this vessel were fighting desperately against the waves as they tried to approach Marion's boat.

Marion had a crew of four men with her, and they panicked when they spotted in the distance armies of sharks, sawfish and moray eels, plus conger eels and stingrays. Now lethal killers were closing in on the fourteen men from the second sunken boat — bull sharks, blue sharks, hammerhead sharks and sawfish leading conger eels, stingrays and moray eels, which were backed up further by octopuses and giant squids. Marion was horrified, but then she ordered her crew to throw their fishing nets overboard so that the men in the sea could climb up on board.

The nets were thrown out into the sea, but the men failed to reach them in time. The vast array of deadly sea creatures exploded to the surface. Marion watched with horror as five men were dragged underwater by octopuses and giant squids, and the octopuses ripped the men apart, pulling the men's limbs off with their powerful tentacles.

All five men were torn to pieces, a horrific fate. Five other giant squids started attacking Marion's boat, and she recounted in her mind the ancient horror stories told by seamen of giant squids dragging ships and boats underwater. Five giant squids measuring thirty to fifty feet in length and width would easily drag this large boat down towards the ocean depths. Nine men in the waves remained, and as the three groups of sharks savaged and ripped to pieces three men, the sawfish tore, disemboweled and dismembered two. The conger eels and moray eels mutilated three men, and the stingrays lashed at the last man with their barbed tails and ejected all their stinging poisons. There was no way Marion could save these fourteen men now… Besides, the sharks were making their way underneath the vessel and ripping at the wood with their razor-sharp teeth and jaws, whilst the giant squids tore the sides and cabin of the vessel with their knifelike tentacles.

Marion raced into the cabin with the four men who were her crew, and they reached for five harpoons which they carried aboard the boat just in case of emergencies like this. For an extreme emergency, there were five electric stun guns which could be pressed against the water-logged sides of the boat so that the water would conduct the electricity through the sea and electrocute any sharks, octopuses, giant squids or other ocean killers that attacked the boat. These primitive killers were extremely sensitive to electric shocks. But the stun guns were only a last resort, for people in the sea, like the eight men from the first boat, would also be electrocuted if the weapons were used.

Marion had been informed by Nacoma that no animals were to be killed or even slightly injured during the Integrity Test, but in an extreme situation like this, all her training went out of the window. She aimed her harpoon at the largest giant squid, focusing the spear towards its eye, then she pulled the trigger and the spear travelled at lightning speed. It hit the giant squid's eye and, with a scream of extreme agony, the giant squid released its hold on the cabin and retreated to the depths below. The other four crewmembers fired into the eyes of the remaining giant squids, and they too roared and retreated, blood gushing from their ruptured eyes. The smell of blood excited the sharks tearing at the boat's bottom, and also aroused the sawfish, conger eels and moray eels.

The giant squids and octopuses started battling furiously with the sharks and ferocious fish, and the ocean was churned red with blood gushing towards the surface from the mutilated bodies and tentacles of the killer fish, octopuses and giant squids. Then the sharks and ocean killers retreated from the area before facing the threat of killer fish which were far larger, more powerful and ferocious than the giant squids. Marion grimaced and turned her face away with horror at seeing the blood of the ocean killers and the fourteen mutilated men, but she had to now save the eight remaining men from the first boat. These men attempted to swim towards the netting hanging from the sides of Marion's boat, but the waves were too strong for them to swim against. But now another danger confronted these men, and Marion picked up on the peril lying 800 metres away.

Numerous great white sharks, tiger sharks and barracudas advanced towards the men.

'Quick, save those men!' Marion yelled. 'I see sharks and barracudas!' The crew had wasted no time in pulling the nets in, and the large, battle-torn boat glided over the rough, choppy water towards the stranded men, but the men increased the danger to themselves by swimming frantically towards the boat when they saw the sharks and barracudas. Marion latched onto this lethal situation straight away and remembered some cardinal rules taught to her by Klaus on what to do when menaced by sharks. According to him, the deadly savagery of sharks can be diffused by staying still in the water, and not splashing or trying to outswim it or making any noise. A human cannot outswim a shark, and splashing or making noise only excites the shark and triggers its predator instinct to attack a scared, panicking victim. Marion had also been informed that staying still in the water fails to provoke a killing response in the predator, for sharks, as a rule, are not bloodthirsty monsters and normally have no interest in attacking or eating humans. Another piece of information Marion had been given was that a human menaced by a shark was in far more danger trying to get out of the water than remaining in the water, because, like a crocodile or an alligator must attack a zebra, antelope or deer trying to get out of the river, a shark must follow its instinct to give chase and attack a human who attempts to climb back into a boat.

This implied that the eight stranded men were safer remaining in the sea, but Marion saw no sense in this whatsoever, and she knew that the barracudas would attack the men whether they remained in the ocean or tried to escape into her boat. Marion felt overwhelming guilt and horror at what had happened to the fourteen men from the second boat, and she was not about to allow these eight men to suffer the same fate.

As the boat raced towards the men, Marion reminded herself that these sharks and barracudas closing in on the men were not demonstrating normal behaviour. The vast majority of humans who had been attacked by sharks had survived becoming the shark's prey, but not without suffering horrific injuries. Surfers or people swimming frantically are always mistaken for prey animals, and when a shark discovers that its victim is a human, in three cases out of five it will abandon the attack. One exception to this rule is when sharks smell blood — which can happen from about half a mile away. In this case, the shark turns psychotic and will ruthlessly attack the human victim until he or she is dead. Marion had also been informed that all these rules and scenarios that applied to sharks also applied to barracudas and other ocean killers. At this moment, the men in the ocean were doing all the wrong things by panicking, screaming and swimming frantically towards the boat.

The sharks and barracudas were closing in on the men with awesome power and lightning speed, so Marion's last chance to save the men would be through the five stun guns in the cabin. The five harpoons had been used up. In the panic and peril of battling with the giant squids, Marion and her four crewmembers had not been able to retrieve the harpoons — they had been carried away over the ocean as the octopuses and giant squids had disappeared with the sawfish, conger eels, moray eels and stingrays, plus the three groups of smaller sharks. Marion knew that ejecting electric shocks into the water from the water-logged sides of her boat would also electrocute the eight men trapped in the waves, but she counted on luck that the men would not die from the electric shocks.

'Get the stun guns!' Marion yelled. 'We'll electrocute the sharks. The men will be more resistant to the electric shocks than the sharks and barracudas. Go now.'

The crewmembers forced the cabin door

that was jammed shut, but the men stranded in the clear, blue water were now surrounded by the sharks and barracudas. At the same time, the boat was speeding towards the stranded men, and Marion muttered, 'Oh my God! Please don't let us be too late!'

The crewmembers continued forcing the door, but it would not break open. The eight men in the sea were petrified when the great whites, tiger sharks and barracudas exploded out of the water and flashed their giant jaws and big, razor-sharp teeth. Marion gulped and her stomach and legs froze up, her heart beating much faster as the enormous sharks gnashed their bone-crushing teeth. They leapt out of the water and lunged for the men, crunching their teeth against the men with evil hatred and lethal rage, whilst the barracudas fastened their fang-like teeth into the last three men with a level of savagery to rival the great white sharks.

To Marion and most other humans, the shark epitomised humankind's ultimate nightmare creature, and Marion again remembered her nightmare on that boat at the beginning of her coma. She had been cornered by a monstrous great white shark, a ferocious tiger shark and three other man-eating sharks that were almost as petrifying as any great white. She watched with horror as the men in the waves were being savaged by the sharks and barracudas, the great whites mauling three men, the tiger sharks mutilating two men and the barracudas dealing several bites to the last three men. Vomit came up into Marion's mouth, but by now her crewmembers had kicked down the door and raced into the cabin, and they had brought the electric stun guns to Marion in a matter of a few seconds.

Marion seized a stun gun, and all five crewmembers pressed the weapons against the water-soaked sides of the boat, waves coming up and touching the electric shocks that were ejected from the probes at the ends of the stun weapons. The electric current passed through the ocean and dealt severe shocks to the enormous sharks and barracudas. They heaved and lurched backwards, abandoning their savage attacks on the eight stranded men. Although the men in the ocean were electrocuted, they were enormously strong and very fit men who could sustain electric shocks due to training they had received in the United States Navy. The sharks and barracudas suffered far worse, and the great white sharks and tiger sharks retreated out into the ocean followed by the barracudas.

'Get those men aboard!' Marion shouted. The weakened naval men climbed the netting by one arm and one leg, now that each of them had lost their second arm and leg to the sharks and barracudas. Marion and her crew helped the men aboard, and Marion turned her face away and closed her hands over her eyes with sheer horror. The horrific injuries the naval men had suffered made her feel sick to her stomach — they had sustained severed legs and arms, torn muscles and fractured ribs and spines. They had lost too much blood from ruptured arteries and blood vessels, and in two minutes they had each passed out and died.

'We couldn't save them,' one crewmember told Marion.

'No!' Marion yelled. 'Our efforts were for nothing!' She suddenly ran towards the side of the boat to throw up. She hoped never to confront sharks or other ocean killers again, but also knew that this was very crucial as part of her training. This was one test she had failed miserably.

* * *

The next situation for Marion was about to test her skills to the limit, and she was determined not to fail the way she had failed to save the twenty-two men from the vicious sharks and ocean killers.

Marion and some tribesmen were in Kenya, in a large steel boat on a river running through the green and brown savanna, the lush, long grass standing to the north and south of the river and the savanna itself bristling with acacia and baobab trees. The water in the river was a combination of blue, green and brown as it mixed in with the mud and clay. Marion was traumatised by her failures during the ocean task, but she buried her distress and trauma deep inside her as she waited for further danger here.

Then peril struck when a horde of Nile

crocodiles dived into the river and closed in on the boat from all sides. Marion spotted the huge reptiles immediately.

'Men — look out!' she shouted at the top of her voice. 'Crocodiles! Crocodiles!'

The men panicked, and there was no meat or fish in the boat to throw to the crocodiles. However, inside the boat's cabin were animal horns carved into musical instruments. Marion had an idea.

'Imitate the calling sounds of hippos, rhinos and buffaloes with these horns!' she commanded. 'Do it now.'

Most of the tribesmen congregated in the cabin and blew violently into the horns, imitating the roaring screams of formidable herbivores, knowing that they were among the crocodile's worst natural enemies. The thunderous chorus and deafening noise of bellowing, roaring, wailing, screaming and squealing numbed Marion's nerves and almost caused her ears to burst. The racket echoed across the savanna but failed to deter the crocodiles. Thirty crocodiles surrounded the boat and hissed with furious hostility, whilst more crocodiles on the riverbank roared in a blood-chilling manner. But Marion battled against her blinding fear and continued imitating wild pig noises and then buffalo sounds. Then an army of large herbivores came to drink at the river, having been drawn towards this stretch of water by the noises, but in order to drink they had to ruthlessly attack and repel the killer reptiles.

Hippos came up from the muddy depths, whilst white rhinos, black rhinos and buffaloes approached the river from the north and south alongside two herds of warthogs and bush pigs. Marion knew that a terrifying battle would occur — and she also knew that she and her men would be caught in the crossfire. Even when the crocodiles were defeated, the herbivores would be equally as deadly, especially hippos who are extremely aggressive and would instinctively attack boats.

The hippos caused chaos with their enraged roars whilst the rhinos were bellowing and the buffaloes were snorting with sheer ferocity. The cavernous mouths of the hippos exposed their fearsome tusks, whilst the rhinos raked their hooves against the ground and lowered their big horns, and the buffaloes shook and tossed their large heads about with their great horns. The wild pigs squealed with hatred, but the bush pigs were larger and fiercer. The crocodiles were hissing, but the rhinos and buffaloes attacked the bloodthirsty reptiles on the riverbank, and, although the crocodiles severely injured four buffaloes, they suffered far worse losses and swiftly retreated upstream.

A pride of lions came to scavenge on the carcasses of the crocodiles, but the warthogs and bush pigs ruthlessly charged the big cats and repelled them, their rasping and squealing striking fear into the lions, for even they respected an adversary as savage as the bush pig.

Now, with the crocodiles and lions fleeing, the herbivores represented a new threat.

'We have no vegetables to give them,' one of the warriors told Marion. 'Giving them vegetables will diffuse their aggression.'

'But we have the elephant horns,' Marion said. 'Elephants are extremely intelligent and less likely to attack us — which gives me an idea. There are two herds of elephants, north and south of us... Get the elephant horns now.'

The warriors raced into the cabin to seize the elephant horns. The boat was trapped in the river, and although it was a strong, steel boat, the hippos would soon destroy the vessel with their giant tusks. The rhinos and buffaloes plunged into the water to join the hippos in attacking the boat whilst the wild pigs stayed on the riverbank to repel any predators who ventured too close.

The hippos and rhinos bellowed loudly enough to shake the savanna and burst the eardrums of the people in the boat, but Marion covered her ears with her hands. The buffaloes then closed in on the boat. Quickly, Marion and the tribesmen blew the elephant horns to imitate the trumpeting noises of elephants, and before long the two herds of giant elephants closed in on the river from the north and south. Marion experienced the utmost relief. The elephants were trumpeting and roaring. Hippos and rhinos were more than a match for elephants in a fight, but the two advancing herds amounted to nearly a hundred elephants — too many for the other herbivores to fight off. Roaring with their humiliating defeat, the rhinos and buffaloes fled from this area joined by the squealing warthogs and bush pigs, leaving only the bellowing hippos in the river. The hippos slowly retreated in both directions as the elephants came to within twenty yards of the river.

Marion knew that, when the other herbivores arrived to repel the crocodiles, one lethal danger would be replaced by another deadly threat. But elephants were amongst the most intelligent of all animals, and were generally friendly and gentle towards humans. The tribesmen cheered Marion, and when the boat landed on the south riverbank, the young woman approached the dominant bull elephant and stroked his trunk.

Now the stage 'saving other people in danger' was over, and Marion had to prepare for the second stage of her Integrity Test. The young brunette walked through another time zone and found herself in another area of Africa.

* * *

Marion began the second stage, 'diffusing aggressive confrontations between animals'. She was in Cameroon in western Africa with Chief Guamo.

'The second stage of the Integrity Test is to diffuse aggressive confrontations between animals,' the chief informed her. 'Part of your training in calming animals down is to prevent them from fighting and killing each other. You may begin.'

Marion suddenly found herself positioned in some bushland between the rainforests of southern Cameroon and some savanna to the north. She was caught up in a war between a pride of lions and a troop of gorillas, including ten males, which were backed up by baboons, drills and mandrills. The lions and lionesses were swelling masses of muscle and brawn. They growled, and then their menacing anger exploded into a thunderous roar that charged the atmosphere.

Marion was petrified.

But the male gorillas were far more formidable. The ten male gorillas were awesome beasts packed solid with massive, muscular arms, barrel-shaped chests and large canine teeth. Gorillas, when they charged, were more terrifying than elephants, rhinos or buffaloes because their faces were very human in their expressions of emotion and anger.

As the lions roared, the gorillas beat their enormous chests with their clubbed fists and bellowed furiously. The baboons screamed, but the drills and mandrills were even more ferocious, their muscular limbs and frames more powerful than a man's and their teeth razor-sharp. A titanic battle was about to occur. In Marion's cloak were six horns that each imitated a different animal: an elephant, a rhino, a buffalo, a hyena, an African hunting dog and a jackal. To the north of her were three herds of elephants, rhinos and buffaloes, but to the south were three packs of hyenas, hunting dogs and jackals. Marion guessed the elephants, rhinos and buffaloes would kill the lions and gorillas because all five species were enemies.

Forgetting the agreement she had made never to harm any animals during the Integrity Test, Marion decided that the hyenas and wild dogs were expendable. The lions, gorillas and baboons would stop fighting each other in order to attack the hyenas and wild dogs. Marion blew the hyena horn, then the hunting dog and jackal horns. The three packs of hyenas, hunting dogs and jackals cantered across the savanna to attack the lions and primates, their powerful jaws and serrated teeth fully exposed. The hyenas were laughing manically, the hunting dogs were snarling and the jackals were growling.

Marion immediately regretted her plan, but it was too late to save the canine beasts. The lions and lionesses charged with explosive power and speed, fangs flashing in the sun. The gorillas also hurtled across the savanna whilst the baboons, drills and mandrills attacked the wild dogs with hulking brute strength and ferocity, screaming viciously with dagger-like teeth flashing in the sunlight. The lions savaged many hyenas and hunting dogs, just as the gorillas battered and mauled to death the remaining hyenas, and the baboons, drills and mandrills ripped to pieces the remaining hunting dogs and jackals.

Marion had made an unforgiveable mistake — she should have called the elephants, rhinos and buffaloes — and she now had the deaths of the hyenas and wild dogs on her hands. But she must not worry about this now. She walked through another time zone.

* * *

Marion found herself in the mountain forests of Nepal, and she was caught up in a stand-off between three giant yetis and five Komodo dragons introduced from Indonesia. Marion was intimidated and unnerved by the enormous size of the yetis and Komodo dragons. The yetis were close in size to rhinos or elephants, their strength and power were awesome and their dark brown fur contained silvery-grey tips so they resembled a male silverback gorilla. Their chests, legs and arms bristled with enormous muscles and were greater in size than the chest and legs of the biggest polar bear or Kodiak bear. Their clubbed fists could kill an elephant with five fearsome blows, and their huge canine teeth could tear a yak to pieces. The Komodo dragons were also huge, with primitive eyes and razor-sharp teeth and claws.

Marion knew that a battle was imminent, so she reached for the elephant horn in her pocket and blew into it. Within a minute, twenty enormous elephants came charging through the mountain forest, their huge ears outspread and their trunks flailing between their formidable tusks as their heads were raised.

The elephants were trumpeting loudly, and the Komodo dragons fled in panic, but the elephants and yetis were friendly with each other. Joining the elephants to keep the peace were two huge male rhinos.

Marion had passed the second stage of the Integrity Test.

* * *

Marion had travelled to join Chong Lee, Mao Sing and Sun Ying, and they were soon joined by ten other Buddhist and Hindu priests.

'Now to begin the third stage of the Integrity Test,' Chong Lee told her, 'in which you will save people guilty of evil.'

'What is the point of saving people guilty of evil?' Marion wanted to know. 'If they're evil, then they deserve to die.'

'If you take that line, then you become one of them,' Chong Lee rebuked her. 'Nobody deserves to die, no matter how evil and wicked they are. If you save them, then you are better than them. They will be punished in ways that are far more effective than taking their lives.'

'I see,' Marion said, though she was still doubtful. 'Okay, what do I have to do first?'

'We will be transported to India at the end of

the Second World War,' Mao Sing explained. 'Some Japanese war criminals guilty of atrocities against civilians and allied prisoners of war have been sentenced by the Gurkhas from Nepal to be killed by four Siberian tigers, five Bengal tigers, five leopards, three black panthers and three clouded leopards. Our task is to pacify these big cats with meditation, exploiting the natural hatred between the big cats. Now — let's begin.'

* * *

Marion and the thirteen Buddhist and Hindu priests passed through another time zone.

They found themselves in the enclosure where the Japanese war criminals had been thrown to the big cats. The Gurkha soldiers were watching intensely. Four barred enclosures were opened, releasing the Siberian tigers, then the Bengal tigers, then the leopards and black panthers, and lastly the clouded leopards. Marion and the Buddhist and Hindu priests were terrified, but also confident in diffusing the aggression of the big cats with meditation. The Japanese soldiers were screaming and yelling; this was the ultimate humiliation and degradation for Japanese war criminals, who believed that the only honourable way to die was in battle, not as prisoners of war about to be devoured by big cats.

As the great cats emerged from their enclosures, Marion remembered her training in the arena in Nepal with meditation where, alongside facing an angry horse and a sullen bull, she had to confront a huge, enraged lion and a massive tiger. It was true that she had succeeded in appeasing them — but they were only *two* big cats then, not *twenty*.

Marion suddenly remembered the Bible story of Daniel in the lion's den. The lions would not kill Daniel because he showed no fear and had faith that God was protecting him. Marion also knew how circus trainers commanded the respect of lions and tigers with their voices, chairs and whips. But these were wild beasts, not tame animals.

Marion knew she had to use all her training to stay calm and controlled in this situation, but the screams of the Japanese people were not making her task any easier. The tigers were massive brutes of awesome power, their huge, striped bodies rippling with thick muscle, and their snarls exposed the full length of their lethal fangs. The leopards and black panthers showed no other instinct than to kill without mercy. The clouded leopards were intimidating as they growled with devilish fury in their eyes. Marion shuddered before the big cats, her heart pounding and her courage wavering. Marion and the priests started waving their arms and relaxing their expressions as they fixed their eyes on the big cats but avoided eye contact. Marion forced her whole body to relax, for she knew all too well how easily an animal could smell fear. If she gave in to terror now, she, the priests and the Japanese soldiers would be mauled and devoured by the cats. The psychotic roaring of the tigers exploded again like thunder, echoing through and shaking the jungle, and the leopards snarled and hissed as their menacing eyes glared at the priests and Marion with a cold hatred. The big cats circled the humans, but they were still wary of each other. For this reason, Marion was not deterred by their vicious aggression. She called to the Shaolin Temple and power flowed into her from the temple as Grand Master Chong Lee stood beside her and spoke to her.

'Focus your mind,' Chong Lee told her calmly.

Focusing her mind became second nature as Marion allowed the power to strengthen her body until she felt strong and fresh again, and she smiled as she waved her arms and glanced at the furious tigers. Cautious and wary of each other, the Siberian and Bengal tigers retreated into the two tiger enclosures, and Marion approached the tigers as they calmed down. They eventually fell asleep in the enclosures.

Seeing the more dominant tigers succumb, the three clouded leopards began to follow suit, retreating towards another enclosure. Despite their deadly savagery and venomous hissing, these clouded leopards had an instinctive fear of humankind and respected people who showed no fear themselves.

The leopards and black panthers were far harder to tame, and they closed in on the humans, still growling and displaying their sharp fangs and claws. They seemed to be ready for the kill, their vicious eyes blazing. But Marion did not give in. Chong Lee spoke to her again, reinforcing the confidence and power of her mind over her body and the power of the Shaolin Temple, and she approached the leopards and black panthers with a relaxed body, a calm face and focused eyes. She ignored their rage, and this unnerved the big cats. Seeing no fear in her, they too retreated into the other enclosures and subsequently fell asleep.

Marion sighed and fell against the wall of the main enclosure, overcome with relief. She was sweating and felt very sick. A couple of the Japanese prisoners threw up, and another wet themselves.

The Gurkhas opened the enclosures and released the Japanese soldiers, plus Marion and the priests. They returned the Japanese soldiers' swords to them, and, dishonoured by their humiliation, the Japanese committed suicide by falling onto their swords.

Marion was sickened by this spectacle and had to run into the headquarters of the Gurkha sergeant before vomiting in the toilet to relieve her tormenting nausea. She flushed the toilet, ran to the sink, flicked on the tap and raised a handful of fresh, cold water to her mouth. She shook her head and swirled the water around before spitting it back out. She repeated this twice before turning off the tap and leaving the headquarters.

Along with utter revulsion at how the Japanese had gruesomely committed suicide, Marion found it ironic that her task had been to save these evil men only so they would take their own lives to escape a bitter humiliation. But at least she had not descended to their level by allowing them to be devoured by the big cats. Her conscience was clear.

The Gurkhas cheered for Marion as she emerged out of the headquarters, and the sergeant and the three Shaolin priests approached her.

'You can leave,' the sergeant ordered her evenly.

'Can you feed the big cats and then release them?' Marion asked. 'The war is over. The big cats have done their job, and their true home is the jungle.'

'I suppose I can,' the sergeant agreed.

On his orders, large chunks of meat were thrown to the big cats before they were to be set free, and then Marion left for another time zone in order to begin her second task.

* * *

Marion found herself alone in Tibet, her task being to protect two prostitutes from two snow leopards. These women had been whores who had used men for their own greedy ends, and the villagers had bound and gagged the women, leaving them outside the snow leopards' lair to give the big cats an easy meal.

Marion was carrying a sack with chunks of

meat inside, which had been given to her by the Shaolin priests, and she darted towards the prostitutes in order to protect them.

Then, with a soft snarl, the two snow leopards emerged from their lair.

Marion stood rooted to the spot, dread chilling her already cold body as her stomach churned and her mind froze with fear. Marion was in real danger, but she knew from previous training how food could pacify hungry animals and would divert the snow leopards from killing the two prostitutes. She reached into her sack, produced the two massive chunks of dried beef and threw them to the big cats. She passed a third chunk of beef to the snow leopards for them to give to the three cubs. The snow leopards calmed slightly and began chewing on the two chunks of dried beef, leaving the third, smaller chunk to their cubs, which padded out of the lair at the smell of the meat. They fed on the third chunk of beef, ignoring the humans.

Marion loosened the ropes that tied the women's wrists and freed them before removing their gags. The prostitutes got up and thanked Marion for saving their lives, and the three women hugged each other.

Marion suddenly heard a voice in her head that told her that her third task was to protect three murderers in Nepal from three Asian bears. Gritting her teeth grimly, she said goodbye to the two prostitutes and was transported into another time zone.

* * *

Marion found herself in the mountain forests of Nepal, and she knew with horror how the Himalayan black bear, the sloth bear and the sun bear were almost as ferocious as the North American bears... And Marion was in a forest teaming with tigers and bears. Previous experience had taught Marion that facing tigers in Nepal and bears in North America and Europe was terrifying enough, but confronting the Asian bears was to be equally as unnerving.

Marion saw the three murderers bound and gagged against a tree, having been condemned to death by their tribe for rape and murder. She felt utter revulsion towards their crimes but knew that the correct form of justice was to drag them through the Nepalese legal system and sentence them to life imprisonment, not the more barbaric penalty of death.

Marion stood in front of the three men as they groaned through their gags, and then the three Asian bears came hurtling through the undergrowth, the Himalayan black bear roaring savagely, the sloth bear growling with furious hostility and the sun bear snarling with rage. This experience numbed Marion's mind with extreme terror. However, like the Kodiak bear, the grizzly bear, the American black bear and the brown bear, these Asian bears were all enemies. The Himalayan black bear would prey on the sloth bear and the sun bear, and both smaller bears were wary and fearful of each other. Marion was gambling with her life by trying to diffuse their savagery whilst taking advantage of their mutual hatred.

The bears lumbered to a halt only three yards from Marion. She raised her hands, relaxed her face and held her breath. The bears hesitated and growled with vicious rage towards each other, the sloth bear and the sun bear ganging up against the larger black bear. The two of them would kill or repel the black bear before turning on each other.

Marion refused to be afraid. She gently raised her arms again, slanted her eyes and then sat in the lotus position, deep in prayer. The bears were calmed by her lack of fear, and left her and the murderers and rapists alone.

Marion was roused by the arrival of the police who wanted to take the murderers away to stand trial in Kathmandu.

'Thank you, Marion,' the police chief said gratefully, as he and two other policemen approached her from their squad van. 'We'll drag these men through the legal system and sentence them to life imprisonment for rape and murder.'

The uniformed men untied the three killers, removed their gags and slipped handcuffs onto their wrists before locking them in their van. Marion waved farewell to the police before she was alone with the bears, who were still cautious of each other. The black bear lumbered towards a mountain cave with incredible power and speed, whilst the sloth bear made its way towards the nearby river and the sun bear scaled a tree to join its mate and their cubs. Despite her fear of all bears, Marion felt that none of the Asian bears really deserved their aggressive image as vicious man-killers.

The third stage of the Integrity Test was over, and now she had to prepare for the fourth.

* * *

Marion faced Chief Guamo, Chong Lee and Nacoma on the imaginary border between Africa, Asia and Canada.

'In the fourth stage of the Integrity Test, you will need to be prepared to use physical force if necessary,' Guamo told her. 'And the first task of this stage will take place on the imaginary border between Africa and India, where you will face a honey badger and several smaller wild cats of these countries.'

'But I thought no animals are to be harmed or killed,' Marion objected. 'There's been too much bloodshed already! I've killed many animals so far on this test, and that's really heavy on my conscience. I have no intention of injuring or killing another animal.'

'You can use reasonable force without injuring or killing the animals,' Chong Lee said, 'by using your common sense, plus weapons that won't deal injury or death to the animals concerned.'

'Okay, Grand Master,' Marion said reluctantly.

'But before that, we'll show you how different tribes in South America, North America and the Pacific Islands pacify dangerous animals with their calming methods,' Nacoma suggested. 'And then how people in Europe use weapons to scare off deadly predators rather than injuring or killing them. Watch...'

Nacoma conjured a vision so that Marion could witness the use of physical force against Europe's most dangerous animals without these creatures being harmed. In Byelorussia a herd of wild boars gored four careless tourists who approached the wild pigs too closely, but the park rangers sprayed the wild boars with jets of water from hoses and the deadly wild boars fled. Then a wolf, a wolverine and a lynx attacked three farmers who defended their sheep against the fierce predators, but the wolf and the lynx were very fearful of the wolverine and also each other. This gave the farmers time to reach for their rifles — but rather than kill the predators, the farmers pumped three shots into the air and the terrifying, deafening noise of this gunfire put the wolf, the wolverine and the lynx to flight. On both occasions neither the wild boars nor the predators had been harmed when the humans had resorted to physical force. Marion knew she must follow this example.

* * *

Marion was soon transported through time zones and found herself on the imaginary border between Africa and India. It seemed that her next task was to protect some sheep from a honey badger and four wild cats.

Moving in alongside the honey badger came the lynx-like caracal and the serval, whilst stalking from the jungle in India were the Asian golden cat and the jungle cat. Mao Sing had informed Marion that the smaller feral cats were deadly adversaries if cornered, and she could now see what he meant.

All five smaller predators hissed, spat and snarled with greater ferocity than a feral cat or common badger, their sinuous bodies tense as they prepared to lunge towards Marion. They circled her, closing in for the kill. Honey badgers were by far the most powerful and savage of them all; they had been known to kill venomous snakes, pythons and even buffaloes that were several times their size and weight. Foam spilled from its black lips as they creased in a vicious snarl. The caracal, the golden cat and the jungle cat matched the clouded leopard in sheer ferocity and were almost as scary as any leopard or black panther.

All four smaller cats snarled at Marion, who was trembling. She had to think fast. Positioned behind her were the crocodile organs, a sack with very little magic sleeping powder and a hunting rifle. She had to use minimal force. Using the organs would result in death to the five killers, which was not the result she wanted, but there was too little sleeping powder to knock out all of them. Besides, she would have no time to use the powder, for they would all attack her at the same time. They were closing in now, the honey badger leading the others. The third weapon was the rifle which was obviously designed to kill.

Marion thought for a moment, remembering the vision in Byelorussia where the farmers had scared away the wolf, the lynx and the wolverine. She suddenly seized the rifle, squeezed the trigger and fired the gun into the air. All five predators were so petrified that they fled towards the savanna and the jungle. Marion had saved the sheep!

* * *

Marion had been transported to the imaginary border between Canada and Europe, where her next task was to break up a battle over a deer carcass between two warring groups of mustelids. This deer had been killed by a wolf or coyote pack before they had finished their share of the carcass and left the remains to the scavengers. From Europe came three packs of weasels, stoats and polecats, backed up by a family of ferrets, and from both Europe and Canada came three groups of pine martens, beech martens and fishers and a pack of mink. All eight species were cunning, bloodthirsty killers with the vicious nature of the much larger wolverine. On the other side were the American badger, the common badger and the feral cat, all three of them large and aggressive enough to defy the army of smaller mustelids. All three had the same malice and devilish hatred in their faces. The American badger matched the common badger's size and strength, with the savagery of the weasel, the stoat and the mink, whilst the common badger could injure a large dog and the feral cat was as vicious and cunning as any lynx or bobcat.

Both sides hissed like bobcats, raising their tails and arching their backs, but Marion was equipped with a hose and prepared to spray the opposing armies with water. She walked towards the tap at the wall and immediately flicked it on, and as both sides ruthlessly attacked each other she sprayed them with a powerful jet of water and they were soaked. The cat and the two badgers turned to attack Marion, but she sprayed their faces and took all the fighting spirit out of them. Feral cats and badgers hated water, and so too did weasels and stoats, and these deadly killers fled. But the mink, polecats and martens were inhabitants of rivers or trees, polecats and martens being just as proficient at swimming as mink, and they were not deterred by water. They charged towards Marion, but she swiftly sprayed them with just as much ruthlessness, taking all the fight out of them. The polecats, pine martens and beech martens fled with the fishers and mink, and all five packs of mustelids joined the weasels, stoats and ferrets in darting through the grass. Marion had diffused a deadly situation with no more force than spraying the aggressors with water. Then she heard Nacoma's voice calling to her inside her head.

'What is it, Nacoma?' Marion asked.

'Your last and most dangerous task is to use tranquilliser weapons on eight of North America's deadly predators,' he announced. 'They will be united together rather than enemies of each other, for they are possessed by evil spirits. Do you remember when you used sleep grenades to knock out those Komodo dragons and crocodiles in Nepal?'

'I do remember,' Marion said. 'They were united by evil spirits, and the big cats, dholes and jackals were united by noble spirits. And the predators I am about to face are united by evil spirits, I assume?'

'That is right,' Nacoma told her. 'The situation will be in a warehouse and a shed in Canada, and the predators you face will be a puma, a wolf, a coyote, a fox and a dog, which will be backed up by a wolverine, a lynx and a bobcat. Their evil spirits have united them. So you must be as smart and cunning as they are. Good luck, Marion.'

'I'll need it,' Marion remarked half-heartedly.

* * *

Marion made her way through another time zone and found herself at the entrance to a warehouse in Alberta. She could hear the hideous noises of a puma screaming, a wolf growling, a coyote and a dog snarling and a fox barking — not to mention the noises the wolverine, the lynx and the bobcat were making. These vicious cries of fury and hatred echoed around her mind, and she cautiously peeked into the warehouse. She caught sight of the predators — but they also caught sight of her.

They stalked stealthily through the doorway, all eight beasts being large killers bristling with muscle and sinew.

The puma leading the other beasts was massive with rippling muscles, evil eyes, ferocious fangs, and cruel claws shaped like medieval instruments of torture. Of the four wild dogs, the wolf was the most vicious and dangerous, his eyes sinister, his teeth jagged. The dog was a powerfully built bull mastiff. Bull mastiffs tend to have very friendly temperaments until they become feral like this one. The fox was a very large mountain fox and the coyote was slightly larger yet just as fierce. The most savage and fearless of the eight killers was the wolverine.

All the beasts were very cunning. The lynx and the bobcat moved to cut off Marion's escape route whilst the puma and the other beasts headed towards her. Marion panicked and ran into the warehouse, heading for the second floor. She burst into a room, reached the far window and caught hold of her first tranquilliser weapon in her cloak — the sleep gun. The wolf and the coyote had made their way up the stairs and now confronted her alongside the fox and the dog. All four large beasts were positioned three yards away from her, growling and snapping with fury.

Suddenly, the dog lunged towards Marion with brute power and speed, but she sprayed sleeping gas towards it in mid air and it crashed against the window and fell to the floor.

The coyote and the fox hurled themselves at Marion, but she sprayed two more jets of gas from the sleep gun and they soon joined the dog on the floor, unconscious. The wolf then bunched up its muscles and leapt at her, but she leapt aside and the beast crashed against the window and fell into the corner.

But it was still conscious.

The wolf stood and shook itself before charging again, lunging towards the young woman. Marion sprayed another blast of sleeping gas into the wolf's face, and its heavy body crashed against her upper body with a sickening thud before it finally fell to the floor, out cold.

The impact winded Marion and she collapsed against the floor. Gasping, she yanked open the window, leapt onto the ledge and caught sight of a strong, steel pipe descending along the warehouse wall from the roof down to the ground. But she knew, with a chill in her stomach, that she still had to face the puma, the wolverine, the lynx and the bobcat.

Marion silently climbed down the pipe and then dropped to the floor. She barely had chance to regain her breath when the lynx, the bobcat and the wolverine came charging towards her with lightning speed from around a corner. Their savage snarls were chilling and Marion ran as fast as possible towards the nearby shed. She threw herself across the doorway and tried to slam the door, but it wouldn't shut completely, and she knew the killer cats would easily slip through the gap in the doorway. She looked around wildly, wondering what to do.

Marion spotted a ladder leading towards an opening in the roof and she climbed it a fast as she could with hurt ribs. She reached the hole and climbed through it, and then glanced down into the shed to discover that the wolverine, the lynx and the bobcat were already inside. Their piercing eyes glared up at her with a burning hatred, and she very nearly lost her nerve.

The lynx had its front paws on the bottom rung of the ladder, so Marion swiftly seized the sleep grenade in her cloak, pulled the pin out and threw it through the opening into the shed. The grenade exploded with little force and released a cloud of sleeping gas, choking the wolverine, the lynx and the bobcat. All three were knocked out in seconds.

Marion dropped down from the shed's roof towards the snow and then ran for the warehouse. There was only the puma remaining.

Marion grabbed the sleep gun again, which contained a dart with a sleeping drug powerful enough to knock unconscious an animal of the puma's size. She was through the doorway, and stared at the stairs, but from behind some crates came the puma. Marion froze with terror. The puma snarled, but Marion refused to be intimidated. She raised the sleep gun and, as the puma raced towards her, she fired, and the tranquilliser dart penetrated the puma's shoulder. The puma hurled himself towards Marion, but she dropped to the floor and the puma's attack failed to find its mark. Marion worried that the drug was not strong enough to knock out the big cat, so she ran into a corner and reached for some sleeping powder. The puma raced towards her with spitfire speed and Marion flung the powder into its face. The puma ploughed into her, curled up in a ball and in ten seconds was unconscious. Marion sighed with relief and cursed. 'The situations I get into!' she muttered, shaking her head.

The evil spirits in the eight predators had now been destroyed, and they came round and nuzzled Marion with respect and affection. Marion had survived, and her smiling face broke into a huge grin.

Suddenly, Nacoma and his four warriors appeared from nowhere and approached her.

'You have yet to pass the fifth stage of the Integrity Test, but you will be in no danger,' Nacoma said.

'What does the fifth stage involve?' she asked, her eyes sharp with anxiety.

'Forgiveness of animals who have wronged you,' Nacoma replied. 'For it is only by forgiving these animals that you will truly be at peace with nature. These animals are both predators of Germany's Bavarian Forest — and I don't mean bears or wolverines. I mean the she-wolf which attacked you when you were fifteen and the mountain foxes which killed your two terriers, Mavis and Mildew. Here they are.'

'Now… I am ready to forgive,' Marion said slowly. She looked at the aged she-wolf and her pack, and said, 'I forgive you, wolf.' Then she turned to face the five large foxes that had killed her dogs. 'I forgive you,' she repeated.

'And now,' Nacoma concluded. 'You have earned yourself the right to be my guest of honour at the banquet in our reservation. Then you can get some sleep before leaving for the Canadian Arctic around Hudson Bay.'

'Thank you,' Marion said joyfully.

CHAPTER 10

After Marion had attended the banquet, she approached Nacoma sadly.

Nacoma picked up on her mood right away. He fixed his gaze into her face with his wise, intelligent eyes and asked, 'What's wrong, Marion?'

'When I was with my four crewmembers on that boat off the coast of California,' Marion began, 'I forgot what you had told me that no animals were to be harmed. Not only were the giant squids and other ocean predators killed in the subsequent battle after the five of us blinded them with our harpoons, but we failed to save all twenty-two naval men from the two sunken boats. They were all killed. When I had finally decided to use the stun guns, it was too late. The sailors' rules dictated that the stun guns must only ever be used as a last resort, in case people trapped in the ocean were electrocuted. But the voltage in a stun gun is very rarely powerful enough to kill a human. I should have used my judgement and used the stun guns as a first resort instead of the harpoons. I broke my agreement never to harm any animals, and I failed to save twenty-two men from a gruesome death from the sharks, barracudas and other ocean killers. And the whole situation in Cameroon was... awful. I failed again...' She broke off, tears running down her face.

'It is terrible that you made that mistake,' Nacoma said, 'but you must let go of your guilt. These were errors of judgement. But animals live by the law of nature: kill or be killed. You did not intend to kill those wild dogs, and you felt guilty afterwards. That shows you have a conscience, and I bet you will never make the same mistake again. You believed you were doing the right thing — anybody could have made the mistakes you have made.'

'That's easy for you to say,' Marion said heavily, wiping a tear from her cheek. 'But that doesn't make my mistakes any easier to live with.'

'Get some sleep,' Nacoma said gently. 'You'll feel much better in the morning.'

Marion climbed into bed and wrapped herself underneath the animal furs. She was crying, her mind full of guilt.

As she fell asleep, Marion dreamed of all the animals she had encountered in the Integrity Test; they all lived in absolute harmony with humans, and seemed a lot more tolerant of each other, too. She found herself wishing that the animal world really was like this, instead of wild animals living at each other's expense, but she knew all too well this would never be a reality. Not even humans could live in peace with each other.

* * *

Marion awoke and discovered she could not remember a single detail about what happened during the Integrity Test. Nacoma had cast a spell on her to make her forget her terrible mistakes, so she no longer harboured remorse about the three tasks that had gone tragically wrong.

Nacoma and Klaus entered the wigwam, and her husband passed a bowl of venison soup towards her.

'Thanks, Klaus,' she said. 'I need a light meal.'

'Nacoma's wife made it,' he replied, smiling at her. 'Venison soup.'

'I'll enjoy it,' Marion enthused.

'Today is a special day,' Nacoma said. 'You are leaving for the Canadian Arctic to overcome your terror of polar bears, the largest and most formidable of all land carnivores.'

'I'll adapt the same rule with polar bears as I have with grizzlies and black bears,' Marion began. 'Give them respect and space and don't make any sudden movements.'

'You have been taught well,' Klaus said happily.

Nacoma cast a spell and Marion suddenly found herself in the Arctic, by Hudson Bay. She shivered and took in her surroundings; there was a small village nearby, so she headed briskly towards it.

As she walked, Marion saw a thick sheet of ice spread over the sea and then cut southwards, leaving a stretch of water in between this ice and the land four hundred yards to the west. On the ice facing westwards, a huge polar bear was staring at the land. Two other polar bears surfaced. The three polar bears approached Marion, and they appeared loveable and friendly. But Marion made no mistake about their nature. They were the largest and most dangerous of all bears — even grizzlies. Klaus had once told her that other bears could be scared off, bluffed or fooled into not attacking humans, but not polar bears. The polar bear was also the most intelligent and cunning of all bears; it could run faster than a caribou, and its size, strength and power were such that it would easily kill a bearded seal or even a walrus with one or two devastating blows from its massive paws. In the Arctic, only killer whales, walruses and musk oxen could stand up to an attack by polar bears. Marion was amazed by the sheer size of these three polar bears on the ice, and Klaus had also informed her that polar bears were two to three times the size of lions and tigers, weighing in at 1,000 to 1,500 pounds.

Marion took another glance towards the Inuit village and then advanced towards the igloos. A man came out to greet her. He was a tall, rugged man of fifty-three with long grey hair tinged with black.

'Hello, Marion, I am Aram,' the man said. 'You have come at last.'

'I have,' Marion replied. 'It is bitterly cold here.'

'Then come into my igloo where it is nice and warm,' Aram suggested.

They made their way inside, and Marion greeted Aram's wife as she cooked them a hot stew made from the meat of a caribou. Aram began to introduce Marion to the Inuit spiritualism surrounding the polar bear.

'The polar bear has been given a terrifying reputation by modern people from America and Europe who don't really understand them,' Aram told Marion. 'But we natives understand them far better and recognise them for the gentle giants they are. Cases of people being attacked or killed by polar bears are very rare, but one should still treat them with respect and caution, and give them plenty of space. Although they are gentle giants, they are still carnivorous predators and can be unpredictable and extremely dangerous. You do not take liberties with polar bears.'

'Do you hunt polar bears?' Marion asked.

'We used to hunt them for their flesh and blubber,' Aram said. 'But not anymore. The polar bear is now a vulnerable species, protected by the Government of Canada and the Governments of Alaska, Russia, Finland, Sweden and Norway — the areas around the Arctic where polar bears are found. We natives are having to adapt to the modern world. Fortunately, the Canadians have set aside land for us and our wildlife. But oil companies want to drill for oil in Alaska and

Canada, and if this were to happen, it would destroy the Arctic wilderness and its wildlife. Conservationists have been campaigning for years to prevent this. Global warming is also melting the polar ice caps, and although most nations in the world have cut down on pollution and greenhouse gasses, which erode the ozone layer, the Americans have generally failed to do this.'

'I sympathise with you, as I also sympathise with the Native North American peoples,' Marion said softly. 'Their culture is also dying out, and the natural world is in far more danger now than it has ever been before. But more people understand the need for conservation now than they did twenty years ago.'

'You're right, Marion,' Aram said, nodding. 'But going back to the spiritualism of polar bears... It's true that my people used to hunt polar bears, but we lived in balance with the polar bear and never endangered the species. We learned from the polar bear how to kill a sleeping walrus with a block of ice or stone, and also how to build igloos of ice and snow. Take a look...'

Aram raised his hands and a spell exposed the scene of a polar bear killing a walrus with a boulder, and then the polar bear building a den under ice and snow.

'Inuits hunted polar bears for more than food and clothing,' Aram continued. 'We hunted these bears to prove our manhood. And there are many tales of the polar bear's strength, wisdom, cunning and ferocity. There is also the superstition that the polar bear's claws keep away the evil spirit called lightning. Take another look…'

Aram conjured another vision, and they saw a polar bear's claws scaring off the lightning so that it did not strike the Arctic when a rainstorm raged. Then they witnessed polar bears savagely attacking igloos to kill Inuits trapped inside.

Aram cleared his throat. 'To the Inuits, the polar bear is a shaman of profound wisdom who will readily communicate with the spirit world. However, although the polar bear is a god and a shaman, it still has to face the same icy, cold weather, plus the chilling rain, wind and snow. And, somewhere out there, there is a mythical village of spirit polar bears. My people believe that polar bears are so intelligent and wise that they will never be killed, but only by being killed by an Inuit hunter will the polar bear be ready for the next world in the afterlife.'

In the next vision, Marion saw the village of spirit bears. 'This is fascinating,' Marion said, gasping. 'I want to hear more.'

'After the hunters have killed polar bears, they respect the souls or spirits of these bears for four days for males and five days for females,' Aram informed her. 'During that time, no work is permitted in the Inuit community. The finest men's tools are placed near the male bear skins and women's tools near the hides of female bears. In some villages, like this one, the bladders of bears are thought to contain the *inua* — the spirit — so they are blown up like balloons, painted and then hung up in the main lodge. The *inua* is given food and water, and then the bladders are pushed through holes in the ice. The dead polar bears are treated with great respect, worship and veneration. When their spirits leave their bodies, they report this kind treatment to the village of polar bears, so these live polar bears are eager to be hunted and killed by my people.'

'I see,' Marion said, revelling in the new information.

'In Alaska,' Aram continued, 'there are tales of Kokogiak, the ten-legged polar bear which is the savage monster of the Arctic ice pack and threatens death to any hunters who find or see him. Kokogiak is five times larger than a normal polar bear…'

Marion saw a vision of Kokogiak devouring a hunter after tearing him to pieces with all ten paws, claws and teeth as well.

'Back in Canada, we Inuits believe that the Mother of Bears gives human and polar bear shamans the ability to look into the spirit world. This not only relates to polar bears, but also to grizzlies and black bears on the Canadian tundra and to brown bears on the tundra of Scandinavia. That is all the spiritualism there is on polar bears. But killer whales and walruses are also deadly predators, and there is worship and spiritualism surrounding them, if you'd like to hear more?'

'Go on,' Marion said eagerly.

Aram smiled. 'Killer whales have virtually never attacked humans, but walruses have made a few attacks,' he explained. 'But like polar bears, they are intelligent and normally gentle giants. Whales, killer whales and walruses used to be hunted by my people. Mythology says how walruses include sea monsters, like the whale-elephant, the seahorse and the sea cow. My people also call the walrus the Old Man of the Ice Floes because of its moustache-like whiskers. Another superstition states that the walrus is a "monstrous swine" which uses its tusks to climb to the top of a cliff and then roll down into the ocean. We believe that seals and walruses were originally the severed fingers of the sea spirit who keeps all game creatures at the bottom of the ocean to be hunted for their food and fur. Like polar bears, the seals and walruses permit themselves to be hunted and killed by us. We throw walrus bladders containing their souls or spirits back into the ocean where they will be reincarnated as creatures which will again offer themselves as prey. But killer whales were very rarely hunted, unlike the true whales. When hunting whales and killer whales, my people used to wear a magic charm with a picture of a whale on it for good luck. As with polar bears, seals and walruses, we have profound respect for the intelligence and wisdom of whales and killer whales. We hold ceremonies for these whales, during which we decorate our canoes with scenes of hunters attacking the creatures.'

'I see,' Marion said in amazement.

'I almost forgot — there is one last aspect of polar bear spiritualism that I must tell you about,' Aram said quickly. 'When an old man dies, we leave his body inside an igloo and wait for a polar bear to approach the dead man and eat him. If we then kill the polar bear, the old man's spirit will be rekindled.'

'But you mustn't kill the polar bear,' Marion begged the old man. 'That's murder. A polar bear is a beautiful and noble animal.'

'Then how will the old man's soul live on as a human?' Aram asked.

'The Great Spirit or God will decide the fate of the old man,' Marion said. 'I know that ancient tribal beliefs and attitudes have to be respected, but I cannot allow your people to kill a polar bear. The old man's spirit will live on in Heaven, whether you kill a polar bear or not. I was once terrified of bears and other dangerous animals, but I now have a strong urge to protect them.'

'Then come outside the igloo with me and we may be able to prevent my people from killing a polar bear,' Aram said, pointing.

They both rose from the floor of animal skins and headed out of the igloo. They saw some of the villagers closing in on a polar bear after it had eaten an old man who had died. They were armed with harpoons.

Marion ran towards the men as fast as her legs would allow. 'Stop, don't kill him!' she yelled. She pushed two men aside and stood between the men and the polar bear.

'What are you doing?' one of the men shouted. 'This polar bear will kill you!'

But with Marion obstructing their line of fire, they lowered their weapons. The polar bear lowered its head, and its growls were far worse than those of a Kodiak bear or a grizzly. Its shoulders were at least a metre in width, its paws were larger than a lion's, its long claws were black and razor-sharp, and foam and saliva sprayed from its powerful jaws as it snarled. Its creamy coat was beautiful, but Marion experienced only sheer terror and panic at being so close to the beast.

The polar bear roared again with a thunderous noise that shook the igloos and caused the villagers to freeze with terror. Three other equally enormous polar bears joined the first, growling and grunting.

'Oh n-no,' Marion stammered, but she gulped, and nausea tormented her throat as she fought to swallow her fear and allowed the power and energy of her mind to control her body.

Her terror gradually disappeared and she approached the polar bear which had eaten the old man. Fighting her instinct to run away — which would have been a fatal mistake — she drew on the Great Spirit and used meditation to pacify the polar bears. The bellowing polar bears were taken aback by her lack of fear; they were accustomed to their prey showing it and either fighting or running away, but

Marion maintained her composure, and the villagers joined in to appease the other three polar bears with their own version of native meditation. Marion stood to the side of the leading polar bear and caressed the bear's right shoulder and enormous head, and she sang a song to calm it down. The polar bears turned tail and lumbered away onto the tundra. The villagers turned sharply towards Marion, insane anger taking over.

'Why did you put yourself in danger like that?!' one of the men scolded her. 'That was very brave, but reckless and stupid. Those polar bears could've ripped you to pieces!'

'Don't be angry with her!' Aram cried. 'You were about to kill the polar bear who fed on the old man, but Marion here respected the polar bear's right to live. We are living in a changing world where animal rights are regarded as very important. And the first of Marion's last three tests was to pacify this polar bear and save its life. Be angry with me, for I sent her to save the polar bear.'

The villagers hesitated, before the team leader turned to both Marion and Aram. 'Then we make it our pledge never to kill another polar bear,' he said humbly. 'We accept that polar bears are protected animals with as much right to live as we do. We lay down our pledge.'

The other villagers cheered, and Marion fixed her beaming smile towards Aram, her gaze focused onto his intelligent eyes.

'Your second test,' he told her, 'is to diffuse

an oncoming battle between two schools of killer whales and walruses. This will be in the sea of Hudson Bay, so you'll need a large boat. The boat will contain three enormous chunks of whale meat for the three killer whales and a hundred pieces of fish for the walruses. There will be terrible danger in store for you, Marion. So you must dislodge the whale chunks and fish pieces as soon as possible, then get to safety.'

'Why are the killer whales and walruses fighting?' Marion wanted to know.

'Because the killer whales are preying on the walruses and the walruses are defending themselves,' Aram said. 'But we don't want either the walruses or killer whales harmed.'

'I understand,' Marion replied. Her gaze was fixed towards a pack of polar bears watching the ocean from the tundra, joined by five grizzlies, four black bears and six wolves.

The men guided Marion to a large boat, and she climbed into the vessel with twelve men before those on the shore pushed the vessel into the sky-blue waters of Hudson Bay. The twelve men in the boat used their oars to pull the boat forwards through the ocean, and after half an hour the vessel approached three ravenous killer whales preparing to attack and kill their prey of thirty fearsome walruses. Killer whales are so savage that a school of them can rip a much larger whale to pieces. These beautiful black and white killing machines are more than a match for walruses, polar bears and even sharks.

This battle involved thirty walruses against three killer whales. Dread chilled Marion's blood so that her stomach and legs turned to jelly, and adrenalin raced through her, forcing her heart to beat much faster. She knew that as soon as the boat was between the killer whales and walruses, she and the men must hurl the whale meat and fish pieces into the sea. The icy waves pummelled the massive boat as a gale screeched and whistled against the sails and the blue water leapt, churned and thrashed, like lava boiling from an erupting volcano.

Marion had heard exaggerated horror stories about killer whales attacking humans, but she knew that the truth about killer whales was not so macabre. Even when severely provoked by men in boats, killer whales prefer to flee to safety. This applies with equal truth to walruses — although, cases have occurred of humans being chased and gored by the beasts. A walrus can move faster on land or ice than a human athlete, and its long tusks would deal terrible wounds to a human if given the chance.

Her companions pulled the ocean-battered vessel between the walruses and killer whales, and Marion's heart dropped to her stomach as her adrenalin raced through her. The killer whales exploded out of the sky-blue water and bellowed, their shining bodies thrashing about and splashing icy water over the boat. Their gaping jaws opened like caverns, exposing their dreaded teeth.

Marion was freezing, but she summoned the courage to order the Inuits to throw the whale meat and fish into the water.

'Okay, throw the whale meat now!' she screamed with a chill in her husky German accent. The twelve men grabbed the enormous chunks of whale meat and ejected them over the boat's side with all their brute strength, hurling the three massive carcasses into the water. Marion prayed that this would distract the killer whales and keep them from smashing the boat or devouring the walruses.

'Now throw the fish overboard to the walruses!' Marion yelled, and the men caught hold of the baskets of fish and threw at least a hundred fish pieces into the thrashing, bubbling water that churned with the huge walruses. The killer whales attacked the chunks of whale meat just as the walruses thrashed through the water in a feeding frenzy, devouring the fish pieces, and the smell of whale meat, fish and blood, combined with the moist, salty aroma of the air and the ocean, made Marion feel sick. She leaned towards the side of the boat and spewed to the point where her stomach ached with hellish agony and she had to take deep breaths of the ice-cold air. One of the men came up to her.

'Are you okay?' he asked.

'I will be when we get back to land,' she said with great effort.

'Then we'll turn the boat and head off home,' he replied reassuringly. He yelled a command to his men and the boat was steered round and pulled by oars towards the land overlooking Hudson Bay.

The killer whales had disappeared underwater with the whale carcasses, this easy supply of meat reducing their incentive to attack the walruses, and the walruses had made short work of the fish pieces before swimming in the opposite direction. Very soon, Marion and the others reached land, but she felt too sick and exhausted to brag about how such a hostile encounter between the killer whales and walruses had been diffused.

Marion ambled towards Aram's igloo, tucked herself under the caribou-skin blankets and succumbed to sleep. Aram fondled her dark hair and caressed her shoulder as she slept. He knew that her third and last test would be by far her most dangerous ordeal, and he prayed to the Great Spirit to guide her in her time of deadly peril.

* * *

Marion lay awake for most of the night and was anxious and apprehensive about her last test. When dawn broke, she found Aram and asked, 'What will my last test be?'

'It will be by far your most deadly ordeal, even worse than the confrontation between the killer whales and walruses,' Aram explained. 'It will take place in Byelorussia, Europe, on its western border with Poland and the Baltic states. You will face many of Europe's dangerous animals — herbivores and predators united by evil spirits — and the only way to kill their evil spirits is with tranquilliser weapons. And you know by now what these weapons are?'

'I do,' Marion said shakily.

'You must use your intelligence and skill,' Aram told her. 'I have asked the Great Spirit to guide you.'

Marion slept for almost ten hours during the day to prepare herself for the last task. She dreamed of numerous lethal creatures attacking humans, each attack having a different motive. In all these cases, humans were at fault, for they had infringed on the animals' habitats with their modern development or provoked the animals in other ways, indicating to Marion that no animals would attack her if left to themselves.

Her dream began in Africa, where big game hunters were suddenly charged by a massive herd of zebras and giraffes. There were far too many animals for the men's rifles to massacre, and the formidable herbivores kicked and trampled the men under an onslaught of flailing legs and hooves. In a nearby river, boats intruded on the territory of hippos and crocodiles, but the hippos crushed the boats with their tusks and cavernous mouths, and then both hippos and crocodiles mauled or devoured the men in the water. As the crocodiles made easy meals of the injured men, the hippos were at peace with the elephants, rhinos and buffaloes.

The dream switched to a zoo in California,

America, where eight cheetahs savagely attacked their five keepers due to the men trusting these cheetahs too much. All animals which had lost their fear of man through being kept by humans were more dangerous than wild animals who feared man. Cheetahs were no exception, and, like lions, tigers, leopards and jaguars, cheetahs could turn vicious and inflict severe injuries on humans with their razor-sharp claws and deadly fangs. The five zookeepers ended up in the Los Angeles Hospital covered in ripping claw and puncture wounds.

Marion then found herself, still dreaming, in the Arctic Ocean near Hudson Bay. Oilmen in boats surveyed the sea in their determination to establish oil wells, but killer whales and walruses ploughed into the large boats and mauled the men in the water after the boats sank, whilst bearded seals, fur seals and sea lions repeated this attack against the smaller boats and savaged the men underwater as viciously as the killer whales and walruses had. On the tundra, three groups of polar bears, musk oxen and caribou attacked workmen near oilrigs, the polar bears slaughtering most of the men inside the buildings and the herbivores goring those who fled outside to escape from the polar bears. Marion knew this was only a nightmare, but she could not escape from the dream, for the purpose of it was to indicate that humans were almost always at fault when they fell victim to deadly creatures.

All these violent attacks were provoked by humans in some way. Marion needed reassurance that normally these animals were no threat to humans or herself, and so her mind conjured some positive images. Off the coast of California, divers swam with great white sharks and tiger sharks. Tourists photographed grizzlies and black bears from their vehicles, taking care not to feed the bears as this would make them aggressive. Naturalists and zoologists studied herds of bison, moose and bighorn sheep, and the massive herbivores refrained from attacking because the men kept themselves at a safe distance. This gave Marion enormous reassurance.

Darkness overcame Marion as she fell into a deeper, dreamless sleep.

* * *

Marion awoke in a strange room on the second floor of a warehouse. She was very frightened and confused, but she knew she had to fight her fear and dread.

Marion assumed she was in Byelorussia, so she got up and looked around. She was wearing jeans, a shirt and a jumper, and in her belt were two sleep grenades and a container with magic sleeping powder inside. Flanking the belt as they were positioned above her hips were two holsters, one with a sleep gun and the other containing a tranquilliser pistol already loaded with a drug dart.

Slightly more confident now that she knew

she had a means of self-defence, Marion walked slowly out onto a landing on the second floor that met some stairs leading down to the ground floor. She suddenly felt the ghostly presence of birds of prey behind her, and saw a group of fierce mustelids in front of her. Coming into her view from the stairs onto the landing were the common badger and the feral cat leading three packs of weasels, stoats and ferrets and two large families of polecats and pine martens. Marion gritted her teeth and spun round to spot the three birds of prey on a beam: an eagle, a hawk and an owl. The snarls of the weasels and stoats were fearsome, but the cat's venomous hissing and the badger's vicious growling tormented Marion even more. Then the owl, the hawk and the eagle screeched, sending shivers down her spine. The five packs of weasels charged with spitfire speed towards Marion, ready to wear her down with dozens of bite wounds, but she reached into the container of sleeping powder, raised the substance to her mouth and blew the powder everywhere. The weasels and stoats were all knocked unconscious, followed by the polecats and pine martens. But then the badger and the feral cat also charged, and the eagle, the hawk and the owl swooped towards the young woman. Marion fearfully remembered tales of how owls and hawks had torn peoples' eyes out and mutilated their faces, but there was no way she was going to let that happen to her. Not if she could help it.

Marion ducked and the fearsome birds skimmed over her head, then the owl circled around and ripped at Marion's face with its terrible talons, narrowly missing her eye, and she cried out in agony. At the same time, she felt the badger clawing and biting at her slender legs with its powerful claws and vice-like teeth, and the cat fastening all four sets of claws and fangs into her left arm. The agony in her legs and arm was unbearable, and with the cat immobilising her left arm, she could only use her right one to fight off the owl. She seized the owl's legs and wrenched it away from her face, its talons dripping blood. The eagle was clawing her back and the hawk was tearing at her hair and scalp. Ignoring them, Marion caught hold of the cat by the neck and violently flung it eight feet away before kicking desperately at the badger. Grabbing two handfuls of powder, she threw it into their faces, and both the cat and the badger were knocked out cold in seconds. She grabbed more of the powder and blew it into the faces of the owl and the hawk, and both birds dropped to the floor, but the eagle's talons were still ripping through her jumper and clawing her back.

The eagle suddenly changed tack and swooped towards her face, copying the attacks of the hawk and the owl. Taking more of the powder in her right hand, Marion blew the substance towards the eagle and it too fell to the floor. Marion was in agony and covered in blood and wounds, but she managed to climb into the attic room. As she knelt in the attic, she looked down onto the landing, the bannister overlooking the main warehouse and the bales of straw below, and an idea quickly came to her. A drop of blood dripped down onto the landing and she quickly withdrew her head to stop the blood giving away her position to the larger predators.

A brown bear and a wolf led a fox, a dog, a wolverine and a lynx up the steps onto the landing, and these killers examined the unconscious bodies of the other animals. The wolf licked blood off the floor, which had poured from Marion's injuries, and then growled savagely. Marion gulped, her eyes big with terror as she stared down again. In the warehouse downstairs, she also saw an elk and a wild boar leading a bull, an ox, a horse, a donkey, a mule, a billy goat and a ram. Then Marion saw the bear and the wolf head towards the door to the room in which she had slept, before they turned round just as the fox, the dog, the wolverine and the lynx circled the landing directly below the opening to the attic. They had seen Marion peeping through the opening, and she was now cornered and more petrified than ever. She grabbed a grenade from her belt, pulled out the pin and dropped it through the attic's opening towards the landing. It exploded with little force so that the predators would not be harmed. The gas engulfed the dog, the fox, the wolverine and the lynx so that all four killers were knocked unconscious. But the bear and the wolf had retreated out of harm's way.

Marion pulled her jumper up over her face so as not to breathe in the gas, then hurtled towards the landing, leapt over the bannister and fell towards the bales of hay. The gas steamed between the bear and the wolf on one side and the stairs to the other, so that the beasts delayed charging towards the woman for fear of breathing in the gas themselves. This gave Marion time to confront the nine herbivores led by the elk and the wild boar. All of them except the goat and the ram were enormous beasts rippling with hard muscle, but even the goat and the ram were large and deadly, with horns almost as big as those of the bull and the ox. Through her blind terror, Marion seized the other grenade, ripped out the pin and threw it. The grenade exploded with a billowing of gas, and the feral herbivores collapsed to the floor.

By now, the bear and the wolf had closed in, their jagged teeth and black claws glinting and their eyes rolling in fury. They charged towards Marion with awesome power and speed. Marion grabbed the two pistols from their holsters, sprayed some sleeping gas into the bear's face so that he crashed to the ground and was unconscious in seconds, and at the same time pumped a tranquilliser dart into the wolf's shoulder. The wolf lunged, but missed the young woman, then fell to the floor and lay beside the bear, out cold.

Marion took some deep breaths, relieved that the ordeal was now over, but her injuries were hurting more than ever.

Klaus, Aram and Nacoma suddenly appeared in the doorway. Marion leapt off the hay and ran into her husband's arms. He embraced her and fondled her hair before all four of them watched the animals recovering from being out cold, their evil spirits now destroyed. Marion and Klaus laughed, and then stroked the heads of the bear, the wolf and the wild boar before Marion turned and smiled at Aram and Nacoma.

'Your work in this dreamworld is done,' Nacoma said gently.

'You may return to the real world,' Aram added, smiling.

'Goodbye,' Marion and Klaus replied.

Marion hugged the two men, whispering, 'And thank you.'

CHAPTER 11

Marion emerged from her coma three minutes later at Regensburg Hospital, and Klaus and both their families greeted Marion.

'Boy, am I glad to see you!' Marion exclaimed.

'And we're glad to see you,' Klaus gushed, and then laughed. 'How are you feeling? I've missed you so much. Did you have any dreams in your coma?'

'A little shaky, but otherwise fine. I've missed you too!' Marion said, smiling weakly. 'And yeah, you bet I dreamed!' she added, then spent five hours recounting her long dream to Klaus and the two families. They found it impossible to believe that, during the time Marion had spent in her coma, she had overcome her phobia of wild animals.

'How about you and I go on holiday to the Bavarian Forest?' Marion suggested to Klaus. 'That's after I've been discharged from hospital. How many more days' vacation do we have left before we return to work at the zoo?'

Klaus stared at her for a few moments, mouth slightly agape. Then he cleared his throat. 'Um... five days,' he replied. 'The doctors did a wonderful job of mending your arm and your leg. But your ribs are still broken. Are they still hurting or can you breathe okay?'

'My breathing is fine,' Marion told him. 'That plaster cast mended my ribs, and I have no brain damage as a result of that road accident. My face is healed.'

'That's good to hear,' Marion's mother, Rachel, enthused.

'Then we'll go to the Bavarian Forest,' Klaus decided. 'If you're sure you've overcome your terrors.'

'I'm sure,' Marion replied.

* * *

The following day, Klaus drove both himself and Marian from Regensburg Hospital eastwards towards the Bavarian Forest, the jewel of southern Germany. As they stopped outside the forest boundary, they came upon the national park ranger armed with a rifle at the checkpoint.

'Hello there, folks,' he said. 'I'm sorry about your two terriers, Mavis and Mildew.'

'You heard about that?' Marion said sadly. 'Well, I've forgiven the five mountain foxes who killed my dogs. I have also forgiven that she-wolf who attacked me when I was fifteen.'

'I see a change in you,' the ranger told Marion, his eyes filled with wonder. 'Up until a week ago, you were terrified of forests, and the dangerous animals inside these ones. Now you seem positively happy to be here.'

'It's a long story,' Marion told him.

'She has overcome her phobias,' Klaus informed the ranger.

'That's great to hear, but I'm afraid you have come at a bad time,' the ranger said. 'Two days ago, a young woman was killed by a wolf in this forest. The beeper on this tagged wolf came up on our computer screens and proved that the wolf was from a pack living in the Bohemian Forest. But this wolf had crossed the boundary from the Bohemian Forest into the Bavarian Forest and attacked this woman as she explored with her husband and children. The wolf was a large male and extremely savage, so the woman stood no chance. We presume that the Bohemian Forest pack expelled this wolf and he is now roaming the Bavarian Forest. Be very vigilant when camping in the forest or on the meadows nearby. And don't leave any food lying around.'

'We'll take your advice,' Klaus said. 'I trust that's the only beast we have to watch out for?'

'Well, red deer and roe deer will run away from you, but you have to beware of wild boars. With the exception of this male wolf that killed the woman, other wolves, feral dogs and lynxes are no threat to humans. And there are no bears in Germany, though part of me longs for the day they return to these forests.'

'We have a large axe in the boot of our car in case that wolf or any wild animals attack us,' Klaus said confidently. 'But we'll be extremely careful. Can we go into the forest now?'

'You may, but at your own risk.'

'I've wanted to visit the German forests for a long time, and where better than the Bavarian Forest?' Marion enthused. 'I'm not about to allow a rogue wolf to spoil our holiday.'

'We'll take the risk,' Klaus said, smiling at his wife's brave new attitude.

'It's your lives — and your funerals,' the ranger warned them. 'Have an enjoyable and safe holiday.'

Klaus drove past the ranger, and then they were deep in the forest. It was a pleasure to know that some of Europe's wilderness areas had been left untamed and unspoilt, even in a modern industrial country like Germany.

Marion and Klaus camped outside a farm in the forest, which was quiet and tranquil. The couple slept through the night, with the moon and stars gleaming down upon the trees, thickets and meadows.

* * *

The next morning, Marion and Klaus awoke and left their tent. They found themselves surrounded by five farm beasts; a bull and an ox stood in front of the farm whilst a horse, a donkey and a mule were nearer the forest trees. Marion rose to her feet, adopted a submissive body posture and sang a song to the bull and the ox, pacifying the beasts. Klaus gently patted the horse, the donkey and the mule. Eventually, all of the farm beasts retreated towards the farm they had come from.

Then Marion had a hallucination of that male wolf glaring at her with cold, evil eyes which epitomised his ruthless hatred of humans — the same wolf which had killed that young woman a few days back. Marion was shaking, her eyes big and sharp with terror, but then the wolf disappeared.

'What's wrong?' Klaus snapped. 'You look like you saw a ghost.'

'I thought I saw a wolf,' Marion whispered, her face white. 'But there's no wolf.'

Klaus laughed. 'It's bad enough we faced a bull and an ox alongside a horse, a donkey and a mule, and then ten wild boars! The last thing we need is to worry about a wolf. Come on, let's head for the river.'

Marion and Klaus were close to the river when they saw some swans tending to their young. The males were helping out the females, and the dominant male swan was feeding the cygnets. He was the tallest of the swans, with beautiful, white plumage and a long neck; his eyes and beak barely showed a smile of happiness. At that moment, a large mountain fox was lurking through the vegetation to steal one of the young, and in the sky an eagle, a hawk and a falcon were hovering, watching their young targets. The swans took off into the air to drive off the birds of prey, and this distraction served the fox well.

'He's going to kill the young,' Marion said worriedly. 'I hate this.'

'Quiet now,' Klaus whispered, though he didn't like the situation either.

The fox darted along the riverbank and snatched a young cygnet in its jaws, but the swans saw this and mobbed him. Despite the fox's great size and strength, it was heavily outnumbered. It was forced to release the cygnet, and then it fled into the long grass.

'Let's go over and feed them,' Marion suggested to Klaus.

'No,' Klaus objected. 'A swan can break your arm.'

'As long as we don't act rashly we will be fine,' Marion said. She reached into her rucksack, broke up a ham sandwich and fed a piece to the swan before throwing the rest in the water for other birds to squabble over.

Marion and Klaus decided to head further over the meadows, and took a long hike through the south-western quarter of the vast forest, twice stopping at village cafés to have a proper lunch and a cup of tea. Then, when they reached the meadows again, they decided to make camp. They consumed their sandwiches and cans of lager, and finally succumbed to a much-needed sleep.

* * *

'No!'

Marion awoke in her tent, bathed in sweat. She was shaking with terror, and her outburst disturbed her husband's sleep.

'What is it?' Klaus cried.

'I had a nightmare!' Marion gasped. 'About the wolf that killed that woman — it was growling at me!'

'Okay, calm down,' Klaus told her. 'It's all right.'

'But what if the wolf is targeting us? Maybe the vision at the farm and then this dream are a warning to us to be on our guard.'

'Maybe you're right,' Klaus said slowly.

'Can I sleep with that axe beside me?' Marion enquired. 'The axe in your rucksack. That way, I'll defend myself or you can protect me if the wolf does attack one of us.'

'If it makes you feel safer,' Klaus replied. 'Let's sleep for three more hours and then we'll head for our car in the forest clearing. The sooner we leave here, the safer we'll be.'

The young couple succumbed to another long sleep as the night was about to falter to the onset of dawn.

* * *

Marion awoke at first light and went to find some water to drink from the river before ambling back towards the tent. A fearsome noise reached her ears and sent a shock through her mind — the snarling of a savage beast. Then she heard Klaus crying out in agony.

'Oh my God!' Marion exclaimed, running until she caught sight of the tent again. 'Klaus! Klaus! I'm coming!' she yelled.

She immediately saw that Klaus was vainly trying to fight off that male wolf, but the wolf was extremely powerful and savage. Its fangs and shearing teeth ripped at his shirt and shredded his stomach, rending muscle and sending blood gushing from his belly. Klaus covered the wounds with his arms and rolled up in a ball, but the snarling beast sank its teeth into his arm and shoulder, ripping his shirt and tearing flesh away. No arteries or blood vessels had been ruptured, but it was only a matter of time before Klaus would lose too much blood. Time was running out fast. Klaus appeared to be numbed with shock and he was weakening.

Marion by this time had yanked the axe from inside the tent and charged towards the wolf with all her wiry power and speed. Her old terror of wolves threatened to return, but she pressed it deep down within her and transformed the fear into rage.

The wolf continued to rip through flesh and fracture bones, but Marion summoned all her energy, raised the axe and swung it down in a sweeping arc, landing the steel blade square into the wolf's back. The wolf yelped in agony as his spine was splintered by the blow, and then Marion smashed a powerful kick into the beast's ribs, sending it reeling. As the wolf lay paralysed by the axe-blow to his spine, Marion raised the axe again and hacked at the wolf's head, splitting his skull in two and killing him outright.

Panting, she dropped the axe and then lowered herself to her knees in order to tend to her husband, who was writhing around on the ground and crying out in agony at his terrible wounds.

'Oh my God!' Marion cried out. 'You'll be okay, Klaus, stay with me. You're in shock from loss of blood, but it seems that no arteries or blood vessels were punctured, thank God. I'll take you to the car, drive us both to the ranger's station, call an ambulance and apply First Aid to your injuries.'

'You k-killed a wolf... single-handedly?' Klaus groaned, biting back pain. He tried to look up at her but his eyes were unfocused. 'You... have guts, young lady.'

* * *

Back at the ranger's station, to avoid infection, the ranger applied antiseptic cream to Klaus's injuries and then placed bandages around the wounds. To treat Klaus for shock, Marion helped him to the ground and gently raised his legs to prop them against a chair. At the same time, the ranger's wife phoned Regensburg Hospital for an ambulance.

After about twenty minutes, the ambulance arrived and took Klaus and Marion to the hospital. The park ranger followed the ambulance in his truck to make a statement to the appropriate officials.

At the hospital, Marion sat anxiously in the waiting room whilst Klaus was being treated in intensive care. She had to remind herself that this wolf was only a wild animal following its natural instinct to kill prey. Unusually, this particular wolf had learned to attack and kill humans, seemingly on a whim. Marion also reminded herself that wolf attacks were incredibly rare. She knew that she'd had no choice but to kill the wolf; it had been in self-defence.

She just had to hope her husband would recover.

* * *

Canada.

The puma's savage roar was combined with the wolf's eerie howls, the barks of the coyote and the fox, the blood-chilling hissing of the wolverine, and the malicious growls of the lynx and the bobcat. Despite her paralysing terror, Marion raised her arms and then descended into the lotus position. Through her use of native forms of meditation, it was not long before the seven large predators were appeased.

Once Marion's task was complete, and the beasts were calmed, Guamo, Chiaguar, Nacoma, Aram and the rest of her friends joined her to celebrate. The wild beasts approached the humans, their faces conveying no hatred...

Marion awoke in her bed and heard Klaus clattering about in the kitchen. His injuries had healed and he had been home for a month now. She smiled and climbed out of bed to enter the kitchen.

'Klaus, what are you doing?' she asked.

'Making some hot chocolate for you,' Klaus replied, passing her a steaming mug. 'This will help you to sleep better.'

'Thank you, darling,' Marion said gratefully. 'But I've had plenty of sleep, and now I'm ready for work. I've had another wonderful dream. Do you want to hear about it?'

Klaus nodded eagerly and they sat down at the kitchen table.

A new day had begun for Marion.

AUTHOR PROFILE

Michael Elia was born in Southampton in 1968. He has Asperger's syndrome and Tourette's syndrome and lives in Berkshire in shared accommodation for people with autism. Michael was educated at Eynsham's Bartholomew School in Oxfordshire, received further education at Oxpens College and has recently finished a course at Reading College.

Fear of the Unknown is his fourth novel, as he has previously written *Nature's Revenge*, A *Trio of Cartels* and *Web of Crime*. Michael has recently written five other novels, which have yet to be published.

Publisher Information

Rowanvale Books

Rowanvale Books provides publishing services to independent authors, writers and poets all over the globe. We deliver a personal, honest and efficient service that allows authors to see their work published, while remaining in control of the process and retaining their creativity. By making publishing services available to authors in a cost-effective and ethical way, we at Rowanvale Books hope to ensure that the local, national and international community benefits from a steady stream of good quality literature.

For more information about us, our authors or our publications, please get in touch.

www.rowanvalebooks.com
info@rowanvalebooks.com